THE CTHULHU ENCRYPTION

A ROMANCE OF PIRACY

BRIAN STABLEFORD

THE BORGO PRESS

MMXI

THE CTHULHU ENCRYPTION

FIRST EDITION

Published by Wildside Press LLC

www.wildsidebooks.com

THE CTHULHU ENCRYPTION

Borgo Press Fiction by BRIAN STABLEFORD

Alien Abduction: The Wiltshire Revelations
The Best of Both Worlds and Other Ambiguous Tales
Beyond the Colors of Darkness and Other Exotica
Changelings and Other Metaphoric Tales
Complications and Other Stories
The Cosmic Perspective and Other Black Comedies
The Cthulhu Encryption: A Romance of Piracy
The Cure for Love and Other Tales of the Biotech Revolution
The Dragon Man: A Novel of the Future
The Eleventh Hour
The Fenris Device (Hooded Swan #5)
Firefly: A Novel of the Far Future
Les Fleurs du Mal: A Tale of the Biotech Revolution
The Gardens of Tantalus and Other Delusions
The Great Chain of Being and Other Tales of the Biotech Revolution
Halycon Drift (Hooded Swan #1)
The Haunted Bookshop and Other Apparitions
In the Flesh and Other Tales of the Biotech Revolution
The Innsmouth Heritage and Other Sequels
Kiss the Goat
Luscinia: A Romance of Nightingales and Roses
The Mad Trist: A Romance of Bibliomania
The Moment of Truth: A Novel of the Future
An Oasis of Horror: Decadent Tales and Contes Cruels
The Paradise Game (Hooded Swan #4)
The Plurality of Worlds: A Sixteenth-Century Space Opera
Prelude to Eternity: A Romance of the First Time Machine
Promised Land (Hooded Swan #3)
The Quintessence of August: A Romance of Possession
The Return of the Djinn and Other Black Melodramas
Rhapsody in Black (Hooded Swan #2)
Salome and Other Decadent Fantasies
The Tree of Life and Other Tales of the Biotech Revolution
The Undead: A Tale of the Biotech Revolution
Valdemar's Daughter: A Romance of Mesmerism
The World Beyond: A Sequel to S. Fowler Wright's The World Below
Xeno's Paradox: A Tale of the Biotech Revolution
Zombies Don't Cry: A Tale of the Biotech Revolution

DEDICATION

For Elaine

CONTENTS

AUTHOR'S NOTE

THIS STORY IS THE fifth in a sequence; although the story is independent and self-contained, some reference is inevitably made to the earlier elements of the series. "The Legacy of Erich Zann" can be found in a Perilous Press volume in company with a short novel from outside the series, *The Womb of Time*, while *Valdemar's Daughter* and *The Mad Trist* make up the two halves of a Borgo Press/Wildside Press double. *The Quintessence of August* is also published by Borgo/Wildside.

I was first struck by the potential narrative utility of the wordplay fundamental to this story when I heard it deployed in a fascinating paper by Minwen Huang of the University of Leipzig, "The Haunted House of Science Fiction: Modern Ghosts, Crypts and Technologies," presented at the inaugural conference of the Gesellschaft für Fantastikforschung in Hamburg in 2010. I am very grateful to Ms. Huang for making the full text of the paper available to me, in order that I could plunder it piratically.

"Captain England having sided so much to Captain Mackra's Interest, was a Means of making him many Enemies among the Crew; they thinking that such good Usage was inconsistent with their Polity, because it looked like procuring Favour at the Aggravation of their Crimes; therefore upon Imagination or Report, that Captain Mackra was fitting out against them, with the Company's Force, he was soon abdicated or pulled out of his Government and marooned on the island of Mauritius....

"Angria is a famous Indian Pyrate, of considerable Strength and Territories, that gives continual Disturbance to the European (and especially the English) Trade: His chief Hold is Callaba, not many leagues from Bombay, and has one Island in sight of that Port, whereby he gains frequent Opportunities of annoying the Company. It would not be so insuperable a Difficulty to suppress him, if the Shallowness of the Water did not prevent Ships of War from coming nigh; and a better Art he has, of bribing the Mogul's Ministers for Protection, when he finds an Enemy too powerful...."

Captain Charles Johnson, Chapter V of
A General History of the Pyrates (1724)

"J'ai lu monsieur Leuret, le sage de Bicêtre
"Et j'ignore pas qu'un poète est un fou."
[I've read Monsieur Leuret, the sage of Bicêtre
And I'm not unaware that all poets are mad.]
Victor Hugo *La Légende des siècles, deuxième série* (1877)

"Ph'nglui mglw'nath Cthulhu R'lyeh wgah'nagl fhtagn"
[In his house at R'lyeh, dead Cthulhu waits dreaming]
Reported phonetic version of the chant of
Cthulhu-"worshippers", as reproduced in H. P. Lovecraft,
"The Call of Cthulhu" (1928)

CHAPTER ONE
THE CRYPTOGRAM

THERE WAS A PERIOD of time, between the Autumn of 1846 and the revolution of 1848, when my regular meetings with Auguste Dupin—which almost invariably took place in my house, a far more comfortable and readily-accessible location than his apartment—were so frequently complicated by the supplementation of a third party that I almost began thinking of us as a threesome rather than a pair. I could not help borrowing an image from a recent popular *feuilleton* by referring to us, strictly in the privacy of my own mind, as "the three musketeers"—although I ought to stress that we were by no means violent individuals.

The third party in question could not always be with us, for he was in great demand as a physician, while we were supposedly men of leisure—though certainly no idlers—but for a while, he was present nearly as often as he was absent at our conversational evenings. The man in question was the mesmerist Pierre Chapelain, who had become a regular visitor to my house in late August and early September 1846, when I had suffered a bad bout of heatstroke.

The interval in question was a time of conspicuous rivalries, of which the long battle fought for the public's attention by the clamorous *feuilletonists* Monsieur Dumas and Monsieur Sue seemed an apt symbol. Since the man who now styled himself the Baron Du Potet de Sennevoy seemed to have thrown in his lot with the self-styled Comte de Saint-Germain and Jana Valdemar to form an allegedly-unholy trinity at the heart of the

Harmonic Philosophical Society of Paris, it seemed only appropriate—to me, at least—that his chief rival as a contemporary mesmerist, Chapelain, should have formed a complementary alliance with Dupin and myself, whom Fate had cast as scholars of a more skeptical and less personally-ambitious kind.

The tacit rivalry between Du Potet and Chapelain was a recomplication of the long-standing dispute between the two principal schools of mesmeric theory, the spiritualists and the physiologists. That distinction had become somewhat obsolete as conceptual boundaries had shifted; no one seemed certain any longer as to what such terms as "spirit" and "soul" ought to imply, and notions of the relationship between the human mind and body had shifted considerably since René Descartes had drawn such a clear-cut distinction. Du Potet had apparently started out as a physiologist, convinced that the phenomena of "animal magnetism" were physical in nature and subject to analysis by positivist scientific methods, but now appeared to be a convert not merely to the spiritualist conviction that the mind, or soul, had an independent existence of its own but to the thesis that ancient magic and modern mesmerism were essentially the same thing, essentially ungraspable by positivist thought and action but capable, if mastered, of enormous power. Chapelain had always a much more pragmatic approach, less interested in theory than in the workability and utility of mesmeric practices in the diagnosis and treatment of illness. He remained a conscientious agnostic on such questions as whether various forms of "hallucination" were merely the mental side-effects of bodily occurrences, or whether there really were "diseases of the mind" that not only lacked physical causes but might generate physical side-effects, as the newly-fashionable jargon put it, "psychosomatically."

I mention that question in particular because it was the one that had been exercising Dupin and myself before the mesmerist's late arrival, on the evening on which all three of us became collectively involved in what turned out to be the most bizarre of all our "adventures": occasions when Dupin and I were forced by circumstance to desert mere philosophical discussion for actual confrontation with what I continued, stubbornly, to regard as "the supernatural." Dupin was, of course, equally stubborn in maintaining that there could be no such thing: that everything that happened, however out of the ordinary it might seem to timid human experience, must be regarded as natural, and must be fitted, somehow, into the coherent order of the universe—or, at he preferred to put it, "the plenum."

The fact that we had been discussing hallucination that day came to seem anticipatory when Chapelain finally arrived in my smoking-room, in a state of apparent exhaustion and evident exasperation. He had spent a highly stressful day at Bicêtre, where he was often summoned to consultations by the director, François Leuret. He had come directly from the asylum, without having gone home to bathe and change his clothes, so he still retained something of the reek of the place, which could not be covered up by any kind of eau-de-cologne or disinfectant fluid. Chapelain apologized for the slight offensive odor, and expressed the hope that he was not similarly tainted with an imperceptible but far more dangerous "miasma of madness."

Even though it was late October, and the night air was taking on a distinct chill, I opened a window—although, to be perfectly honest, the smoke from our well-exercised tobacco-pipes and the crackling log fire, imperfectly drawn into the sullen Parisian air by my chimney, not only drowned out Chapelain's faint indecency with its sap-sweet and carbon-sour mélange but provided even more incentive to improve the circulation. The faint whiff of Bicêtre was a minor player in the olfactory cacophony.

Bicêtre had once been a hell-hole in which incarcerated madmen—and madwomen—were kept in appalling conditions, direly abused and routinely exhibited to tourists who went to mock them and marvel at their afflictions. That had been in pre-Revolutionary days, however (the Revolution of 1789, that is), and ever since Philippe Pinel had taken over the institution in 1793, attempts had been made to introduce a more humane regime. Leuret had taken over where Pinel had left off, and although he still used cold showers as a punitive measure to control unruly inmates, the main thrust of the institution was now to care for its inmates and, where possible, to improve the state of their health. Under Leuret's supervision, there were now educational classes, music and dancing at Bicêtre, and physicians like Chapelain made regular visits to attempt diagnosis and treatment of cases that seemed tractable, or at least capable of some amelioration. The results of these good intentions would doubtless have been much better had the institution not been so direly overcrowded, but there was, alas, no shortage of demand for places in the various asylums of Paris.

I was not surprised by Chapelain's distressed appearance, for I knew how seriously he took his work. People who regard mesmerists as mere charlatans may suppose that there is no real labor involved in entrancing patients, interrogating them in a somniloquistic state as to the causes of their ailments, and attempting to exert the power of suggestion upon those ailments, but I had seen Chapelain at work, and I knew that it not only involved exhausting effort but was frequently harrowing. It sometimes seemed to me that when he succeeded in relieving the pain and distress of his patients, he did so by accepting that burden into himself, and that when he went to Bicêtre, Charenton or the Saltpêtrière he sometimes placed himself in real danger of being infected by the tide of madness that surged through the worst wards of those establishments: the wards where patients doomed to die were stored while they awaited the arrival of the reaper. It was not hard to deduce that Chapelain had spent time in some such ward that day.

I hastened to pour him a stiff glass of brandy as he slumped into what was now recognized as "his" armchair, and I instructed my cook to make him an omelette. Although Dupin has insisted that I sent back the cook and valet that the Comte de Saint-German had "lent" me following my bout of illness, I had grown so used to the care they had lavished upon me while I was still incapable of caring for myself that I had immediately hired replacements: a married couple, Breton in origin, named Bihan.

Dupin could not help but approve of them because Madame Bihan was a cousin of his concierge, Madame Lacuzon—an old gorgon who had become legendary in Paris for her ability to force unwelcome callers into hectic retreat by the power of her stare alone.

"I take it that your treatments did not go well today, my friend," I said to him, when he had eaten the omelette and progressed to his second glass of brandy.

"That is a matter of opinion, alas," he replied, with a sigh, wriggling in order to mold the cushions of the armchair to his relaxed body.

"Have you had another argument with Monsieur Leuret?" Dupin asked, trying to feign sympathy.

"Yes, I have," the mesmerist confirmed, "although I really don't know why, given that the woman is dying, and Leuret knows as well as I do that we can do nothing for her except try to make her comfortable."

"Which is doubtless very difficult," I put in, having no need to feign my own sympathy.

"Not in this particular instance—provided that my approach to the problem is licensed. Alas, Leuret disapproves of my endeavor on principle, and is insistent that I am proceeding in the wrong direction."

"Please explain," said Dupin, who did not approve of beating around bushes.

"The patient is dying of syphilis. She might have a fortnight to live, a month at the very most, and laudanum is limited in its power to dull her pain, although I have prescribed a regular dose in order to obtain what advantage can be had. She is, however, unusually amenable to entrancement. Indeed, I am half-convinced that she was already in a trance of some sort before I saw her for the first time, a week ago. I had no difficulty in entrancing her a little more deeply—upon which, without any prompting, she lost herself spontaneously in a pleasant dream of her own manufacture: a childish fantasy compounded from fragments of folklore and romance. I have encountered such fantasies before, especially in patients who have previously been mesmerized, as this one clearly has. I could have tried to go even deeper, to attempt to discover what lay behind the fantasy, but that seemed pointless to me. Given that the dream seemed to comfort her, and relieve her distress to some degree, I thought the best thing to do was to let her enjoy it—and so I decided not to bring her out of the trance. Leuret objected at the time, but not strenuously. When I went back today, however...."

We already knew, by courtesy of past conversations, that Leuret believed that his primary duty was to attempt to cure madness. He was endeavoring to build a taxonomy of madness, in terms of various categories of hallucinatory obsession, and had become increasingly insistent in the conviction that the only responsible curative strategy was to make every effort to dispel hallucinations and bring his patients "down to earth" or "back to reality." I could understand, therefore, why he might have a principled objection to Chapelain's encouragement of a delusion—although I could also understand Chapelain's readiness to do that, if it might serve to relieve the distress of a woman who was bound to die.

"Why have Leuret's objections become stronger?" Dupin asked, when Chapelain's momentary abandonment of his account seemed likely to drag on indefinitely as he savored his brandy and took a long draught on his pipe.

"Primarily, because he believes that the woman's fantasy is upsetting some of the other patients. It seemed harmlessly pleasant to me, but certain kinds of people are apt to find hints of diabolism in everything, and it does not take much to win women of unprepossessing appearance a reputation for witchcraft—as you know very well, Monsieur Dupin, given what is said about your concierge by people whom she turns away. You might expect women vulnerable to such accusations themselves to be more sympathetic, but...well, Bicêtre being what it is....

"The specific problem, according to Leuret, is that the fantasy has had a strange psychosomatic effect, in bringing out a patch of inflammation on her skin. Given that she's syphilitic, that isn't unduly surprising, and Leuret's interpretation is that the design is an amateurish tattoo that had faded, but has now been caused to stand out again by the progress of the disease. The thing is not very big, and it's situated on her back, between her shoulder-blades, so there's no reason why any of the other patients should ever have seen it if the orderlies hadn't drawn attention to it, but...at any rate, some other madwoman has identified it as a 'Devil's mark,' and that has caused whispers.

"Apparently, there have been nightmares, demonic sightings...but this is a death-watch ward at Bicêtre, for God's sake. When has it ever been free of nightmares and demonic sightings? For once, however, Leuret has found a scapegoat, and it is me. By leaving the poor woman to enjoy her comforting hallucination, I have apparently made the atmosphere in the ward even more infectious than it was before—and when I refused to bring her out of her kindly entrancement today, Leuret become quite angry. I stuck to my refusal, though. I will not bring a patient back to agony, to face death in the cold light of reality, while she has a mental refuge in which to insulate herself from that horror. It is her refuge, not mine—I have not supplied any of its imagery. Until she does die, though, I expect it will be a bone of contention between Leuret and myself, which might make him far more reluctant to consult me in future, in spite of his dire need of all the help he can get in making his reforms work."

"Is the woman a prostitute?" Dupin asked.

"Presumably," Chapelain confirmed. "She appears to be her late forties, and undoubtedly contracted the disease long ago. It has now progressed to its tertiary stage—which, as you know, often generates symptoms of madness by itself. It is obvious, too, that she has been subjected in the past to the mercury treatment, which I have always considered to be more likely to do further harm than good. If the disease itself were insufficient to explain her tendency to hallucination, the mercury vapor to which she has been exposed is undoubtedly capable of making up the margin—but the particular hallucination that I assisted her to fabricate seems entirely benign to me. She imagines herself to be the queen of some enchanted underworld, whose king is Oberon—I think she might be English by birth, so that is probably an echo of Shakespeare rather than *Huon of Bordeaux*—and whose personnel is drawn syncretically from various traditional tales and romances."

"Leuret would not approve of that," Dupin observed. So far as I knew, he had never met Leuret, but he had definitely read one of the so-called sage of Bicêtre's books, *Fragmens psychologiques sur la folie*. He had been very interested in its case-studies of hallucination and delusion—especially those in the final section on "terror and damnation."

"Indeed he does not," Chapelain said, with a heartfelt sigh. "I know that you're an admirer of his work, Monsieur Dupin, as I am myself, but I feel that his attitudes are hardening, unnecessarily and undesirably, in the face of criticism from the dogmatic physiologists at the Saltpêtrière. He disapproves of the preservation of fantastic folklore, especially its use to amuse children. He considers the substance of romance as a species of hallucination, and hence as a species of madness, which would be best eliminated from our society. I had a patient once—a deputé from the Loire valley, a journalist and historian of some repute—who had a very similar view, lumping together all the enemies of progress under the heading "poetic" or "anti-prosaic." Dr. Leuret has a similar distaste for the imaginative in art and literature, regarding Monsieur Nodier's *Smarra* and Monsieur Hugo's *Notre-Dame de Paris* as works direly dangerous to public health. He once looked after Monsieur Hugo's younger brother when he was in Charenton, and considers the great poet no less mad than his unfortunate relative. Indeed, he suspects the elder Hugo of being a noxious source of infection, by virtue of his celebrity. Like Plato, I think Leuret would expel all poets from his ideal Republic, or put them all to death, for the crime of nourishing the excitement of the mind rather than sternly promoting the calm of reason. I was always sure, personally, that Plato had his tongue in his cheek when he wrote that—he was an accomplished romancer himself, after all—but Dr. Leuret seems to be serious now that he is becoming more cantankerous. That, too, is a factor in his reaction to this particular case."

"There is no genius without a hint of madness," I observed, quoting Aristotle. "Modern psychologists and artists seem to be in agreement about that—Joseph Moreau did not lack for volunteers when he started to conduct experiments in hallucination using Oriental drugs. Hugo's acolyte Gautier was one of the most enthusiastic, I believe."

"Indeed," said Chapelain, with a sigh. "Actually, Monsieur Dupin, there is one aspect of the present case with which you might be able to help me. At the very least, it might be of some slight interest to you."

So saying, he reached into the inside pocket of his frock-coat and brought out a piece of paper, which he showed to Dupin and myself. Inscribed on the paper was an array of forty-nine characters, symmetrically arrayed in seven groups of seven to form a square. If the characters were letters, they did not belong to any alphabet that I could recognize.

After a preliminary glance, Dupin took hold of the paper and studied it more attentively. There was a frown on his face that I assumed to be a frown of puzzlement and concentration.

After fifteen or twenty seconds of profound silence, Chapelian said: "Well, Monsieur Dupin—do you know what it means?"

"No," Dupin admitted—but he was quick to add: "But I know, in a general sense, what it *is*."

"And what is it?" Chapelain asked.

"A cryptogram."

"You mean, a coded message of some kind," I put in. "Those symbols stand for letters of the alphabet, which, when the correct substitutions are made, spell out a text in Latin, French or whatever?"

I had, of course, read my American correspondent's excellent tale "The Gold Bug," in which a coded message of that kind leads to treasure buried by the infamous pirate Captain Kidd.

Tales of pirate treasure were very much in vogue in Paris in 1846, because the second phase of the rivalry between Monsieur Sue and Monsieur Dumas had spawned Dumas' relentlessly melodramatic tale of the *Comte de Monte Cristo*, who had set out to take revenge upon the enemies that had confined him to the Château d'If after enriching himself fabulously with such a treasure.

"That is the vulgar understanding of a cryptogram," Dupin confirmed, with such naked contempt in his voice that I felt momentarily ashamed for having innocently suggested it.

"That's my understanding too," Chapelain put in, loyally. "If there's a more sophisticated one, it has escaped my notice."

"That might well be to your credit," Dupin admitted, "for the other meaning is one that is more likely to recommend itself to the Baron Du Potet, now that he is haunting the bookshops of Paris for esoteric tomes of all sorts." The edge in his voice suggested that he did not appreciate the extra competition, give that there were more than enough bibliomaniacs in Paris already—not to mention those in the provinces, who occasionally mounted voracious raids on the bookshops of Paris.

"So tell us," I said, a trifle sharply. "What is a cryptogram, to intellectuals of a *less vulgar* stripe?"

"Originally," Dupin said, "a cryptogram was a particular kind of magic spell. The format has been cheapened by overmuch imitation, of course—you can see magical squares of this sort, almost invariably manifesting the same seven-by-seven formation—in numerous alchemical texts and so-called grimoires. Many of those attempt to adapt the format to a Christian context to which it is ill-fitted, while others pretend—always falsely, so far as I can tell—to be the most celebrated legendary original."

"What *legendary original* is that?" Chapelain queried, the hint of impatience in his voice not entirely due to his heavy day at Bicêtre.

"The so-called Key, or Seal, of Solomon—the instrument with which the great king is said to have bound the demons that once supposedly ravaged the earth: the djinn, as Arab folklore calls them."

"Ah!" said Chapelain. He seemed slightly disappointed. I could understand why: the *Clavicule Salomonis* was one of the so-called "forbidden books" on Dupin's shelves—or, to be perfectly accurate, two of them, for he had two entirely distinct tomes bearing that title, both of them printed in the sixteenth century. The mere fact of their having been printed robbed them of any real claim they had to be considered esoteric, while the fact that various distinct versions existed illustrated the sad truth that the occult *monde* in which the likes of the Comte de Saint-Germain and Mademoiselle Valdemar moved was awash with such optimistic fakes.

"Perhaps that's the real one," I quipped, nodding my head in the direction of the piece of paper that Dupin was holding.

"Perhaps it is," he said, sarcastically. "But it has been scribbled on modern note-paper with a steel-nibbed pen, in a rather slapdash manner, so I would beg leave to doubt it, even if Dr. Chapelain had not found it in the possession of a mercury-addled syphilitic whore who suffers from bizarre hallucinations."

Chapelain took some slight offence at that, presumably on behalf of his patient. He was a good and humane man, who did his best for all his patients, whether they came to consult him from the aristocratic houses of Faubourg Saint-Germain or somehow came to his attention in the dire wards of Bicêtre.

"That's not the original," of course," he said, mildly. "That's a copy made this afternoon by Dr. Leuret—but you're correct about the steel nib. Fine detective work, that."

Dupin smiled, wryly. "You should have brought the original," he said, in a tone of mild reproof, "but I accept the rebuke."

"That would have been somewhat impractical, although not actually impossible," Chapelain countered. I could tell from his tone that he had a revelation up his sleeve with which he hoped to put Dupin's nose ever so slightly out of joint.

"Is it hewn in stone then?" Dupin asked, lightly.

"No," said Chapelain. "It's inscribed on the woman's back— that's the pattern of the inflammation to which I referred, although the version you're holding is considerably larger than the original, which is no more than five centimetres across. As I said, Leuret thinks that it was tattooed a long time ago, but it certainly wasn't done in any inking parlor in Paris or Le Havre, and I beg leave to doubt that it was contrived with a steel needle."

"Ah!" said Dupin thoughtfully. "That *is* intriguing, as further complications go. It's far more intricate, is it not, than the growths and birthmarks that are usually identified as the Devil's marks? Have you asked her what it is?"

"No—I'm not even sure that she was aware of its presence until the wretched orderlies drew attention to it. I dare say, though, that she would me more likely to attributed it to King Oberon's magic than the Devil's…or Merlin's." His voice seemed slightly strangled as he pronounced the last name. He did not wait to be asked a question before adding: "She calls me Merlin, having adapted me into her fantasy."

"Of course," Dupin observed, in a tranquil tone. "What does she call Leuret?"

"She calls him the Mahatma—but she refuses to associate him with a character in her consolatory Underworld. As I said, I think she might be English by birth, but possibly born in India. That would probably have made tales of ancient Britain and Britanny seem even more exotic when they were old to her as a child. Her favorite character seems to be Tristan de Léonais, and that's reflected in what she claims to be her own name. She calls herself Ysolde—Ysolde Leonys. That's L-E-O-N-Y-S, with the stress on the second syllable rather than the first: another clue to her English origin…." He trailed off, having belatedly noticed Dupin's expression, to which puzzlement had returned in full force. "Do you recognize that name?" he added, belatedly.

"Yes," Dupin said. "As it happens, I've heard it mentioned quite recently."

"By whom?" I prompted, when he did not seem inclined to continue—but he was studying the cryptogram again, with a new intensity. "You don't really think it might be the Key of Solomon, do you?" I said, although I felt foolish as soon as the words were out of my mouth.

For once there was no hint of mockery in his response, even though the question was so obviously fatuous. "There's no such thing, strictly speaking," he said. "It's a legend, perverted as well as preserved by virtue of its incorporation into three religions…but it's a legend that might well have *some* foundation in fact. I can't believe for a moment that this might be a copy of one of the cryptograms that gave rise to the legend, but it just might be one of those spun off from it…which are not without interest in more than one antiquarian sense. She was born in India, you said?" The last sentence was couched in a much sharper tone, and addressed to Chapelain.

"I suspect so," Chapelain confirmed, his tone now wary. "Those characters aren't Sanskrit, thought…not, at least, any representation of Sanskrit that I've ever seen."

"No," Dupin agreed," they're not Sanskrit. They're almost certainly improvised to represent phonemes, but if this really is a serious attempt to reproduce, synthesize or fake a cryptogram, it's futile to try to solve it by trying to translate the symbols in such a way that they spell out a message, in Sanskrit, English, Latin, French or any other known language. I'd like to see your Ysolde, Dr. Chapelain, if that's possible."

"She's not really *my* Ysolde," Chapelain said, his tone still very wary. "If she's anyone's, she's Leuret's—but she came to the hospital voluntarily; she wasn't committed by the law. In theory, she's a free agent, although she's in no condition to exercise her freedom."

"So much the better," said Dupin. "If she's free, then she's free to receive visitors. Will Leuret raise any objection?"

"I don't think so. I told him that I would show you the design, and he seemed glad—he knows you by reputation, and not solely on the basis of my remarks. I'm sure that he'll be very interested to know what you make of the design…and what you make of the patient, if you can make anything out of her at all."

"How is it that you recognized her name, Dupin?" I asked my friend, bluntly, when I could get a word in.

"I heard it from Père France," Dupin told us. Père France, whose real name was Thibault, was one on the book-sellers with whom he had regular dealings—a man known to and greatly respected by every bibliophile in Paris. "He asked me whether I knew of any documents signed with that name, or referring to it, perhaps in connection with the name Taylor. He was asking on behalf of one of his provincial customers, a renowned bibliotaph who calls himself Breisz. The collector in question has a keen interest in the Levasseur cryptogram, as well as many other occult matters, and Père France thinks that his enquiry regarding the name Leonys was connected to his interest in that crytogram."

I did not have to ask what a bibliotaph was—it was one of Père France's favourite sarcasms. A bibliotaph is the kind of bibliomaniac who hides his collection away, as if in a tomb. There is, according to the worthy bookseller, no species of miser more secretive or avaricious, and no kind of bibliomaniac less sane—although I doubt that men of that sort frequently end up in the care of men like François Leuret, for it's the kind of eccentricity that requires considerable wealth. Nor did I have to ask why the bibliotaph in question merely "called himself" Breisz; *Breisz* was the Breton word for *Breton*—a far more likely pseudonym than surname. I contented myself, therefore, by asking: "What's the Levasseur cryptogram?"

"I'm surprised that you don't know," Dupin retorted, reverting to type. "Your friend Poe certainly does—he based a story on his legend, although, as a good American, he naturally substituted an American pirate for the French one."

"Captain Kidd, you mean," I said. "In 'The Gold Bug'?"

"Precisely. The idea of coming into possession of a cipher offering directions to a pirate's treasure is hackneyed now, but it was relatively fresh once, and it was in connection with Olivier Levasseur that it was first popularized in France."

"But you can see such clichés any night of the week in the

cheap theaters of the Boulevard du Temple," Chapelain inter-jected. "If poor Ysolde has been a streetwalker for twenty years and more, she's bound to be exceedingly familiar with such fare—but there's nothing about pirates in her fantasies, which are of an altogether more fabulous stripe."

"Pirates are fabulous enough in their own right," Dupin assured him. "Especially Olivier Levasseur. You must have heard of him in your youth, although the name has clearly slipped your memory now."

"You'd better remind me, then," said Chapelain, "if you really think it's relevant."

"I don't know whether it is relevant," Dupin confessed, "but the mere possibility...." He left that sentence hanging, and told us the story instead.

CHAPTER TWO
OUR LADY OF THE CAPE

"Olivier Levasseur," Dupin said, settling into oratorical mode, "was a seaman who obtained a *lettre de marque* from Louis XIV in order that he might serve as a privateer during the War of the Spanish Succession. When the war ended in 1714 he was ordered to return to France, but, like numerous other privateers, he elected to continue his new way of life instead, originally joining a Caribbean pirate fleet commanded by the Englishman Benjamin Hornigold. Hornigold was soon recruited by the English government to hunt down his former peers, however, and Levasseur found it diplomatic to remove himself from his treacherous ally's reach.

"Levasseur took his ship to the east coast of Africa, where there were moderately rich pickings by virtue of the booming slave trade. His attention was soon diverted further eastwards, because the increasing British activity in India and thriving trade with the Far East were making the Indian Ocean much busier. The area was dangerous for European pirates, however, because a native pirate fleet based in India had a virtual monopoly. It was commanded by a warlord named Angria, who had a fortress in Callaba, not far from Bombay, and the support of the Mogul. When the British East India Company lost patience and became determined to put a stop to Angria's activities he seems to have made some kind of clandestine treaty with them, whereby he was licensed to plunder Portuguese, French and Dutch ships to his heart's content, with a ready market for his prizes. In order to find a measure of safety in numbers, Levasseur joined forced with the English pirate Edward England—who has a chapter dedicated to him in Captain Johnson's famous history of piracy—and the two of them established a base on an island near Madagascar early in 1721. Whether they made any kind of agreement with Angria, no one knows—but he does not seem to have attacked them, as he surely could have done.

"Johnson is unclear as to the details, but Edward England was deposed from his command by one of his subsidiary captains, John Taylor, apparently for attempting to forge a treaty of his own with the East India Company via one of its captains that the pirates had captured. Taylor marooned England on Mauritius; he is said to have escaped, but he disappeared from the historical record thereafter.

"In collaboration with Taylor, Levasseur then made the single biggest capture ever attained by any pirate anywhere, when the two of them captured the Portuguese galleon *Nossa Senhora del Cabo*—*Our Lady of the Cape*, in English—which was carrying the Bishop and Viceroy of Goa home to Lisbon, with the respective fortunes they had made by colonial plunder. The haul was so massive than when the routine division of gold, silver and gems was made between all the members of the various pirate crews—who must have numbered more than a hundred—each man is said received a fortune worth more than a million francs in today's money. Taylor and Levasseur, as captains, obtained an extra share, which was largely made up of goods other than metals and precious stones. Levasseur, however, took the most celebrated artefact: the so-called Flaming Cross of Goa—a church ornament made with gold plundered from the Indian continent.

"So much is fact. You will forgive me, however, if I digress into speculation. The pirates' only thought, at that moment, must have been to retire from their exacting profession and live in luxury on the booty they had seized—but that was not an easy thing to do. You have both read *Le Comte de Monte Cristo*, of course—another tale partly based on the legend of

Levasseur—and were no doubt seduced by the idea of Edmond Dantès employing his discovered hoard to establish a brilliant new identity for himself, but can you imagine how difficult that would have been to accomplish in reality, especially for the common seamen in the pirate crews? Imagine a hundred uncouth mariners, who had never been anything but poor and dissolute, suddenly in possession of gold, silver and diamonds worth more than a million francs apiece—and every one of them liable to be hung if they were found in possession of such goods or ever identified as a pirate!

"Where could they go? How could the pirates hold on to or spend their fortune without attracting the attention of the law—or, even worse, other murderous robbers! Remember that their rival Angria, based on the far side of the India Ocean, had a fleet of his own, which far outnumbered theirs. How could they not only escape that sort of predation, but establish new identities for themselves, and convert their weighty holdings into property and paper: title-deeds, bonds and share-certificates that would guarantee them a princely income? Could they rely on old friends and distant family-members, given the attendant risks? Could they negotiate on successful terms with money-changers, merchants and bankers—the legalized pirates of modern civilization, no less ruthless than the seaborne kind? How many of that hundred-and-some, do you suppose, can have lived long enough to derive the comfort and joy for which they had so long yearned from their gains? Perhaps one...or none at all.

"The only two men who could possibly have been in a position, in terms of their knowledge, experience and social contacts, to carry through any such project were the two captains, Levasseur and Taylor—but Taylor himself was an upstart sailor, who had recently got rid of his own former commander, Edward England. Levasseur was the man who was most likely to succeed in making productive use of his amazing wealth—and I presume that most of his crewmen stayed with him, eager to follow his lead. Levasseur wanted, and certainly tried, to return to France. It is recorded that he attempted to take advantage of an amnesty offered to repentant pirates by the French state—but in exchange for the amnesty, the state wanted his booty, and he was not prepared to hand it over. He left France again, and apparently attempted to settle in the Seychelles, but he could not hide for long. He was eventually captured there, returned to Paris, and hanged in 1830. The bulk of his treasure, however, remained hidden perhaps secreted while he was in France, or perhaps hidden in the Seychelles; at any rate, it was not recovered.

"At this point in the story, legend takes over. What legend says is that Levasseur wore a locket of some sort around his neck, in which there was a piece of paper, on which a cryptogram was inscribed. On his way to be hanged, Levasseur is reported to have thrown that locket into the crowd, saying that his fortune would belong to anyone who could solve its mystery. The locket was never seen again, although pieces of paper turn up from time to time, bearing what is claimed to be the original or a copy of the cryptogram contained therein. It is the principal Parisian equivalent of the maps hawked to credulous individuals in the Americas, supposedly showing the location of Blackbeard's loot or Captain Kidd's. At any rate, legend holds that there is a vast hoard of gold, silver and gems still buried somewhere, in France, the Seychelles, or some other island in the Indian Ocean."

"But you doubt it?" I queried.

"I do. We do not know how much of his fortune Levasseur might have lost to theft, or traded away, while he was still alive, and we would not necessarily know if anyone had found it after his death, if they were wise enough to conduct themselves discreetly. Gold can vanish with surprising alacrity, when the voracious scent it. Levasseur was nicknamed *La Buse*—the buzzard—but the moment he became rich, he was competing with eagles. Levesseur lived for more than eight years after the capture of the Portuguese treasure-ship, and he must have spent or lost a considerable fraction of his wealth. In all likelihood, he and his crewmen did bury some of it, probably in more than one location—but a further hundred and twenty years has passed since then. Any surviving crewmen surely returned to the sites they knew, and might well have given information to others in a less melodramatic fashion than Levasseur is reputed to have done. The chances of any such treasure meaning where it was buried to this day are, to my mind, very slim. On the other hand…it is not merely the Flaming Cross of Goa and the gold coins that have not been seen again."

"What else?" asked Chapelain, who was clearly fascinated by the story. I was enraptured myself, but I got up to close the window nevertheless, having found that the cold draught of night air was becoming irritating.

"The versions of the legend repeated in the cabarets of the Marais and the theaters of the Boulevard du Temple," Dupin continued, "naturally make no mention of anything but gold, silver and precious stones—but when their counterparts are whispered by the *bouquinistes* of the Seine, or among the stacks of Père France's shop, they take on a slightly different complexion. Money is only money, after all—a game of numbers—but the Bishop of Goa's book collection is another matter."

"Ah!" I said, realizing that we were now getting to the heart of the problem, in Dupin's view. If, one day, he were ever to stumble upon an iron-bound sea-chest full of gold, silver diamonds and rubies, in some forsaken cranny of the Parisian *carrières*—it was impossible to imagine him on a desert island in the Seychelles—he would very likely sigh over the inconvenience and distraction that its disposal would cause him; but if, at the bottom of the chest, there were some Medieval manuscript illegibly scribbled in an arcane script….*that* would make his eyes shine.

"The bishop was a churchman and a scholar of sorts, as well as a merciless plunderer," Dupin continued. "He is reputed to have amassed a collection of Sanskrit manuscripts second to none while he was supposedly in charge of the spiritual welfare of the subcontinent's Catholic converts—and he is also reputed to have had a substantial quantity of Latin and Greek texts, some of them stolen from the British East India Company, whose burgeoning commercial empire surrounds and threatens Goa. British ships sometimes fall victim to Spanish and Portuguese pirates, of course as well as *vice versa*—but the most interesting fragment of the rumors attached to the Bishop's priceless collection concern books stolen from the very heart of England, by a very ingenious Portuguese sneak-thief: from the library of John Dee himself, which was supposedly lost when a mob stormed his house in Mortlake and supposedly burned the bulk of it."

"Dee the wizard?" I queried. "The man who was duped by a confidence-trickster who claimed to be able to talk to angels by means of a black stone?"

"Such is his posthumous reputation," Dupin confirmed. "In the same way that every great scientist prior to the Age of Enlightenment attracted suspicions of wizardry by virtue of his abstruse intelligence and arcane interests—but with an extra and more vital factor, in Dee's case."

"Which was?" asked Chapelain. He was extremely tired, and seemed hardly to be able to keep his eyes open, now that the brandy and tobacco he had consumed were taking effect, but he was utterly fascinated, and determined to pursue Dupin's study to the end.

"Dee and his initial collaborator, Leonard Digges, were the finest mathematicians in England in their day," Dupin continued, "and were also passionately interested in astronomy and optical science—the keys to successful navigation. Nowadays, of course, we take the instrumentations of navigation—charts, sextants, octants, compasses, telescopes and marine chronometers—entirely for granted, but most of those aids were uninvented in the sixteenth century, and those that were known could not be fully exploited. We do not know to this day how many of them Digges and Dee devised, because all the discoveries they made were secrets of great value, carefully hoarded in order go preserve England's naval advantages for as long as humanly possible. Digges had the misfortune to meddle too intrusively in politics, and was ruined, but that only made Dee all the more precious, not merely to the Royal Navy but, perhaps more importantly, to the Guild of Merchant Adventurers and the founders of the joint-stock company that became the British East India Company. He provided their manuals of navigation and their training programs, and played a vital role in allowing the British East India Company to overtake and eventually obliterate the rival Dutch East India Company and the Portuguese commercial concerns operating out of Goa. There was no one more vital than John Dee to the maintenance of Britain's empire of the waves—and England's enemies knew that, even though most of his own countrymen were ignorant of the fact, and many were stupid enough to fear and loathe him for his education and enterprise.

"There is no doubt that a mob did attack Dee's house during his absence, that they overcame the guards posted to look after it, and that they attempted to burn it to the ground—but who commissioned that mob, and what became of those manuscripts that did not perish in the fire, we do not know. Dee was visiting the continent at the time, and immediately went to the court of the Holy Roman Emperor in Prague, probably because he thought the Emperor might be able to help him to discover what had become of the manuscripts, and perhaps to recover some of the most precious ones. He lingered in Prague for some time, but his hopes appear to have been dashed; he returned to England empty-handed, having abandoned any further questing to his associate Edward Kelley—the skryer who supposedly talked to angels. Dee could not possibly go to Lisbon, of course, although Elizabeth doubtless made what use she could of her spies in that enemy capital on his behalf. The books that remained in England eventually ended up in the British Museum, but the ones that did not were probably the most precious of all."

"And what were they?" Chapelain asked.

"They included the core of Roger Bacon's manuscript collection, which Dee had acquired. That would have included two of the three lost books of Sanchuniathon. numerous alchemical and magical texts, including at least two versions of the *Clavicule Salomonis*. There was also said to be a copy of a text known as the *Necronomicon*, which Dee had attempted to translate from Latin into English, although the Latin translation had been made from a Greek translation of a text allegedly first written in Arabic, and was doubtless hopelessly corrupt. In addition to the Bacon inheritance, the lost texts undoubtedly included some of Dee's own manuscripts, including the originals of his navigational manuals, and the only known copy of one of his own collections of cryptograms, the so-called *Claves Demonicae*. A copy of its counterpart, the *Claves Angelicae*, survived, although it is probably a reconstruction, and very likely defective. I have seen a copy of the copy, and have studied the cryptograms it contains, which are in the same seven-by-seven format as the one I have here, but use markedly different symbols, probably devised by Dee or Kelley, and are opaque as to their meaning."

He had not given the piece of paper that Chapelain had shown him back to the mesmerist, and now seemed inclined to hang on to it, but he raised it indicatively as he spoke the final sentence. Chapelain peered at it again, in a bleary-eyed fashion implying that he could no longer bring it properly into focus.

Trying to connect up the pieces of the puzzle, I said: "So you think that the cryptogram in Levasseur's possession, which he threw into the crowd when he was hanged, might have come from one of Dee's books, which ended up in Goa via Lisbon, after being stolen from London? And you think that the cryptogram tattooed on Chapelain's dying whore might be the same one?"

"As to those matters, I still have a scrupulously open mind," Dupin said, in his usual infuriating manner, "but with regard to the question of whether there might be some connection, I am certainly prepared to take an interest—enough interest, at least, to make it worth my while to visit Bicêtre first thing in the morning, if that can be arranged."

"But I still don't see what connection there can possibly be between my patient and Olivier Levasseur," Chapelain objected, wearily.

"Nor can I," said Dupin, "but Levasseur was caught and hanged. John Taylor was never found. Captain Johnson wrote his book too soon to make any comment on his eventual fate, but other sources report, vaguely, that he settled in India. If that is true, he must have had help. If his friends belonged to the East India Company—which seems the likeliest possibility—they surely demanded a large tribute in gold and diamonds in return for their help, and certainly had the institutional means to redistribute such produce without attraction undue attention. At any rate, there was no evidential trace of him for a long time, and so far as I know, no one has the slightest idea of the circumstances in which he lived or died—but now, unless I am linking the information you have gleaned about your patient to Père France's enquiry in an overly fanciful manner, there is a provincial bibliophile who possesses some indication that the name Taylor assumed when it become impolitic to be John Taylor any longer, might have been...."

"Leonys," I put in swiftly, eager to claim what little credit I could for deductive acumen. "Hence the bibliotaph's speculative linkage of the two names."

"Exactly," Dupin confirmed.

"You think my patient might be this John Taylor's descendant, four or five generations removed?" Chapelain queried. "Or do you think she might have acquired the name by marriage to one of the pirate's descendants?

"I am in no position to judge, as yet—but the possibility seems to be worth investigating."

"A pity, in either case," Chapelain went on, "that it's the wrong pirate—the one who never came to France—although I suppose that they might both have had a copy of the cryptogram, and might each have tried to preserve it in his own way. If she had the key to a fortune in gold and gems inscribed on her back, though, she'd hardly have ended up as a streetwalker in the gutters of Paris. It's all too tenuous, in any case—probably the merest of coincidences."

"But you said before that she might not even have known that the inscription was there," I reminded him, "and if she had, she surely would not have had the key to the cipher."

"As I remarked previously," Dupin observed, patiently, "fortunes can disappear with remarkable rapidity, when one does not have the wherewithal to husband them and help them grow. In the course of the five generations the separate us from the seizure of *Our Lady of the Cape*, even a million francs might evaporate."

"And manuscripts might rot, especially in the torrid climes of India," I put in, causing him to wince.

"That's true," he admitted. "Speech and script are only a little less transient than dreams, alas...unless one takes great care to preserve them. Even signs and symbols hewn in stone eventually fade away before the forces of erosion...but with the aid of copyists, some things do survive, only gradually corrupted over hundred, or even thousands of years...and even dreams sometimes recur."

"So you really think this woman might have been...let's call it tattooed, until I can figure out exactly what was done...in the interests of preserving this...magic spell...for want of a more reliable kind of copying?" Chapelain was clearly finding that hard to swallow.

"I have an open mind," Dupin repeated, "and no particular expectations, but you know how hard it is for me to resist a puzzle, and this"—again he held up the copy of the cryptogram—"is now a very intriguing puzzle, even if it has only become so by virtue of my fanciful elaborations. Will you take me to Bicêtre in the morning, in order that I might investigate the matter further?"

I frowned slightly at that, because he had said *I*, not *us*.

"I have a consultation at nine, and another at ten," Chapelain replied. "I might be free by noon, though. I doubt that Leuret will object to my turning up without an appointment, in spite of our little spat. At the end of the day, he needs my help desperately if he is to impose any order at all on the chaos of his crowded wards. Shall I meet you here, or at your apartment?"

"Here," Dupin said—and my frown cleared. He had, after all, no intention of excluding me from what promised to be an intriguing adventure.

"If all three of us are going, we'll have to take a fiacre," Chapelain observed. "My fly can only carry two."

Dupin did not even hesitate. "We will take a fiacre," he said.

Mention of the fly seemed to remind Chapelain that he was extremely tired, and he stood up to go. I fetched his coat, hat and stick myself, not having quite accustomed myself to the fact that I now had a manservant to take care of such things in my stead, for whom I only had to ring. Naturally, the doctor volunteered to drop Dupin off at his apartment on the way—although it was not "on the way" in a strictly geographical sense—and Dupin naturally accepted.

"I'll see you in the morning," Chapelain said to me, as he bid me goodnight. "Noon, at the latest."

"I'll be here," I promised.

"So will I," Dupin put in. He had put the cryptogram in his jacket pocket, and I suspected that he would be poring over it for hours when he got back, comparing it to those in his esoteric texts in the hope of finding clues to its origin and meaning.

When they had gone, I went to my own bookshelves and pulled out the latest issues of the *Bulletin du Bibliophile*, and hunted through them in search of any reference to Roger Bacon, John Dee, the Bishop of Goa, the Key of Solomon or a text called the *Necronomicon*. There was nothing, so I allowed myself to the sidetracked by loving accounts of rare incunabular editions of *Ars Moriendi* and *Theuerdank*—which seemed, on the whole, to be saner and more reliable documents than any magic spell scrawled on a streetwalker's pox-scarred back.

CHAPTER THREE
THE SAGE OF BICÊTRE

INEVITABLY, ONCE I had written my diary—a longer entry than I had made for a month—and taken myself off to bed, I immediately thought of a dozen other questions that I ought to have raised regarding cryptograms, grimoires and buried treasures, but I figured that they could wait until morning, and went to sleep peacefully enough. If I had any dreams, I forgot them as soon as I woke up, before I could scribble so much so a single note about their content.

I do have a tendency to forget dreams easily—even those I have while awake, which François Leuret would call hallucinations and identify as preliminary signs of madness—and that is now the principal reason why I am making such records as this one, based on diary entries made at the time. The entries themselves are insufficient, for memories require reinforcement if they are to survive, and narrative coherency too. Poe is long dead, alas, so I no longer have anyone to whom I might confide my raw materials; I have no alternative but to do such work as might be done myself.

I hoped that Dupin would come early, so that I could ask him to clarify certain murky issues before Chapelain arrived, but I assume that he was carrying out preliminary research of his own, and not in the pages of the *Bulletin du Bibliophile*. In the end, he turned up less than five minutes before Chapelain arrived, even though Chapelain was not far in advance of the time he had specified as the latest moment of his arrival. At least I remembered to let Bihan answer the door. I had to keep reminding myself not to think of him as "Monsieur Bihan," even though it was permissible to continue thinking of Madame Bihan as "Madame Bihan."

My problems in dealing with servants did not arise from my being American—there had been plenty of servants around when I was growing up in Boston or living in New York—but rather from a private awkwardness. I had sometimes been tempted ask Chapelain about it, but I always refrained, lest doing so should somehow elevate it to the rank of a "symptom." Chapelain was not an alienist, strictly speaking, but every mesmerist is continually confronted with problems of mental illness, especially since the reform of the lunatic asylums has usurped madness, very forcefully, as a medical problem. I had suffered hallucinations enough in my time to have some slight fear of my sanity being bought into question.

We live in a strange world; although I could make no particular claims on my own behalf, I was always well aware of the paradoxicality of the fact that Auguste Dupin, who was surely the sanest man in the world, and a Chevalier de la Légion d'honneur to boot, was often called mad by the ignorant, simply because of his intelligence, his scholarly interests, his open mind and the awesome power of his imagination. I had not read Leuret's *Fragmens* myself, but I had read other works of a similar stripe, and I was well aware that he was not the only man in Paris to consider the supposed madness of poets and artists to be in direct proportion to their imaginative power, and dreaded to think what his opinion might have been of my good friend Poe.

Once we were settled in the fiacre, the opportunity was there to fill in some of the gaps left by the previous evening's conversation, but Dupin was rarely as talkative in the mornings as he was in the evenings, darkness rather than daylight being his true element, and I could sense his resistance. He probably had not slept for more than an hour, although I judged from his lack of exuberance that he had made little or no progress in deciphering the cryptogram. He was also impatient to see the mysterious ex-Queen of the Underworld for himself, and examine the inscription that Chapelain was strangely reluctant to call a tattoo, and his impatience further augmented his peevishness.

In any case, Bicêtre is less than four kilometers south of the Boulevard Saint-Germain, and once we had got to the end of the Boulevard Saint-Michel and passed through the *barrière* the roads were relatively clear in that direction, so the journey time was too short to allow any detailed discussion.

I was content to wait and see how matters developed, gearing myself up to meet the so-called sage of Bicêtre and see his reformed empire for the first time. The morning had started cold, but now that the sun was up, relatively uninhibited by cloud, the temperature had become quite mild, and the journey was pleasant enough. It is not until one passes the *barrière* that one realizes how stale the air in Paris is, by comparison with that of the surrounding countryside.

What immediately struck me about Dr. Leuret, when we were eventually introduced to him, was that he did not seem to be a well man himself. He was in his mid-forties and sufficiently robust in his build, but he did not seem to me to be the kind of man likely to attain his allotted threescore years and ten. His complexion was sallow, his hair and beard already three-quarters grey, and his eyes slightly jaundiced. His career, I imagined, had taken a heavy toll on him. One cannot spend one's life in the company of the terminally-diseased without becoming corrupted oneself. He was, however, nervously active and clearly very interested to meet us...or, at least, to meet Auguste Dupin.

"I've heard a great deal about you, Monsieur," he told Dupin. "Pierre is always quoting your opinions—he certainly holds them in higher esteem than my own, and, if I measure him rightly, higher than Esquirol's or Lélut's." Esquirol had long been the guiding star of the Saltpêtrière and a leading pioneer of modern psyhological analysis; Lélut's was the leading name in that specialism since Esquirol's death

"I'm merely a layman," Dupin assured him, although I could see him swelling slightly with pride under the influence of the compliment. "I never had the honor of meting Dr. Esquirol, alas, and remain in awe of Dr. Lélut, whose *Du demon de Socrate* is one of the most fascinating philosophical texts of recent years….along with your own *Fragmens*, of course." He knew how to pay a compliment when the occasion warranted it, and the recipients of his flattery rarely noticed his oddly mechanical manner of delivery.

"Our case-studies do seem to have been markedly different," Leuret remarked. "My good friend Monsieur Groix tells me that he has often consulted you in mysterious criminal matters."

"Occasionally," Dupin admitted. His dealings with the Prefect of Police were mysterious in themselves, and I was surprised to hear that Groix had mentioned them at all—but I assumed that Leuret was exaggerating slightly, for effect.

"I have looked after some famous murderers in my time," the alienist said, "But that was when I was at Charenton. Things have changed at Bicêtre, mercifully. I hope you will be impressed."

The formalities over, the tour began. Leuret did not want to take us to the ward where Ysolde Leonys was confined without showing off his reforms in advance, so we visited the music room first, and called in on two of the educational classes then in progress—although the latter seemed to involve little more than elementary lessons in reading and simple arithmetic. Dupin was impatient, and Chapelain had to invoke all his diplomatic talents to persuade Leuret to escort us to the relevant ward in reasonable time.

When we did reach the ward, I must confess that I had something of a shock. Having heard so much about Pinel's reforms and Leuret's continuation of them, I had not expected the sight to be quite so horrific. Leuret was quick to point out how well-lighted the room was, and what facilities had been made for its ventilation, but the fact that the high windows were better than mere slits and that ventilation-shafts had been excavated in the outer wall did not seem to me to have made overmuch impact on the prevailing odors of excrement and putrefaction—which could hardly have been less than powerful, considering the crowded state of the ward. Had there been half as many beds, there might have been some slight hope of maintaining fugitive standards of cleanliness, but there was no way that an army of laundresses could have kept up with the task confronting them.

Leuret hastened to tell us how unfortunate and inconvenient it was that so many individuals on the threshold of death either beat a path to his door or were dumped there. "But what can I do?" He said, mournfully. "Other people may turn them away, but ours is the last resort. We have to take them in and accommodate them as best we can. The other wards are much better than this one, even though they too are overcrowded. Paris is a huge city...."

And you have no Heracles to clean your Augean stables," Dupin said, as sympathetically as he could. "You are doing a heroic job, Dr. Leuret, in impossible circumstances. That is the truest heroism of them all."

I will concede that there was no screaming going on at the moment when we appeared, and relatively little sobbing and whimpering—but that, I suspect, was because our arrival provided a welcome distraction, and provoked a great deal of interest, from the patients and orderlies alike. There was certainly a great deal of agitation. Even though our arrival at the hospital had been unannounced, we had been there long enough for all manner of rumors to go around, and I doubt that there was anyone on the ward who did not know by now that two more respectable gentlemen had come to contemplate the mystery that was Ysolde Leonys. I suspected that the celebrity would not increase her popularity, and would probably lead to an amplification of the prevailing whispers of diabolism.

The women on the ward were, almost without exception, quiet and docile; their agitation was almost entirely confined to hardly-audible inarticulate muttering and ill-suppressed quivering. Whether that was due to the fact that they were heavily dosed with laudanum, the everpresence of patrolling orderlies, or merely the fact that most of them were in such an obvious state of total despair that it was a wonder their hearts could still muster the energy to beat, I could not tell. The great majority were old, although I suspect that some of them looked a great deal older than strict chronology might have implied—but that was presumably an effect of the sorting process by which they had been allocated to the ward rather than a statistical summary of the hospital's population as a whole.

Dupin was not a man to let his emotions show, and he did not react to the initial sight of the ward with any evident expression of horror, but I knew him well, and I could see the tightening of his facial muscles as he controlled himself. I knew that he was affected, perhaps more deeply than I was, by the sheer ugliness and hopelessness of the situation. I could see that Chapelain was nervous about what Dupin might say, and perhaps a little ashamed of the fact that he had so long grown used to such sights himself that they no longer had any measurable effect on him.

All Dupin said, however, was: "Which bed is it?"

Leuret led us to the bed in question. It was no different from any of the others, although it was placed—evidently by design—in a corner, and there seemed to be nothing to distinguish the woman lying on it. The single thin and filthy blanket with which her body was covered did not conceal its emaciation, and the syphilitic sores on her face did not, alas, mark her condition out as significantly worse than that of her neighbors to the one side where she had neighbors—indeed, the woman in the next bed was unconscious, and seemed likely to die at any moment.

Ysolde Leonys' eyes were also closed, and she seemed to be unaware of our presence at first, but I did not get the impression that she was actually asleep. She seemed, rather, to be removing herself mentally from her environment, refusing to admit that she was where she actually was.

Leuret stepped forward first, and tried to attract her attention. He addressed her, with scrupulous politeness, as "Mademoiselle

Leonys."

She did not open her eyes. Then Chapelain stepped forward and spoke, reminding her that he had visited her yesterday, and telling her that he had brought other visitors to see her. That must have piqued her drowsy curiosity. She could not have been expecting visitors, and cannot have had any others, save for visiting alienists.

When she opened her eyes, only by a crack, at first, she looked at Chapelain first. "Merlin," she said, as if the two syllables were explanation enough of his presence. Then her gaze alighted on me. She looked at me in the strangest way, as if weighing me up and trying to place me. Finally, she murmured: "Tom."

As soon as she had named me, she glanced back at Chapelain, and smiled, apparently in gratitude. Leuret was still trying to attract her attention, and was so close as to obstruct her view somewhat, but she paid him no heed at all, trying to look past him.

Dupin had to move sideways in order to let her have a clear sight of him, and was clearly hoping for some sort of reaction when she did—but he could not possibly have expected the nature or intensity of the reaction he got.

Her face changed completely—so completely that it seemed to me to be more than a mere change of expression, although it could not, in logical terms, have been anything more. One often says of people, carelessly, that "their eyes lit up," but it seemed to me that her eyes really did acquire a literal illumination, perhaps caused by a sudden surge of her latent fever. I cannot say that she smiled again, but a new life of some sort suddenly entered into her, and a new consciousness too.

"Tristan!" she said. "They told me you would come, but I hardly dared believe...I thought I would need to die first...or am I dead?"

Dr. Leuret wanted to assure her that she was not dead as yet, but Chapelain took hold of his arm and drew him gently back, bidding him to be silent in some private non-verbal language known to alienists. Chapelain only wanted to give Dupin more room to be seen, but Dupin took advantage of the cleared space actually to kneel down by the bed.

I would not have set my knee upon that miry floor unless literally forced—and I do not think of myself as an unusually fastidious man—but when Dupin is gripped by fascination, mere matters of dirt become irrelevant…and the fact that the woman had addressed him as "Tristan" had very obviously caught his attention.

I knew, without Leuret or Chapelain having to tell me, that the woman was still in the mesmeric trance in which Chaplain had left her, and that she was obviously hallucinating. I guessed that Leuret's first impulse, on observing the fact, was to try to dispel the hallucination and return her to reality—but he had probably tried to do that before, after Chapelain had left, and failed. My sympathies, however, were with Chapelain, and with Dupin. Looking at that dismal wreck of a woman, hovering on the brink of death, I thought it kinder by far to leave her hallucinated until she actually passed away, and to pander to her illusion if the opportunity arose.

Dupin was no mere pander, however; he had questions to ask, and was already prepared to improvise in the manner of his interrogation. "Who told you that I would come?" was the first.

"The angels," she replied. "But I dared not trust them…they have told me so many lies."

"I am here, though," he said, "and you are not yet dead. Did I not promise to come?" That was obviously a guess, but I could see why he had made it.

"Yes," she replied, "but that was so long ago…so long ago… and I thought that I would have to die. Have you really come to take me away from this place? Have you come to take me back to the Underworld?" Her expression clouded then, and she added: "But Oberon might not permit that…he might kill us both…even though I have surely been punished enough."

Dupin had no difficulty avoiding the question as to whether his intention was to take her to some phantom underworld.

"Does it matter where you are?" he asked, probably not quite able to bring himself to say *we*. Even in the interest of a scientific investigation.

"No," she answered. "Not any more. There's no good place to die. But will they let you stay here, Tristan? This is not your world."

"Oddly enough," he said, contributing a smile of sorts, "I seem to have mislaid my world, and cannot quite remember where I left it. Do you find yourself forgetting things, Ysolde?"

She brought her hand out from beneath the paltry cover, and reached out toward him. I would have had extreme difficulty in doing so, but I think, in the circumstances, that I could have taken it. Dupin did so with no apparent hesitation. The handclasp seemed almost to electrify her, or whatever was possessing her. She brightened even further.

"Oh yes," she said. "I forget so much...sometimes, I wish I could forget so much more...but not you, Tristan...never the year in which I was the faithless Queen of the Underworld. I have been punished enough for that, have I not? Oh, you do not know, Tristan...at least, I pray that you do not know...or would pray, if I had a God to pray to...any god but Oberon...."

Chapelain, I could see, was fascinated. Even Leuret seemed a little interested in the content of the hallucination, even though he considered that his vocation—his very purpose in life—was to take arms against such strange afflictions and drag his patients back to reality, kicking and screaming if necessary, and with cruel deluges of cold water if the necessity seemed absolute.

"Oberon has forgiven you now, Ysolde," Dupin told her. "There is to be no further punishment."

"But you," she murmured, her voice becoming fainter in spite of the seeming revivification of her flesh. "What has he done to you...you faded away...I was sure that he had taken you back, to kill you."

"I'm here, am I not?" Dupin said. "Whatever has been done is done, and is over...but for one thing. Do you remember the legend inscribed on your flesh, Ysolde?"

"Oh yes," she said, he voice regarding a little of its force. "My flesh forgot, for a while, but my inner self never did...I never could...but let's not speak of that, Tristan. We have so much more...."

"Indeed we have," said Dupin, "but there are things I need to know. Do you know what the inscription *says*, Ysolde. Can you pronounce it?"

"No one can," she replied. "Except perhaps Oberon...."

It was, I think, a frank denial on her part. She meant what she said. She had no intention of attempting to pronounce anything...but there seemed to be some kind of contest going on between her flesh and her consciousness, which was no mere side-effect of the great pox. She fell silent, but there was something inside her that would not tolerate silence. Her madness was layered; there was something behind or beneath her comforting legendary fantasy that did not want to let her rest easy. Perhaps something within her did not believe that she had, as yet, been punished *enough*.

She was, I think, stricken unconscious *before* her lips moved—but her lips moved, nevertheless.

She was right, though. *Nobody* could have pronounced the mock-syllables that whatever was in her wanted to pronounce. The nonsense was strangely memorable, but it was utter nonsense. Had I not had occasion to hear it several more times in the course of the next few days, I would never have been able to scribble the various representations of it that enable me to reproduce it, very approximately, here and now.

What her lips said, as far as I can estimate it, was: "*Ph'nglui mglw'nat Cthulhu R'laiyeh wgah'ngl fhtaign.*" Each individual letter in that written version, however, needs to be pronounced as a distinct syllable, no matter what the conventions of English orthography might imply as to their pronunciation in combination.

Dupin dropped the sick woman's hand as if he had suddenly realized that he was holding a venomous snake by the tail. I could feel the eyes of half a hundred patients and half a dozen orderlies fixed upon us, as if we were players on a stage, at some crucial point in a melodramatic plot. There was audible muttering now, and more violent convulsions, to which the orderlies were slow to respond.

It did not matter that "Tristan" had dropped "Ysolde's" hand, for she was already oblivious—but not certainly not dead. Her face seemed to be on fire—and I suspected that her whole body might be streaked with scarlet as well.

Dupin stood up and turned to Chapelain. "Will you help me turn her over," he said. "I need to see the inscription on her back."

Leuret had had enough. "I must protest, Monsieur Dupin," he said. "I cannot pretend to know what you are doing, but I really do not think that this is helping my patient in the least. I know that there is a school of thought that advises humoring patients in their hallucinations, and it is a method that I have tried myself in the hope of achieving further insights into their condition, but I have found it wanting as a means of helping patients to recover their sanity. We must not lose sight of our objective in treating the mentally ill, which is to dispel their hallucinations and return them to a safe and secure grasp of reality."

"Forgive me, Dr. Leuret," Dupin replied, smoothly, "if what I am doing seems unorthodox, or even offensive—but I really am trying to act in your patient's interest…and my ultimate objective, as always, is to make sure that reality continues to maintain a safe and secure grasp of *us*."

He should not have added that last remark, in my opinion, but he never could resist the temptation of clever wordplay. The sage of Bicêtre was not yet in a position to accuse him of madness, though, no matter what suspicions he might have formed.

In the meantime, Chapelain had chosen his own side, and for the time being, it was not Leuret's. He removed the blanket covering the stricken woman, and helped Dupin to roll her over, as gently as possible. Then, with as much reverence and decency as could be contrived, in the circumstances—which was not a great deal—he displaced the shift that was her only garment to reveal a square array of characters inscribed on her back.

They seemed very tiny—certainly much smaller than the magnified version on the piece of paper in Dupin's pocket. A casual glance from a distance would not have identified anything other than a pattern of grazes, which might have been made by raking fingernails, were there no so many of them.

Dupin, however, was not content to look at them from a distance. He pored over them intently, and then took the piece of paper out of his pocket in order to determine whether it was an accurate transcription. I could not help leaning over too; nor could Chapelain.

I could see immediately why Chapelain had demurred in the matter of calling the inscription a tattoo, even though I could not imagine any other process by which the forty-nine symbols could have been incorporated into her flesh. They *looked* as if they had been written beneath the surface of her skin in blood—arterial blood, for they were red, not blue—but that was impossible, so the appearance was clearly deceptive.

Dupin obviously wanted to continue his comparison, but he was also aware that the situation was problematic in more ways than one. Abruptly, he put the paper away, got to his feet again and stood aside, in order to allow Chapelain to return the slight shred of decency that the poor woman had left. I was slightly surprised that he seemed to be surrendering so easily to the pressure of convention, but only temporarily.

"Have you ever seen anything like that before, Monsieur Dupin?" Chapelain was quick to ask, as soon as he stood up again.

"Not exactly," Dupin replied, curtly but scrupulously. "We must procure her a cloak, at least—she cannot travel like this."

"Travel?" repeated Chapelain and Leuret, as one—and the only reason that my voice was absent from the chorus was that I could only mouth the echo silently.

"You cannot take her away, Monsieur Dupin," Leuret continued. "I could not possibly allow that. She is my patient.

You have no authority."

"Forgive me, Dr. Leuret," said Dupin, in what was probably intended to be his most soothing tone, "I know that you have done, and are doing, an enormous amount of good here, and you have my every sympathy and support in your heroic endeavors—but you cannot plausibly contend that any patient would be better off in surroundings like this than in a clean room of her own, with the personal attention of a physician of the ability of Dr. Chapelain. You are one man, with a mere handful of assistants and nearly a thousand patients to care for. You only know me by reputation, but Monsieur Groix will vouch for me as well as Dr. Chapelain, and they will both assure you that I am a trustworthy man. Your patient will come to no harm in my custody—no more harm than she is doomed to suffer anyway, given that she is dying—and will certainly be more comfortable. Dr. Chapelain told me last night that she is here voluntarily, and remains a free agent, with no legal constraint obliging her to remain. You heard her, just a few minutes ago, express a clear desire that I should take her away. That is what I intend to do, and I hope and expect that you will raise no objection, because you can clearly see that it is for the best."

While Leuret stood there dumbfounded I looked at Chapelain, and he met my eyes. We both knew that undertakings were being offered on our behalf, and that demands would shortly be made of us, of a frankly excessive nature and urgency, but neither of us said a word. He was the Chevalier Auguste Dupin—when he made firm decisions, it was not for lesser men to contest them.

François Leuret did not want to cast himself as a lesser man, but he was no fool. He could see the inevitable when it was staring him in the eyes, and he was sage enough to capitulate with it. When he finally replied, it was to say: "Where do you intend taking her?"

My heart had already sunk; there was no surprise in the answer, when it came.

"To my friend's house, just south of the Boulevard Saint-Germain, near Saint-Germain-des-Prés," he replied.

Absurdly, the only objection I was able to raise, on the spot, was: "What about the servants?"

"I will send you my concierge, to help install her," he said, as if that were an answer to all possible objections. It probably was. Madame Lacuzon was not a person to tolerate objections, and her cousin—my cook—was as terrified of her as everyone else.

Chapelain said nothing. He, after all, was going to gain from the arrangement too. My house was a good deal closer to his own residence than Bicêtre, and if he were to attend to the patient at all—as he clearly was, now that his curiosity had been thoroughly piqued—it would be infinitely more comfortable and convenient for him to do so in my house than in the filthy ward at the asylum.

That thought might have occurred to Leuret, too. "In all conscience," the sage of Bicêtre said, "I must continue to monitor the patient, and make sure that everything possible is being done for her. She is a free agent, but I am not; I have an obligation."

"You will be welcome to see her whenever you wish, Dr. Leuret," Dupin told him. "Indeed, Dr. Chapelain and I will be very glad of your advice as to how best to make her comfortable during the last days of her life."

Leuret could hardly have failed to notice that there was a tacit challenge in that silky remark, but he must already have deduced that Dupin had no intention of seeking to "cure" Ysolde Leonys of her hallucination—and he must have known, too, that there was little point in attempting to bring a dying madwoman back to reality merely in the hope that she might die sane. I suspected that it was an argument that he had not only broached but exhausted when he had become annoyed with Chapelain the day before.

In the end, all that the asylum director said was: "I cannot in all conscience oppose a move that will make the ward less crowded. I have every confidence in Dr. Chapelain's ability to care for the patient as well as anyone else in Paris. But I do think that you owe me an explanation of your conduct. What is the meaning of the symbols tattooed on Madame Leonys' back, and why are you so interested in them?"

"I do, indeed, owe you an explanation," Dupin conceded, looking round at the host of eyes that were upon him "but it will, of necessity, be a long one. Might I suggest that you call at my friend's house his evening—or some other evening, if tonight is inconvenient—in order that we can discuss the matter at our leisure?"

His presumption did not stop there; he left me to give Leuret my address, arrange a time for his visit that evening and swear him to the utmost secrecy with regard to what had just happened, while he and Chapelain returned their attention to unconscious woman.

Having procured a batter blanket, for want of a good cloak, they had the ward orderlies place her on a stretcher and take her out to the fiacre, which was waiting for us at the gate.

"A remarkable man, Monsieur Dupin," Leuret observed, looking at me with a hint of sympathy, as I left the ward behind the, taking a deep breath of the slightly-less fetid air in the corridor as soon as the door was closed.

"Very," I agreed.

"I feel it only fair to warn you," he said, "that in my opinion, what you are doing is dangerous."

"Why?" I asked. "The woman is dying. If Chapelain can ease her final days, that is all to the good—and whether or not my friend can assuage his raging thirst for enlightenment in regard to the mystery she presents, his investigation can do her no harm."

"I did not mean that it is dangerous for *her*," he said. "I meant that it is dangerous for *you*—and I shall be glad to explain why when I visit your home tonight, for I have no time at present."

And with that—having taking what slight revenge he could for Dupin's cavalier treatment of him—he stalked away in the direction of his office.

CHAPTER FOUR
DUPIN PLAYS TRISTAN

YSOLDE LEONYS DID not recover consciousness before we had carried her into my house and installed her in what had once been Dupin's own bedroom, in the days when he had lived with me in my rented house. He was as good as his word; we had picked up his concierge, Madame Lacuzon, on the way, and she had climbed into the cab—even though there was no room for her on the cushions—without a flicker of protest at the fact that she might be thought derelict in her own duties

I had known Dupin so long that I was almost accustomed to the gorgon's intimidating presence, and was nowadays able to look in her direction if not actually to meet her eyes. I was astonished to notice, from the corner of my eye, that when Dupin told her the woman's name, her expression shifted slightly, almost as if she had recognized the name—but I could not imagine that Dupin had discussed any matter with his concierge that might have led to his mentioning it before.

I had to give the coachman a larger tip than usual to make up for the fact that, in spite of the clean blanket, the madwoman's temporary presence in his vehicle had left it considerably more malodorous than usual. I have to admit, though, that Madame Lacuzon's presence as Dupin's auxiliary set aside any possibility that my servants might rebel in deed, word or expression against what was asked of them, and the gorgon pitched in with a will when she and her cousin were obliged to tackle the awkward task of cleaning the woman up sufficiently to be accommodated in clean sheets.

Dupin stayed to supervise the eventual installation—and perhaps to take a further peek at the symbols in her flesh. I saw no such necessity, having already done my part, and took Chapelain into the smoking-room for a stiff brandy.

"Well," I said to him, "I must say that this is *most* unexpected. Have you the slightest idea what Dupin is up to?"

"Not the slightest," Chapelain confirmed, with a sigh, "but it is fascinating, is it not? From what I have been able to observe over the last year or two, Monsieur Dupin is a veritable magnet for strange occurrences—and I must say that you do not seem at all surprised by this bizarre sequence of events."

"I think I'm immune to astonishment now, where Monsieur Dupin is concerned," I told him. "You're right—fate does seem to have singled him out as a target for strange events. Fate...or the angels. She *is* mad, isn't she?"

"Utterly," Chapelain confirmed. "I must confess, though, to some anxiety regarding this latest development. I had hoped that I had entranced her sufficiently to allow her to remain lost in her dream of Oberon, Merlin, Tristan and the like—where she seems reasonably content, in spite of her anxieties about being punished. If she sinks of her own accord into some further and more nightmarish dream-arena, however, I might have difficulty returning her to any kind of illusory stability. I have no idea what she was trying to say when that fit came upon her, but it sounded truly horrible. Monsieur Dupin seemed to recognize it, though, if not to understand it. Have you heard anything like it before?"

"No," I said. "If I had to guess, I'd say that it resembles or recalls something he's reading one of his so-called forbidden books. Not the *Harmonies de l'enfer*, though—I never heard anything less harmonic."

"Nor I," said Chapelain. "That story of the pirate treasure seemed intriguing, mind—although the connection between the pirate Levasseur and Ysolde's cryptogram still seems extremely tenuous to me. This Breisz fellow might have expressed an

interest in the name Leonys for some reason entirely uncon-
nected with his interest in the Levasseur cryptogram."

"I can see why Dupin was struck by the coincidence, though,"
I observed. "You know how inquisitive he is when his attention
is caught by something like that. He cannot rest until he finds a
satisfactory explanation—or becomes satisfied that the coincidence is of no significance at all."

"True," Chapelain admitted. "He will want me to entrance
her again, I presume, as soon as she wakes—or, given that she
will probably still be entranced, to assist him to interrogate her."

"You may be certain of it," I said. "I wish I could tell you what
he hopes to gain from further intelligence, but I cannot. If the
marks on her back were not tattooed, as you seem to believe, do
you have any idea how they might have been inscribed there?"

"I can only think that it is some strange kind of scar tissue,"
he said "The only other hypothesis that springs to mind seems
too ridiculous."

"The Devil's mark?" I queried.

"Not literally—but I have attended patients, in Bicêtre and
elsewhere, who have manifested bloody symbols of a different
sort, apparently psychosomatically."

"You mean stigmata?" I asked.

"The cases I have seen involved the classic stigmata," he
confirmed.

"But this is far more intricate than vague imprints of Christ's
nails, crown of thorns and spear-wound," I said, although I was
slightly relieved that he had had the same thought as myself,
thus making to seem somewhat less ridiculous than it had while
still unvoiced. "And she surely cannot be manifesting them by
means of some perverted wish-fulfilment."

"Agreed," he said, "but I have read reports in the mesmeric
literature of stigmata-like imprints emerging by an effort of
unconscious will, in response to suggestions planted by a magne-
tizer. Sometimes, if the reports are believable, sketches of faces
have emerged, or even words in Latin, French or German."

"But *forty-nine* tiny symbols, each one intricately designed?"

I queried. "That's surely impossible, for any mesmerist."

He made no comment on my judgment of possibility. "If what the woman's *other voice* said was a diabolical equivalent of speaking in tongues," he observed, soberly, "I have no wish to meet the unholy spirit that inspired it. That one is certainly no paraclete."

The term *paraclete*, I knew, likened the holy spirit to a comforter. "Agreed," I said, in my turn.

He chewed his lip, as if screwing up his courage. "In August," he said, "when Dupin asked me to look after you, it really was a case of heatstroke-induced delirium, was it not? You were not *really* possessed by some vampiric demon, as Saint-German seemed to believe?"

"I wish I could be sure," I told him, not dishonestly.

He turned his head to look at the wall-clock, which was only a few minutes short of chiming four. "I have to go now," he said, abruptly. "Apologize to Dupin for me, and tell him that I'll return as soon as I can—but I have other obligations. I'm willing to entrance the woman for him when I can, and I'll certainly return this evening, when Leuret comes—if only to hear Dupin's explanation of his conduct—but for now...."

"I understand, Doctor," I assured him, and fetched his coat, hat and stick, assuming that Bihan was probably busy.

"It won't have done any good, you know," he said, as we parted, "to swear Leuret to secrecy. He won't say a word, of course—but the orderlies on the ward saw and heard everything. Their gossip will have been repeated all over Paris by this time tomorrow...and it's bound to reach the ears of exactly the people you wouldn't want to hear it."

"I can handle Saint-Germain, if he comes snooping," I assured him.

"I have a suspicion that you might have more than the mystics and would-be magicians of the Harmonic Philosophical Society to deal with this time," was his parting shot.

I had the same suspicion, but I put a brave face on as I bid him *au revoir*.

When I returned to the smoking-room, Dupin was there—without the gorgon, thankfully. I explained Chapelain's absence. He frowned, but made no complaint.

"I'm truly sorry about this imposition, my friend," he said, "but it's a matter of dire necessity."

"So I assumed," I said. "Would you care to tell me why?"

"Of course—but can it possibly wait until this evening, when Leuret comes? That will save me unnecessary repetition—and in any case, I want to go up and sit with her in case she wakes up. If she does, before Chapelain returns, I shall try to interrogate her myself...always provided that she wakes into her dream of the magical underworld rather than...well, rather than whatever else is lurking in the depths of her unconscious mind. I fear that the lady has been sorely abused, perhaps long before she became a whore. There's mention of such things in von Junzt's *Unaussprechlichen Kulten*, but so much of that text is based on traveler's tales that I never believed them. I must find out, if I can, before she dies...and I must take what advantage I can of the fact that she has appointed me her Tristan."

"You intend to play this farce to the end, then, and capitalize on the fact that the poor woman has mistaken you for someone else, in the hope that she might let you in on her secrets?"

"She has not mistaken me for someone else," Dupin pointed out. "Her Tristan of Léonais is a figment of her dream; she has merely invited me to take a part in her fantasy."

That triggered a belated realization. "*That*'s why your concierge seemed to recognize the name Leonys," I said. "Like Chapelain, she took it for an anglicized pronunciation of Léonais—and she's a Breton, like her cousin."

"English folklore usually refers to the mythical equivalent of Léonais as Lyonesse," he said, ever the pedant, "and insists on confusing the forest of that name—which gave its name to the region—with the drowned city of Ys. But the confusion is probably Breton in origin. In parts of Britanny, the forest is more often called Broceliande."

Quibbles of that sort were of no interest to me.

"Do you believe that the inscription on the woman's back really is the Key of Solomon?" I asked him, point-blank.

"No," he said. "It's far worse than that, alas. It's the Cthulhu encryption. Her pronunciation of it was missing the final set of symbols, as Bougainville's version and every other printed version is, but it did not have the abbreviated form of R'laiyeh and one or two of the other syllables differed from the form in which Bougainville recorded them. But this is Paris, not the Pacific wilderness, and Chapelain thinks that the woman was born in India to an English family. How did the inscription get into her flesh, and why was it inscribed there? I need to find out, if I can. Whether she can tell me, or even give me a clue, I don't know—but I have to try. I must go upstairs now—you're welcome to come with me, of course."

He evidently wanted me to go with him. "Then I will," I said, assuming that we could continue the conversation upstairs.

He nodded, as if to thank me. Before we left the room, however, he said: "I've warned Monsieur and Madame Bihan already, but I ought to warn you too—there might be danger, if Leuret's orderlies are slack-mouthed, and anyone takes them seriously. You might want to put a revolver in your pocket...and be careful, if your reflexes get the better of you and you open the door yourself when someone rings.

"Is Madame Lacuzon still here?" I asked.

"For a little while longer, if you don't mind," Dupin said.

"I don't mind, if there's danger. If the Devil himself comes to call, he'll surely not want to argue with *her*."

Dupin smiled wryly. "She looks fearsome, but she has a heart of gold," he said, not very convincingly.

"I expect it has to be gold," I said. "The acid in her veins would surely dissolve any vulgar metal."

As things turned out, though, we had no opportunity for further conversation. As soon as we opened the door to Dupin's old room, Ysolde Leonys opened her eyes.

She looked swiftly around, but did not seem to be in the least astonished to discover that she was not where she had been when she fell unconscious. She lifted the bedclothes briefly to look down at her own body, which was now respectably clad in one of Madame Bihan's capacious nightshirts.

"You kept your promise, Tristan," she said, when she looked back at Dupin. "The angels said you would, but I dared not believe them." She looked at me then, as if wishing that I was not there, so that she might talk to her imagined lover in private.

I thought perhaps I ought to go, in order to allow Dupin to continue with his inquiry under optimum conditions, but he gestured to me to be still.

"I came with a friend," he said. "I could not have found you otherwise. Do you not recognize him?"

In reality, she could not and did not recognize me—but she was far from reality jut now, and fantasy is flexible in so many ways.

"Is it really you, Tom?" she said, after a moment's hesitation. "Tom Linn, the Rhymer?"

"Of course it is," said Dupin, although I knew that he must be smiling inwardly at the notion that I might be a rhymer. As a young man, I had always relied on Poe to make up for my deficiencies in that arena. I would rather have been Huon of Bordeaux, but I suppose it added an extra item of information to our cabinet of curious facts to know that she was familiar with Scottish ballads as well as Breton folklore and romance.

The identification seemed to add another drop to her cup of joy. I only hoped that she was not going to ask me to play or sing. My cello-playing days were behind me forever.

"That was a terrible place you found me in," she said. "But you came regardless, like Orpheus in search of Eurydice— except that this story has a happier ending, or at least a merciful delay. Will Merlin return too? His spells are not as powerful as they once were, but the herbs are soothing."

In the versions of the popular legends with which I was familiar, Merlin had been imprisoned in a tree, Tristan had died and Thomas the Rhymer had returned to his own world only to find that so much time had lapsed during his brief sojourn in fairyland that everyone he had known before was dead. I wasn't entirely sure that her self-induced hallucination was as pleasant as it seemed, even if one set aside the suggestion that something more sinister was concealed beneath it. *Where are you now that we need you, King Arthur?* I wondered. *I wish you were here, instead of this mysterious Oberon—who sounds to me more like Huon's enigmatic accursed dwarf than Shakespeare's counterpart to lovely Titania.*

I had to collect myself, and tell myself not to be silly—but the world of legend is so seductive of thought. How could it be otherwise, since that was the purpose for which it was designed?

Ysolde Leonys' face clouded over suddenly, and she said: "But I do not deserve your succor, Tristan, for I have been wicked and faithless. My punishment has been just."

"No such punishment as yours is just," Dupin assured her—honestly enough, I felt sure. "We must not waste what time we have in dwelling on such thoughts. Let us summon happier memories. Let us talk about your childhood. You were born in India, were you not?"

"My happiest times," she said, "were in the Underworld—with you, Tristan. Ought we not to talk of those?"

"Later," he said, a trifle abruptly—and could not being himself to soften the word with any endearment. "You were happy in India, were you not?"

"Sometimes," she said. "I went to Poona once, in the hills, when my father was there—but I was never happy in Callaba, or in Karla. Karla was a dark place...darker than *our* Underworld, my love."

I had just enough knowledge of India to know that Karla was a cave-system in which a subterranean temple had been constructed, perhaps to some Hindu god or the Buddha."

"What was your surname, Ysolde, before it was changed to Leonys?" Dupin asked.

She seemed uncomfortable, and I wondered whether Dupin was in danger of doing, without wanting to, exactly what Leuret had tried and failed to do: to bring her back to painful reality.

She offered no answer to the question.

"Have you ever heard of Olivier Levasseur, Ysolde?" Dupin asked.

"He was a pirate." She knew more than I did, then—but it was a titbit of information that anyone might have known.

"Have you ever heard of a pirate named John Taylor," Dupin persisted.

Again she looked deeply uncomfortable, and I was sure that she would not answer. Abruptly, however, she said: "Jack Taylor was a *bad man.*"

"Was your father a descendant of John Taylor the pirate?" Dupin asked, doggedly.

She seemed puzzled by that question. "Jack Taylor was a *bad man,*" she repeated—as if it were a phrase that she had heard someone else say, and which had stuck in her mind for some reason.

"Is your father still in India?" Dupin continued.

"He sailed for the South Seas…salt in his blood…darkness in his heart…to raise the Devil…for protection…."

Her voice was fading; I was sure that she was about to fall unconscious again. So was Dupin, for he consented to change the subject.

"Our Underworld was brighter than Karla," he said, tempting a return to kinder fantasy.

"Oh yes," she said, smiling—hideously, alas, for the syphilitic sores about her mouth quite spoiled the normal effect. "I was queen there, for a year and a day, and radiant. Even the angels loved me. I should not have run away…but what would have happened to me had I stayed, when the year and a day was over? What would have become of me?"

I had always thought of Underworlds as gloomy places, but I was not about to protest against her judgment. It was her hallucination, after all.

"Remind me," Dupin said, curiously, "how it was that Oberon came to choose you for his bride."

"Oberon did not choose," she said, in a slightly reproachful one. "Oberon never had a *choice*. Marriages are made in Heaven." She said no more, and it was probably my own imagination, acing alone, but I could not help silently adding: ...*or Hell.*

"Of course," Dupin was quick to agree. "But I chose you, did I not?"

"Did you really?" she answered. "I never knew that. Were some of us free, then? Were we not all driven? But would that not make it *our* fault that things went so badly awry? We have been punished for it, after all...did you say that you had been punished too, my love?"

I couldn't quite remember whether he had or hadn't, but I didn't suppose that it mattered overmuch. Dream logic was firmly in charge here.

"We have been unlucky, Ysolde," Dupin said. "Direly unlucky. Do you know where the manuscripts are?"

"Manuscripts?" she queried, her voice alarmed this time, becoming shrill. "What manuscripts?"

I thought for a moment that he might give her a long lecture on John Dee's importance as a bibliophile and educator of navigators, but he was too impatient for that.

"The pirate's manuscripts," he said. "The manuscripts that your ancestor took from *Our Lady of the Cape.*"

That was probably more reality than she could stand, at present.

"Jack Taylor was a *bad man*," she whispered—and fell asleep.

Dupin was furious. I thought for a moment that he was about to shake her, to make her wake up, but he was only fluttering his hands because he was furious at himself, for mishandling the interrogation. "What a fool I am!" he muttered. "Too clever to play the simpleton, too much the logician to feign affection! It's not as if I had never...." He stopped suddenly and looked at me. "Well," he said, resignedly, "we have one piece of valuable information."

"That Jack Taylor was a *bad man*?" I suggested. "But which one? Her father, or the pirate?"

"One of them, at least," he said, pensively, "seems to have sailed for the South Seas…perhaps to raise the Devil…or perhaps as an explorer."

The last conjecture, I supposed, was his inference, for I had heard nothing in what the woman had said to support it. "An explorer?" I queried. "Looking for what?"

"R'laiyeh," was his terse reply.

"Did he find it, do you think?"

"I hope not," he retorted. "My God, I hope not." Then he stood up. "Food," he said, succinctly. "I need food—and strong coffee."

"I shall have to send the Bihans out in search of supplies," I said. "After all, the sage of Bicêtre is coming to dinner tonight, and we must put on a show. Do you have any conception, Dupin, of how drastically you have upset the pattern of my life?"

He pulled a face—which was quite uncharacteristic of him. "Yes, I have," he said, "and I'm truly sorry."

"But it was a matter of dire necessity," I added, on his behalf.

"And is," he said. "I wish I knew how dire the necessity might become."

"We have faced Nyarlathotep the Crawling Chaos and the Dwellers of the Threshold," I reminded him, "not to mention the Egregore of Parthenope. Will this be very much worse?"

"I don't know," he replied. "I have no idea how Ysolde came to have the Cthulhu encryption engraved into her very flesh, or for what purpose—and I have no idea who or what might come to search for her, once the word spreads that it is manifest. No one in that ward but me could possibly have recognized what she said, of course—but there's enough detail in the story to attract unwelcome attention and curiosity. I only hope that Père France's obsessive bibliotaph is in Brittany just now, not in Paris. Once he scents her name…."

"If it's scent that you're worried about," I observed, "perhaps we should have left her where she was. The keenest bloodhound in the world could not have detected her there."

"I was speaking metaphorically," the notorious pedant said.

"I had already inferred that," I told him. "Let's go downstairs and make our preparations shall we? There's fresh bread in the larder, so we can have a bite to eat as well."

"Tom Linn," he said, "your every word is music."

"My memory's a little sketchy," I said, "but didn't Thomas the Rhymer's story end tragically—just like Tristan's?"

"Folklore is full of sticky ends," he told me. "And yet, somehow, fairyland always seems so pleasant and peaceful in modern dreams and hallucinations. Perhaps Monsieur Leuret can explain the psychology of that to us, after dinner tonight."

"Perhaps," I agreed.

CHAPTER FIVE
A PHILOSOPHICAL
DISAGREEMENT

LEURET ARRIVED VERY punctually at seven o'clock, scrupulously well-dressed and very self-composed. I got the impression that he was glad to be away from Bicêtre, and did not often have the opportunity. I could understand why, even though he was a gentleman through and through, and I fully expected him to by an amiable dinner-companion. The kinds of people who plan dinner-parties as a matter of routine would probably think twice about inviting the director of a lunatic asylum as a guest—especially a reformist who might wax lyrical about the humane treatment of the insane, or the danger posed to the cause of progress by Romantic poets and story-tellers.

Chapelain was late, and did not arrive until near quarter past, but that did not delay the serving of the soup unduly. Madame Lacuzon was still in the house, "helping out," but she had been appointed to sit with the sleeping Ysolde Leonys, leaving the preparation of the meal and the actual serving to the Bihans— who did a very creditable job, in my opinion, given that it was not a kind of service to which they were accustomed. The soup was first-rate, and the *magret de canard* served as the centrepiece of the entrée was not far short of excellent. I blessed the circumstances that had led me to hire servants, for I dread to think what the meal might have amounted to had I still been living alone.

As convention required, the talk prior to the serving of the coffee—for which we would retire to the smoking-room—was conspicuously general, light and polite. That was in spite of the impatience of all concerned, and I have to admit that it carried a certain underlying edge by virtue of a measurable tension between Leuret and Chapelain, on the one hand, and Leuret and Dupin, on the other. The first two obviously respected one another, and would probably have been unhesitating in naming one another as good friends, but the philosophical differences between them had been further sharpened by the day's extraordinary events, while the second two did not, as yet, know quite what to make of one another.

As the soirée's host, I suppose I might and ought to have deflected the conversation away from any matters likely to prove controversial, but given that Leuret was an exceedingly determined psychologist, Chapelain an exceedingly devoted mesmerist physician and that Auguste Dupin was exceedingly eager to involve himself in their differences of opinion, it would have needed a conversationalist far more talented than myself to deviate them in the slightest.

As I have said before, the mid-1840s was a time of rivalries, when intellectual battle-lines were being drawn and forces readying themselves for conflict. Bellicosity of every kind was in the Parisian air just then, even though it was to be more than a year before actual barricades went up in the streets and political Revolution reared its hoary head yet again, condemning Louis-Philippe's *juste milieu* to the dustbin of history.

In such times as that, essentially petty disputes can sometimes become exaggerated, to such an extent that when one looks back at them ten for twelve years later—as I am doing now—it is not easy to see what all the fuss was about. Fundamentally, Leuret and Chapelain were on the same side, allies in the same long war of attrition, but they could not quite see eye to eye in matters of tactics and strategy. They were not supposed to discuss their patients in front of laymen—even expert laymen like Dupin—but there was a loophole in that particular barricade when the patients in question had public reputations and could be discussed in their public roles. Leuret had to know that Honoré de Balzac was Chapelain's patient, and that Chapelain had treated other notable writers in the past, just as Chapelain knew full well that Leuret had looked after Victor Hugo's brother when he was at Charenton, and must have met the great man on numerous occasions—but that did not prevent them from discussing the great men's published works, nor from incorporating a certain subtext into their discussion.

"I am aware of the prevailing opinion," Leuret said, "that *Notre-Dame de Paris* and *La Peau de Chagrin* are literary masterpieces, and I do not dissent from it, in terms of pure artistry. I will even concede that their employment of hallucination as a theme is full of interest from the viewpoint of psychological science—but that is because they are, in a sense, pathological, and hence dangerous. They do not merely use hallucination as a theme or a device; they are, in themselves, hallucinatory, and thus unhealthy, for their readers as well as their writers."

"There is a sense in which all novels are hallucinatory," Chapelain replied, "even the stubbornly naturalistic novels that Monsieur Balzac began to write when he had laid his Swedenborgian fascinations to rest. But I dispute that literary fantasies, even if they are blatantly and unrepentantly fantastic, are unhealthy. Quite the opposite, in fact; I believe that the two works you cite are more conducive to mental health than injurious to it, not because of their careful moralizing component, but because of the way they engage with and exercise the reader's emotions. The ability to identify with others, to stand imaginatively in their shoes and empathize with their standpoint and feelings, is the key to self-understanding as well as social understanding, and novels help us to do that, not merely by providing a training in the art but by offering us hypothetical identifications that the narrow routines of contemporary social life cannot offer."

"I agree that all novels are essentially hallucinatory," Leuret said, "even those that strive for the utmost naturalism—but their seductiveness is, or at least can be, a dangerous trap. To encourage people to empathize with unreal individuals, even when those individuals are not fanciful or insane, is to encourage a dangerous kind of fantasy. And you must admit, I think, that very many of the characters in novels, however naturalistic they are supposed to be, would be reckoned insane by any competent physician. Do you really believe that it is good for readers to be encouraged to stand in the shoes of madmen and madwomen, as Monsieur Balzac and Monsieur Hugo routinely invite them to do? My own view is that such identification is essentially perilous."

Dupin intervened at this point—but not to deflect the conversation on to safer ground or pour oil on troubled waters. "Do you agree, Dr. Leuret," he asked, "with the common opinion that genius and madness are closely allied?"

"Very much so," Leuret replied, as Dupin must have known that he would, having read the *Fragmens*. "Indeed, I must confess that I agree wholeheartedly with my colleague Dr. Lélut, who considers that genius is but a species of madness, and that many men we consider great, from Socrates onwards, owe their reputations to their hallucinations."

"Which proves, does it not," Chapelain put in, "that hallucinations can be virtuous as well as dangerous—that they have played a key role in human intellectual progress."

"That is to simplify the argument unreasonably," Leuret countered. "The reality is that a man can be capable of solid reasoning as well as hallucination. Consider Isaac Newton, for instance—a man who was very obviously mad, but also a fine logician and mathematician. In the end, his madness got the better of him completely, and he spent the later years of his life trying to indentify and solve ciphers that he believed to be encrypted in the text of Bible, but in his early days, while he was still struggling for sanity, he produced arguments from evidence and mathematical proofs whose objective competence is indubitable. Think what Newton might have achieved, Dr. Chapelain, if only he could have received effective treatment for the madness that ultimately claimed him!"

"You consider logic and mathematics the antithesis of hallucination, then, Dr. Leuret?" Dupin asked.

"Absolutely," said Leuret. "They are provable, and indubitable; they provide us with our firmest grip on the substance of reality. But they are powerful to the exact extent that they are applied to secure, reliable and conscientious observation of the world as it is: the orbits of planets, the behaviour of falling objects, the deflections of rays of light by prisms and lenses. When logic is earnestly applied to false premises—figments of the imagination—the process leads, inexorably, from fancy to further fancy, elaborating extraordinary patterns of delusion that can confuse and ultimately swamp an entire mind, dragging it down into the depths of unalloyed insanity. That is the kind of tragedy that I try, every day, to prevent—but as you saw today, I am fighting against a veritable tide, whose sheer mass of numbers makes even tiny victories inordinately difficult to achieve."

"But if Newton and Socrates were mad," Chapelain interjected, "And owed their genius and greatness in part to their madness, does that not prove that madness can, if only occasionally, be virtuous?"

"I can only repeat what I said before," Leuret retorted. "Imagine what they might have achieved had their sanity been unalloyed with hallucination! If only they could have been cured...."

He seemed enthused by the idea that he might one day have a Socrates or a Newton in his care, to whose flights of fancy he might put a stop. But was not that, in itself, a fantasy, dangerous by his own definition to the balance of his mind?

"You think, therefore, that it was wrong of me to pander to Mademoiselle Leurys' seeming delusions this afternoon?" Dupin said, somewhat careless of convention, as ever.

Leuret did not seem upset by Dupin's originality; he was something of a Revolutionary himself. "I fear, Monsieur Dupin," he said, sententiously, "that I do—I was disappointed in you, I must confess, although I suppose I might have anticipated it, since I had taken Dr. Chapelain to task the day before, for doing exactly the same thing, and he brought you to Bicêtre. I know that the lady is dying, and that it really does not matter in the great scheme of things whether she dies sane or deluded, but there is a principle at stake, and I fear that I can sometimes be overzealous in defending it. I hope you will pardon me for saying so, but I do not think that you are doing the lady any good by bringing her here, even if she will be more comfortable than she could ever be on the ward, if you intend to encourage her fantasies...and I certainly do not think that you are doing yourselves any good."

"You have no need to apologize, Dr. Leuret," Dupin assured him, "for I can agree with you wholeheartedly that it would be better by far if she were be to die sane—but I fear that we do not have that choice. Perhaps the world would be a better place if there were no hallucination in it, and we were all able to be the kind of scientists that Monsieur Comte would like us to be, using mathematics and scrupulous logic to deal with reliable facts gleaned from careful observation—but the fact is that we do not live in such a world, and cannot be people of that kind, no matter how hard we try. We have no choice but to deal with hallucination, and must try to do so wisely. For that reason, I do agree with what Dr. Chapelain says—that the genius of men like Balzac and Hugo is an invaluable resource for men like us."

I did not feel able, even within the scope of my duties as host, to rein in Leuret or Chapelain, but I did think it my duty to exercise some diplomatic restraint over my friend, so I hastened to put in: "But Monsieur Balzac is more than a little mad, is he not? I've only seen Hugo at a distance, but if rumor can be credited, and the evidence of *Notre-Dame de Paris* can be trusted, there more than a little madness in his genius too."

"Dr. Leuret agrees with Dr. Lélut that *all* poets are mad," Chapelain put in, a trifle mischievously. "He thinks the same of all mesmerists, too. Indeed, were he to examine his conscience thoroughly, I think he might be forced to the judgment that there is not a single sane man in all Paris—including himself."

"That is not true, Dr. Chapelain," Leuret replied, in a thoroughly dignified manner, "although I will concede that the vast majority of the sane are those who do not trouble themselves overmuch with the intellectual and moral conundrums that tax men like ourselves—and I will also confess that I sometimes thank God that I am not a genius."

"I'm no genius myself," Chapelain replied, in a more conciliatory tone, "but I will confess that I have difficulty thanking God for it."

All three of us looked at Dupin then, although I doubt that any of us was looking for a confession of lack of genius. "Oh," he said, blithely, "I have no hope of denying, in company like this, that I am mad. Were I to make a claim of sanity, the explanation I promised Dr. Leuret would surely convince him otherwise, and probably Chapelain too. My friend, of course, already knows full well that I am mad."

I shook my head, more in sorrow than anger. "I must confess," I said, "that I cannot see the harm in reading fantastic novels, and even less in listening to nursery tales of magic and chivalry. Such pastimes are delightful, in spite of all the violence and ugliness to which such tales repeatedly play host. Even the insane can surely take as much solace from fairy tales as from dance or music, and I cannot believe that they pose any danger at all to the sane. Hallucinations are not contagious, in the way that measles and smallpox are."

"But they *are* contagious," Leuret insisted. "Not merely in the wards of Bicêtre, but in the drawing-rooms of Paris—they spread like wildfire. You might think that you are safe from their contagion if you refuse belief, insisting that they are *only stories*—but they get into your head, and once there, they alter our thoughts and feelings, for the worse rather than the better. They may seem harmless, but their corruption is all the more insidious in consequence."

No one call him mad for saying that, although I cannot vouch for anyone's private thoughts.

"Dr. Leuret is right, of course," Dupin said. "Legends are contagious, for they are designed to be. And he is right too, to suggest that we underestimate the extent to which they influence our thinking, even when we withhold our belief. When Isaac Newton became convinced that there were cryptograms in Biblical legend, however, and that the whole world is one vast cryptogram, in which all the secrets of Creation lie hidden, he was not entirely wrong. Legend is a species of encryption… although I really ought to explain what I mean by encryption…."

"Indeed you ought," my friend, "I said, for you have promised to do exactly that, in order to explain to us exactly what the Cthulhu encryption is, and why it might be important that it is engraved in Mademoiselle Leonys' flesh…if, indeed, it is. But it is time now for us to move from the dining-room to the smoking-room, into a very different atmosphere."

There were nods all round; all the three of them were enthusiastic to develop the discussion in a more concrete fashion

Even as we stood up from the table, however, the doorbell rang.

Reflexively, I made as if to go and answer it, but Dupin actually put out a hand to stop me, and his grip on my arm was firmer than mere politeness would have required. I heard him mutter: "So soon!" too quietly for the other guests to have heard.

Somewhat to my surprise, as we all paused expectantly, I heard footsteps coming down the stairs; it was Madame Lacuzon, not either of the Bihans, who was going to answer the bell.

I was not sorry about that; as I had told Dupin, I was sure that the Devil himself would not get past that fearsome woman, if she were able to look him in the face.

We all paused, as if petrified, listening for the sound of voices. We heard them, but the front door was too far away for us to make out exactly what was being said, or to have any chance of recognizing the voice of whoever was arguing with Madame Lacuzon.

In the end, I think we all emitted a sigh of restrained relief when, after a long and seemingly pregnant silence, the door closed again. A few second later, Madame Lacuzon appeared in the doorway, bowed politely to the assembled company, and then came to me to hand me a folded piece of paper. Then, without saying a word, she withdrew and went back upstairs to resume her vigil.

I unfolded the note and read it.

> *Dupin's dragon will not let me in*, it read. *It is absolutely imperative that I speak to you, whether Dupin forbids it or not. I will wait in one of the chapels in Saint-Sulpice, all night if necessary. Come when you can. It is a matter of life and death—yours, mine and Dupin's. In this, we are on the same side. Do not fail me.*
>
> *Saint-Germain*

Dupin was looking at me curiously, but I did not hand him the note. I knew well enough what his reaction would be to any approach from Saint-Germain, and I strongly suspected that he might indeed forbid me to go to meet him—but I wanted to make up my own mind about that, and I had never been convinced that the President of the Harmonic Philosophical Society was my enemy, even if he was something of a charlatan and a crook. For that reason, I folded the note again and put it in my pocket, muttering: "Nothing urgent—it can wait until later."

CHAPTER SIX
ENCRYPTION

"You will forgive me, I hope," Dupin said, "if my explanation seems rambling, and a trifle disparate, at least to begin with, but this is a complicated matter." He gathered himself then, holding his pipe just so and sucking on the stem. Then he blew out a cloud of smoke, as if to symbolize the expulsion of thought and fancy that he was about to undertake,

I had gone to open the window slightly, in the hope of clearing the air by some small but substantial margin—but then I spoiled the effect by poking the fire and throwing on another log, which crackled and hissed as its sap seethed and its bark went up in flames.

"When Dr. Chapelain first showed me the cryptogram yesterday," Dupin continued, "my initial reaction was to dismiss it as a matter of no significance, having seen many such scribbles before. I was disinclined to believe that it was a genuine cryptogram, even in the trivial sense that construes encryption as a process of converting information from a readily comprehensible format to an incomprehensible one, by means of a substitution cipher—a process that can as easily be applied to a laundry list as to a message from a political spy or directions to a hidden treasure. Such mundane uses have been common since the days when Athens and Sparta employed spies to report on one another's political intentions by means of scytales, and became rife in such periods of turmoil as the Latin decadence, when early Christians used symbolic and numerological codes

to communicate information that might have facilitated persecution if understood by their enemies.

"Before that, however, the Pythagoreans construed the entire
world as a vast cryptogram in need of deciphering, and they
were the ones who devised the ancestral term whose double
meaning has been carried forward ever since by the word in
question. The literal meaning of encryption is, of course, to
put in a crypt, to *entomb*. The Pythagoreans believed that the
great cryptogram of nature did, indeed, contain much that had
been deliberately buried and concealed. Exactly why this had
been done they were not certain, but they were in no doubt
that various encryptions had been carried out in the immemo-
rial past, and naturally attributed the work to the gods. Most
encryptions, they assumed, had been done for virtuous reasons,
in order to prepare the world for the advent of humankind. The
legend inevitably arose, as a corollary of this assumption, that
a particular individual had taken on the role of sweeping the
world clear of forces that would have been inimical to humans,
entombing them all by means of magic formulae of encryption.
That legend, transfigured within new religious contexts, became
the myth of Solomon imprisoning the demons and setting his
seal upon their prisons—a seal which might be reversed by the
right incantatory key."

"A key whose use implied the ability to make a pact with the
demon thus released?" Leuret queried.

"Some Christian conjurors seem to have believed that,"
Dupin agreed, nodding his head, "although many legends of
that sort warn against potential treachery. Arabic folklore, too,
is profoundly uncertain about the controllability of liberated
djinn, and their likely generosity—but I doubt any encrypted
entities of that sort have ever been properly liberated...."

"As opposed to *improperly* liberated?" I could not resist
putting in—but that only elicited a frown from the pedant.

"There may well be degrees of liberation," he said. "Physical
liberation into the world of matter is one thing; liberation in the
realm of dreams, hallucination and madness might be possible

without that. Indeed, if there are figurative windows in the metaphorical cells where the entities are encrypted, that is the realm on which they look out—and if the entities in the metaphorical tombs can still walk the earth in any measure at all, it is as ghosts and phantoms that they do so, haunting the minds of their privileged seers."

"You are speaking poetically, of course," Leuret observed. Coming from a man whose opinion of poets was as low as his, it was almost a sneer, although his voice was level and its tone polite.

"Of course," Dupin admitted, freely enough. "What other language could I employ but the language of legend, myth and poetry to speak of such matters? We have no science, as yet, with a technical vocabulary equal to the task. If I might continue...?"

"Please do," said our guest of honor.

"Wherever there is an orthodox view, of course," Dupin went on, "it spawns antitheses. Some Pythagoreans inevitably wondered whether the encrypted entities really had been encrypted in order to make the world safer for humankind. Some wondered whether they might simply have been placed in store in order that their eventual release might put an end to the world of humankind—a notion similarly transfigured in the Christian mythos, in the Apocalypse of St. John and similar nightmares. A few, even bolder, wondered whether humans were of any relevance at all, and whether the beings that encrypted others might have been working entirely out of motives of their own. Now that we have a better understanding of human insignificance in a universe vast in time and space, the last-cited possibility has come to seem the most plausible of the three, in purely rational terms.

"The Pythagorean philosophers were exceedingly curious, and some among them undoubtedly endeavored to find answers to such conundrums. The entire cult was, however, secretive by habit and by nature—although the legend is probably false that one of its members was put to death for revealing the existence of irrational numbers—and scant rumor of the greater part of such endeavor was handed down in any manner that has reached our time. Their descendants, the neo-Pythagoreans and neo-Platonists of the Roman Era, were even more secretive, and probably made even more use of ciphers and symbols than the early Christians. Their further descendants, the alchemists and astrologers of the Middle Ages and the Renaissance, continued and intensified the habit, and the modern adherents of the so-called Hermetic Tradition, exemplified by the Inner Circle of the Harmonic Philosophical Society of Paris, now conduct themselves in that fashion as a matter of routine, as much for reasons of intellectual addiction as for any real fear of persecution—although I will admit that the latter pressure has not entirely disappeared, even now."

"Indeed not," murmured Chapelain, who had doubtless experienced a good deal of unreasoned prejudice in his time.

"The Pythagoreans were, of course, intellectually underequipped by comparison with modern philosophers," Dupin went on. "Their science was very primitive, although they did understand the importance of mathematics as an analytical tool. It is, however, a mistake to think that because we have so much more reliable information about the natural world that ancient philosophers were merely ignorant and misled, and that everything they thought they knew has been superseded. The men of the what we now call the Renaissance were acutely aware of the fact that much of the heritage of the ancient world had been lost, if only for the simple reason that so many of the manuscripts in which it had been recorded had fallen victim to decay, vandalism and sheer neglect. It was not until the fall of Byzantium, where a larger fraction of the heritage of Western Europe had been preserved than in Rome itself, that Italian and French scholars were to begin the work of salvage, belatedly copying what they could—and even then the work was highly selective, guided by the Church. To this day, previously-unknown manuscripts are still being discovered in the monasteries and churches of the old Eastern Empire, and that is a process that will doubtless continue long into the twentieth century. The great triumph of printing has been the preservation of much that might otherwise have been lost, even though paper decays as parchment did, and it is not that much harder for a printed edition of five hundred copies to disappear completely than it was for two hundred copies of a manuscript produced by monks or scribes."

"We have national libraries now," Leuret pointed out, "dedicated to the prevention of such losses."

"The ancients had Alexandria," Chapelain interjected. "How many times did it burn? I forget."

Dupin frowned at the interruptions, and continued, more insistently: "The idea that there is an esoteric heritage that has survived alongside the exoteric one—that there are manuscripts that survived the Dark Ages other than in Christian monasteries, or survived in monasteries where they had no right to be, according to the tenets of the Christian orthodoxy—is nowadays derided because so many of the modern documents that claim to be copies of those ancient esoteric sources are obvious fakes. It would, however, be very surprising if there were no such documents at all, or if their custodians had not made efforts to conceal them from Christian persecution exactly as the Christians had tried to preserve their own early secrets from would-be persecutors. Whether the authentic survivals contain anything but intellectual dross—dismissing them as dross is the strategy by which positivists reject them *en masse*—I do not know, but I try my utmost to keep an open mind, and I am proud to follow in the footsteps of men like Roger Bacon and John Dee, who were, before anything else, *bibliomaniacs*: obsessive and relentless book collectors."

You are more than proud, I thought—but did not dare say anything aloud.

"Bacon and Dee were men of genius too," Dupin continued, "and men of conscience, but their first concern, in approaching the matter of ancient manuscripts, was not to judge them as worthy or unworthy, on either religious or scientific grounds, but to accumulate and preserve them. In so doing, they knew that they were running real dangers—that their lives would literally be imperilled by the self-appointed judgers of books—but they did it anyway. Indeed, by virtue of an altogether natural and laudable perversity, they invested more interest in the books that they were forbidden—*literally* forbidden—to read than in those that they were obliged or encouraged to read. They both suffered as a result of that decision, eventually warranting recognition as martyrs, not merely in terms of what became of them materially, but in terms of their posthumous reputations, which were thoroughly blackened with charges of wizardry and diabolism. It has always been safer, in this corrupt world, not to read at all, or, if one must read, to read the books that one is obliged or encouraged to read, or, if one absolutely cannot help being infected with bibliomania, to operate as a bibliotaph: an entomber of one's books, and oneself with them.

"There are, inevitably, all kinds of legends that have grown up around the supposedly forbidden books that reside in various bibliotaphic crypts. Some such texts have even been printed—and the great majority of the ones that have been printed are undoubtedly fakes. Some, however, are more interesting than others. I possess a few of them myself; I dare say that the library of the Harmonic Philosophical Society of Paris includes far more—and I could not begin to hypothesize what serious bibliotaphs like Monsieur Breisz of Brittany, who is something of an esoteric legend in his own lifetime, might possess.

"What I do know, however, is that one of the rarely-seen and most talked-about of all the forbidden books is the so-called *Necronomicon*: an improvised title that implies something like *the book of dead names*. It is a Latin text, but is usually credited to a 'mad Arab' by virtue the frequent allegation that it was originally written in Arabic; its original title is said to have been *Al Azif*, that possibly being the name of a demon in the demon's own language. Although I know of no one who has ever seen a copy of the *Necronomicon*, let alone *Al Azif*, I have heard various rumors of what the text is supposed to contain. As well as a series of cryptograms that were probably cast initially in the seven-by-seven format beloved by the Pythagoreans—their format is said to be only partly preserved in the Latin text—it apparently contains fragments of a narrative, which Dr. Leuret would doubtless consider to be the very acme of madness, and is certainly very fanciful by any standards, although it is not entirely implausible in the context of my own theories regarding the true nature of reality—for which I have evidence of a sort, although it is not evidence likely to convince the followers of August Comte.

"It is getting late, so I will do my best to be brief. In short, I have no sympathy with the recent revival of atomic theory, and the void theory attendant upon it. I am a plenarist, who agrees with Aristotle that the notion of void is essentially abhorrent. The apparent emptiness of space is, in my view, an illusion; all space is full, but its fullness is concealed from us by the fact that the vast bulk of the matter contained in the plenum is inaccessible to our senses. The universe we see, and detect by means of our scientific instruments, is only the merest slice of a vast collection of incompletely-separated slices. Unwittingly, we live in parallel with countless other universes, whose own matter and apparent space is interleaved with our own, but which is inaccessible to our senses. Furthermore, I believe that to be a necessary condition of existence: I do not believe that our universe could exist, and maintain its integrity, were it not part of such a manifold. Were it not for the invisible and intangible matter unavailable to our sensory perception, the visible and tangible matter that is available could not be organized as it is—but that is a side-issue.

"The point is that the separation between the universes is not absolute; there is a certain amount of what might be called *leakage*. This leakage can be physical, but only briefly and temporarily, save for exceptional circumstances that threaten to remove, transfigure or obliterate sectors of universes, and sometimes entire universes. It is more often mental. Insofar as humans have any experience of the other universes, that experience arrives in the form of dreams and hallucinations, for which reason the other universes neighboring ours within the manifold are often referred to in esoteric texts as *the dream-dimensions*. In that context, hallucinations can certainly be contagious— and some of those that are contagious are also toxic, sometimes fatally."

Leuret could not help interrupting there. "I have long been an exponent of the view that there are authentically mental illnesses," he said, "which is to say, diseases of the mind that are by no means mere echoes of physical distress or electrical and chemical events in the brain. The idea that there are kinds of madness that originate outside the individual, however, capable of injection or infusion like a poison, is not one that I can endorse. I think that toying with hallucination is dangerous for sane minds, but the danger comes from within, not without."

"You might be right, Dr. Leuret," Dupin relied. "Indeed, I hope that you are—but I'm not so sure that the distinction between *within* and *without* is as clear as you are trying to draw it. Much of what I have just said is, admittedly, conjecture based on the extrapolation of limited evidence. The remainder of what I have to tell you, I cannot offer as anything more than matters of hallucination and legend—although I do contend that, even if they are no more than that, they have real power to hurt us, and even to destroy us. I feel perfectly sure, Dr. Leuret, that you will not deny, on the basis of your long experience to Charenton and Bicêtre, that hallucination has the power to hurt and destroy us very cruel ways. The only possible dispute there is between us is how best to counter and ameliorate those cruel inflictions, on a case by case basis.

"This, then is what hallucinatory legend has to say. There are entities within the other dimensions that lie close to us in the plenum, and even between the dimensions, that pose a threat to their neighbors, and perhaps to the entire manifold. There are also agents that work to neutralize those threats. You may categorize them as demons and angels, if you care to use that drastically oversimplified and ideologically loaded terminology, but they probably have no interest at all in human beings, and were certainly not specially created merely to afflict or defend us. Our world—the planet Earth, that is—has surely been invaded by those agents in the past, on occasion, and is surely still subject to the threat of further invasions. Indeed, that threat might be intensifying considerably at the present time, for the ironic reason that civilized humans have now evolved, physically and culturally, to the point at which we can begin to investigate and interrogate the underlying processes of dream and hallucination, and the underlying properties of matter.

"Such invasions might well have less practical before there were humans on Earth to dream and think, but the Earth has a very long history—no one knows how long, as yet, but it must be measured in millions of years, if not thousands of millions—and it is possible that there were dreamers and thinkers abroad on its surface before the advent of humankind. At any rate, legends of such invasion were preserved in oral tradition, albeit in corrupted and perhaps encrypted form, long before anyone wrote them down. The narrative that was eventually written down in the text ancestral to the *Necronomicon* describes the temporary invasion of Earth, long before the appearance of humankind, of an entity named Cthulhu. Attempts to describe that extremely alien entity are highly impressionistic, but it is likened to a strange kind of compound of draconian, cephalopod and humanoid characteristics, and there is some suggestion that it might be a compound being, with smaller associates of some kind, sometimes called 'star-spawn' but more frequently named 'shoggoths'. The former name is obviously a recent improvisation, but the latter, like Cthulhu itself, might well be an attempted phonetic rendering of an alien term.

"According to the esoteric legend, Cthulhu's invasion might have been far more destructive than it was. It might have rendered the Earth uninhabitable for the life-forms indigenous to it, but the likelier possibility is that native life would simply have been co-opted as creative material into some vast project of unknown purpose—that being the motive for the invasion. In fact, Cthulhu was prevented from carrying through its project, not by destruction or conclusive banishment, but by a process of encryption. It was, in some fashion that is literal as well as metaphorical, *entombed.* And the mechanism of that entombment was, of course, a cryptogram: the so-called Cthulhu encryption, the ultimate model for the Seal of Solomon.

"According to legend—and I believe that there is at least *some* truth in the legend—that cryptogram has survived into modern times, even though it must initially have been invoked before any human tongue and guiding mind existed to attempt its awkward pronunciation. The key to its survival lies in the translation of the part of the cryptogram that is still to be heard being pronounced by individuals that Louis-Antoine de Bougainville and other explorers have described, not entirely accurately, as 'Cthulhu-worshippers.' You have seen the symbolic form of the cryptogram inscribed in Ysolde Leonys' misfortunate flesh, and you heard her lips attempt to pronounce forty-two of the forty-nine symbols his afternoon. I will not attempt to reproduce her pronunciation, for more reasons than one, but the usual translation derived via Arabic and Latin is: 'In his house at R'lyeh, dead Cthulhu waits dreaming.' The operative word is *dreaming.* Inert and encrypted as it is, presumably dead by any criterion that human physicians could apply, Cthulhu is still dreaming.... and its dreams are capable of interacting with the dreams of human beings. That is how humans came to know of its existence, and such dreams are the source of all that we know about it—not, alas the most reliable one imaginable."

"Why forty-two?" Chapelain put in. "Why did she not voice all forty-nine?"

"Opinions differ," Dupin said. "Presumably, the last seven change the significance of the whole, but no one knows how. If they could be translated, so that the quotation could be completed, we might have a better idea—but the *Necronomicon* is said only to translate the forty-two that are routinely voiced, and the same is presumably true of *Al Azif.*"

"But you're working on a translation yourself?"

"I'm trying to work out how the remaining symbols might be pronounced—and if that leads me to an understanding of their significance, so much the better."

Not necessarily, I thought. *Given the multitudinous uncertainties in your story, it could as easily be so much the worse.*

"Legend is unclear," Dupin continued, stubbornly—hastening his speech slightly now that the end of his discourse was evidently near, "as to whether or not the process of dream-infection by means of which humans have come to know of Clthulhu's existence and nature is accidental or purposive, but legend being what it is, much is made of the suspicion that it is deliberate and malign. If that were the case, it would imply that the ultimate purpose of the infection is the reversal of the entombment, and the liberation of Cthulhu to complete its long-dormant plan for the usurpation and transfiguration of the Earth, including the human species...a transfiguration for which humankind is now allegedly ripe.

"All of this, of course, might be no more than hallucinatory froth, the derivatives of madness—but there are two brute facts with which we have been confronted today. Ysolde Leonys has the Cthulhu encryption engraved in her flesh—and something within her knows how to pronounce the greater part of it. Whether or not the world is in peril, something is definitely happening to *her*: something that I would dearly like to understand, for my benefit as well as hers, and perhaps for the world's.

"And that, Dr. Leuret, in a nutshell, is why I thought it best to remove Mademoiselle Leonys from your custody."

The poetry of Shakespeare inevitably came to mind—to my mind, at any rate—speaking of an individual bounded by a nutshell, who might have been capable nevertheless of imagining himself a king of infinite space, were it not that he had *bad dreams*.

CHAPTER SEVEN
IN SAINT-SULPICE

DR. LEURET UNDOUBTEDLY had more questions to ask Dupin now that his phantasmagorical account was complete. So had Chapelain, I presume. I certainly had. As soon as he had finished speaking, however, Madame Lacuzon came in and hastened to his side, in order to whisper in his ear.

The whisper went on considerably longer than would have been required simply to impart the news that Ysolde Leonys was awake, and I saw Dupin's eyes glance reflexively in my direction, but I was not unduly worried. I had faith enough in Dupin's deductive abilities to know that he would have guessed easily enough who was at the door during dinner, and enough faith in his morals to know that he would not persist in any attempt to forbid me to do whatever I wished, however reluctant he might be to let me go.

As Madame Lacuzon turned to go, Dupin turned to Leuret and said: "Mademoiselle Leonys is awake again. I fear that I did not get very far when I attempted to question her this afternoon, and I would like to call upon Dr. Chapelain's expertise now, if I may. With his assistance, I'm sure that we can make some progress, at least in discovering when and where the Cthulhu inscription was imparted to her flesh—although it might be a good deal harder to figure out how and why. Will you stay to witness the proceedings, Dr. Leuret, no matter how much you might disapprove of their objective?"

"I will, if I may," said Leuret, glancing in my direction for politeness' sake.

"You're very welcome, Dr. Leuret," I told him. "I hope you'll forgive me, though, if I don't join you. I am exceedingly curious to discover what will happen, but Monsieur Dupin will doubtless give me a scrupulously full account when it is convenient. In the meantime, I need to go out for a while."

Dupin looked me full in the face then, but I met his gaze boldly, having steeled myself to do so. How long I could have withstood his gaze had he interrogated or challenged me, I don't know, but in fact he did neither. Indeed, there was nothing forbidding in his stare at all—quite the reverse. He seemed quite glad that I was prepared to take on the burden of gleaning additional information, no matter where it might come from.

All he actually said was: "Be careful, my friend—and be wary." He meant that I needed to be careful in case the wings of rumor had reached other ears than Saint-Germain's and perhaps excited other interest in my house-guest, but also to be wary of anything that Saint-Germain might tell me or ask of me. I nodded in what I hoped would seem a reassuring manner.

My heart was fluttering, though, as I collected my coat, hat and stick and let myself out. There was a stern autumnal chill in the air, darkness having fallen some hours before. I took out my watch, and found that it was nearly midnight; I had not realized that it was so late. The streets were by no means deserted, though; it is not true that Paris never sleeps, but the city does not go to bed early, even in the dead of winter, and is always optimistic in October that a brief Indian summer might yet revive its legendary gaiety for one last fling. The Church of Saint-Sulpice was only five minutes' walk from my house, so there was no need to take a cab and no time to catch a chill.

I must confess that I have never liked Saint-Sulpice. Had I been in the habit of worshipping at all, I would have gone to Saint-Germain-de-Prés, in spite of its raucous bell. Saint-Sulpice is too large and draughty, and its surroundings—especially the square around the new fountain—are so overburdened by commercial enterprise that I cannot imagine that Jesus would have approved. The term *Saint-Sulpicerie* has, of course, become a by-word for religious artefacts of the tawdriest variety. The interior of the Church is far more austere than its immediate surroundings, and the paintings on the walls of genuine artistic merit, but it always seemed to me to be a strangely *louche* environment, whose holiness is patchy at best.

The churches of Paris are never empty, even late at night, but late worshippers tend to cluster in small groups around the altar or the candle-racks, and the secluded side-chapels—especially those lit by a single tokenistic candles, are usually deserted after sunset. That, I imagine, was exactly why the Comte de Saint-Germain had selected it as a convenient meeting-place—convenient for him at least.

It took me some time to locate him—naturally enough, he was in the gloomiest and most isolated place he had been able to locate—but he wanted to be found, so he was on the lookout for me, and beckoned me into his hidey-hole as soon as he caught sight of me. He did at least pull me into the corner of the side-chapel where the candle was, so that we could see one another's faces.

"Thank you for coming," he said. "I feared that I really might have to wait all night, in vain. Did anyone attempt to follow you?"

"I don't know," I confessed.

He pulled a face. "Did Dupin not warn you to be careful?" he asked.

"Yes," I admitted, "but...."

He waved way the impending excuse. "No time," he said. "I have something to give you—but first, I need to convince you that, this time, I really am sincere in wanting to help you. This time, we really are on the same side...and to be perfectly honest, I'm not entirely sorry that it's Dupin who's in the front line. If he needs my help, mind, he only has to ask."

"You've said that before," I reminded him.

"You sound skeptical—but I always mean it."

I could not help thinking of the boy in the moral tale who

cried wolf, and was then eaten because no one came to help when a wolf actually came.

"Come, now," Saint-Germain continued, hurriedly. "I have surely been honest enough in my past dealings with *you* to earn a measure of trust, no matter how determined Dupin is to damn me as a villain. This time, even he will have to admit that he is in my debt."

The words *be wary* were ringing in my ears. "Why do you think Dupin might need help?" I asked, cautiously.

"Because he took a patient out of the asylum at Bicêtre this afternoon, who has manifested the Cthulhu encryption in the form of stigmata. Oh, don't worry—there's not one man in a hundred thousand within the city *enceinte* who could have recognized the cryptogram for what it was from the orderly's drunken description, but the news was bound to reach the Society sooner or later, and it just happened to be sooner. You might have cause to be grateful for that, especially if Dupin can decipher the ultimate line of the incantation—and don't tell me he won't try, for even if he really were the sanest and most virtuous man in the world, as you seem to believe, he can't resist *that* temptation. He'll be determined that he won't recite it, under any circumstances, but there really are some things that it's better not to know...or, if one can't help finding them out, shouldn't be known with out having the right counter-spell already in your possession."

"Counter-spell?" I queried.

"I can't be certain, of course," he said, "but I believe that's what it is. The Society has always held that the Key and the Seal are two different things, not one, as many would-be conjurors seem to have believed in the past. Whether it is or it isn't, it's in the same script as the Encryption Dupin has—and whether he needs it or not to stave off any threat, it will certainly help him decipher the symbols. For that reason alone, he'll be grateful."

So saying, he took a small parcel out of the inside pocket of his frock-coat, and held it out to me. It was a round object, wrapped in a piece of linen.

"What is it?" I asked, refraining as yet from reaching out to take it.

"The Levasseur medallion," he said.

"The pirate's locket?" I queried. "The one with the cryptogram inside?"

"It's not a locket," he said "and the cryptogram is on the outside, not the inside—but apart from that, yes."

"What do you mean?" I said, puzzled.

He sighed. "Rumor always gets things wrong," he said. "It's one of the more perverse laws of nature. Yes, when Levasseur was imprisoned, he was allowed to keep the ornament he wore around his neck, which was thought to be devoid of value by his judges and jailers alike. It was a wooden disk, with a carved image on the front and an array of forty-nine tiny symbols in the back. He probably had no more idea of what those symbols meant than his captors—but the news reached someone who knew something of their significance, in time for that person to attempt to strike a bargain of sorts. The inevitable difficulties of communication via a moronic warder made negotiations difficult, and things moved too quickly for any significant recompense to be arranged, but Levasseur agreed to hand over the medallion. The man who wanted it was unable to secure the prize while Levasseur was in custody, but Levasseur threw it to him while he was on the way to the gallows, making some remark as he did so about the solution to its secret leading to his fortune. It was, I assume, a final jest on his part. The members of the crowd who overheard him—and the guards escorting him, of course—inevitably misunderstood what had happened, and started a thousand fruitless treasure-hunts."

"And who was the man to whom Levasseur threw the medallion?" I demanded.

"Me," said the Comte de Saint-Germain. "But don't tell Dupin that—he won't believe you."

"You in a previous life, you mean?" I queried, skeptically—but I had heard him claim to be immortal, or reincarnated, before, so I was not unduly surprised by his claim.

"Perhaps so," he replied, dismissively. "That doesn't matter. The important thing is that this *is* the Levasseur medallion. It has been the custody of the Society ever since it founding, having been placed in its safe keeping by the Comte de Cagliostro. It has been locked away under Cagliostro's protective seal, but I have felt for some while that the time had come to retrieve it. I'm sending it to Dupin, as I said, because he might well need it—if he can decipher it. If he doesn't need it, of course, or there comes a time when its purpose has been served, I shall want it back. This is a loan, not a gift. And I shall expect gratitude too, to be redeemed in kind. Monsieur Dupin need not accept me as a friend, although I wish he would, but he must stop branding me a villain. In this instance, I repeat, he and I are both on the side of the angels…and I pray that they will appreciate the fact too, for if there is the slightest possibility that Cthulhu might awake from the dream of death…well, we all have our nightmares, do we not? Now, take the damned medallion and *go home*, as swiftly as you can. Be careful."

I finally accepted the package, and carefully put into the inner pocket of my own frock-coat, without unwrapping it.

"Good luck, my friend," Saint-Germain added, in a whisper. He seemed to mean it—but then, he was an expert mesmerist, and probably capable of making an innocent like me believe anything he said.

Unfortunately, he then spoiled the effect by muttering a curse that was far stronger than any mere *Sacré bleu!*

He was looking at something behind me. I turned round.

As an apprentice pedant, I suppose I ought not to say that the blood froze in my veins, but I did obtain a sudden understanding of what the man who invented that phrase might have meant. I really did feel a horridly unpleasant *frisson*, which really did feel as cold as ice.

In terms of the elementary physics of vision, I could hardly see anything at all, for the two silhouettes in the broad doorway of the chapel were little more than dark shadows carved out of slightly-less-intense darkness. The light of the chapel's candle hardy reached them, and the residual glimmer from the main body of the church was fainter than starlight. What I "saw," therefore, I could not *literally* have seen, and must reckon it as a hallucination. At the time, however, I was in no state to make such nice distinctions.

The figures confronting us were vaguely human in outline— as they had to be, since the material bodies they had were certainly human—but whatever was possessing those bodies, in my perception, was not human at all, but far more reminiscent of some slimy octopus or squid. The overall impression it made on my mind was, at least, that of writhing, sticky, inquisitive tentacles. But that was not the whole of the illusion, for if the cephalopod was somehow *inside* the man, there was also something *inside* the cephalopod…or, more accurately, if there was something inhabiting a dimension adjacent to the man that resembled a horrific and loathsome cephalopod, there was something else in a further but still adjacent dimension that was even more horrific and loathsome.

Having heard Dupin's account of the Cthulhu legend not long before, I could not help the word *draconian* springing to mind, and if a dragon really is a kind of worm, with legs, wings and the ability to breathe fire, I suppose that might have been as good a term as any for the impression that further being imparted—but in reality, any attempt to encapsulate it with earthly comparisons was bound to fail. It was unnamable. Indeed, it seemed to me to be unspeakable, or even unthinkable: that it was something beyond the reach, not only of description, but also of conceptualization.

It was not the first time that I had looked into dimensions other than our own, at least in the context of a hallucination, but the horrors I had seen before were not nearly as extreme as this one.

I was petrified, unable to move—at least until Saint-Germain reached out and gripped my arm.

I had always been sceptical about the mesmeric fluid, but I felt its flow then, and knew that the fake Comte was exercising every ounce of his real power.

"They're human insofar as they're more than mere phantoms!" he hissed. "Flesh and blood! Whatever else you see or feel isn't material. They're human—they can be fought, and even killed."

I turned to look at him, primarily in order to tear my eyes away from *them*.

With a flick of the wrist, he split his cane in two—which is to say, he bared the blade of his sword-stick. My cane was, alas, just a stick, and I had not followed Dupin's advice to put a revolver in my pocket. As Saint-Germain put himself *en garde*, I could not believe that it would make much difference that he had a blade while I had only a frail cudgel. I had no doubt that he was a practised fencer, and the blades that the two monsters had in their hands were no longer than his own stubby weapon, but whatever he might say about them, I knew that they were not *entirely* human—and the part that was not was completely immune to the mesmeric thrust of his eyes as well as the brutal thrust of his steel.

I put myself *en garde* too, even though my weapon was wooden, hoping that its extra length might count for something—but when the monsters moved to attack, flowing rather than moving on their feet, I was soon convinced that neither of us stood a chance. Our enemies could doubtless be killed, but I did not think that *we* could kill them—and I did not think that I could hurt one badly enough to keep it at bay.

The weapons clashed as the conflict was engaged: steel against wood and steel against steel. There was more than one contact made, so there was a fight of sorts—perhaps there were even parries and ripostes on our part—but it was to no avail. I felt my stick torn from my grasp, and I heard a blade clatter on the ground, which I knew, without looking, to be Saint-German's sword. We were not stabbed, though, let alone run through—that was not what our adversaries had in mind.

Instead, they closed in on us, backing us up against the cold stone wall of the chapel.

They continued to move forward, blades held wide of their bodies, their arms extended as if to wind around us like tentacles, presumably then to crush us…or perhaps swallow us whole.

Now, I could not help but see the one that was intent on embracing me. Saint-Germain's brief touch had lost its effect; I had no mental insulation whatsoever against the horror, the terror and the sheer disgust of looking into that multidimensional prospect, at a transdimensional creature that could not be given a true name….even though it surely had to be what Dupin had called a *star-spawn*, or a *shoggoth*.

It had time to kill me, but it did not. It was content to press me every more tightly against the wall—until a human hand that was surely not moved by human volition reached for the inside pocket of my frock-coat.

The situation suddenly seemed quite absurd. Monsters from beyond the world operating as common thieves? As *pickpockets*?

Perhaps, I thought, it really was human volition that was moving the hand—that in possessing two footpads abroad in the dark streets for nefarious purposes, the shoggoths had taken possession of their motives as well as their flesh. I had no doubt, though, that the prize for which the hand was reaching was Levasseur's medallion, not my purse or my watch.

It was not only the solid hand that was *reaching*, however—the tentacles that Saint-Germain had assured me were merely phantoms were *reaching* too, into my mind. The footpad, it seemed, did not intend to murder me—but what the effect might be of the shoggoth reaching inside me, I dared not contemplate. I did not want to die, but I wanted even less to be possessed by a demon of that sort.

Just as the probing fingers were about to touch the cloth-swathed medallion, however, and just as I was about to be touched in a far more intimate fashion by the hallucinatory tentacles, perhaps to be kissed by that loathsome worm, *someone spoke*.

I did not know what the voice was saying, and I am certain

that I could not have pronounced whatever it said myself, but someone spoke—and the hallucination was ripped apart.

I do mean *ripped*. It did not fade, or merely vanish: what happened was savage and abrupt.

Suddenly, our attackers were only human—and they were still holding their blades wide, at arm's length.

Instinctively, without even a fragment of intention, I smashed my forehead into the face of the man who was crowding me. I felt and heard the cartilage in his nose break under the impact. I have no idea what Saint-Germain did, but his opponent recoiled too, perhaps not yet unconscious but certainly inconvenienced to such an extent as to be unable to resist when Saint-Germain shoved him away. I did the same to my man—but I think, in all honesty, that they would have collapsed anyway. The ripping apart of their ultradimensional component had delivered an incapacitating shock to their human component.

There was another shadow in the doorway now. "You really ought to be more careful with that medallion, Saint-Germain," said a voice that was not recognizable as the one that had spoken before, although it surely came from the same mouth. "This is not what I would call safe-keeping."

Saint-German laughed—to relieve the tension, not because he was amused. He must have been far more confident than I had been that he could resist possession by the monster, but he had certainly been scared. "Well," he said, "it seems that I owe *you* a debt of gratitude now. I can no longer surrender the medallion to you, though—I have just given it to my friend, in order that he might let Dupin see it."

The other voice laughed too. Then the shadow came toward us—but before the candlelight could fall on the face and show me the stranger's features, he knelt down and put his fingers out to touch the striven footpads.

"They'll live," he said, after a moment or two. "The shoggoths have gone—but what on earth were they doing here? If they wanted the medallion, they could have stolen it a hundred years ago, as soon as Levasseur took it...but they are surely not capable of *wanting* anything at all. The emergence of the encryption in Ysolde's flesh must have attracted their attention, perhaps as a matador's cape draws a bull."

"They intended to possess us," I blurted out.

"Did they?" the mysterious stranger replied. "Well, perhaps they did. In that case, I really did just save your lives, for I doubt that sensitive men like you could have come though that experience unscathed, even if these two can wake up with nothing worse than a headache—and a broken nose, in one instance."

"I fear that you'll have to give him the medallion, my friend," Saint-Germain told me. "I have no strength left with which to fight him, and you've just seen that he's a magician of unusual power. He's been after it for a long time."

"I can be patient a little longer," the shadow murmured, still keeping his features out of the pool of candlelight, although he had risen to his feet again. "It's probably best that Ysolde regains possession of it as soon as possible, if she's in need of protection. Saint-Germain was right to hand it over, albeit that he did so for the wrong reasons...and he might even be correct in thinking that Dupin can decipher the cryptogram. It's a stern test, but I'll be very glad indeed if he can pass it."

"Who are you?" was all I could think of to say, having found the rest of his speech incomprehensible.

"Oh, I'm sorry," Saint-Germain was quick to say. "You two have never met, have you? This is the famous Breton bibliotaph, Monsieur Oberon Breisz. Not his given name, of course."

"Neither of us is wearing his given name tonight, Monsieur de Saint-Germain," said the newcomer, silkily, "but we are who we are, are we not?"

"*Oberon* Breisz," I repeated, dazedly.

"Indeed," said the newcomer—and now he did move forward a little further, so that I could see his features. They seemed rather ordinary, save for their leatheriness. Had he been sun-tanned, I might have taken him for a sailor, but he was very pale...almost pale enough for me to believe that he was a denizen of some uncanny underworld, rather than a mere book-collector.

Except that he could not be a *mere* book-collector, since he knew a spell that could send shoggoths back where they came from, and clearly knew more about Ysolde than a mere reader should have done.

What on Earth is going on? I wondered. It was probably a silly question. Whatever was going on, it was not going on *entirely* on Earth. We might all be lost in a hallucination of some sort, but, one way or another, this business extended into the dream-dimensions, perhaps deeply.

"Thank you for your intervention, Monsieur Breisz," I said. "Although I cannot be certain, now, what would have happened had you not arrived, I was terrified. But how did you come to be here?"

"I followed you from your house," he said. "I hoped that you might give Monsieur Dupin a message for me. I would rather have delivered it myself, but when I saw the witch answer your door...I've encountered her before, when I tried to call on Monsieur Dupin at home. I could have forced my way past her, but I did not think Monsieur Dupin would approve of that, so I told myself to be patient. I am a very patient man, by custom and habit...perhaps a little too patient, if events have now begun to move quickly."

"What message?" I asked, a trifle foolishly.

"Will you tell him that if Ysolde wants to come home, she is more than welcome," Oberon Breisz said, earnestly. "Will you tell him that he is more than welcome in my Underworld too, and that the time has come for him to remember who he really is, and resume his study of the *Necronomicon.*"

"Do you expect him to understand what that means?" I asked.

"Perhaps he will," the bibliotaph said. "If not, he will see it as a puzzle to be solved—and that will intrigue him all the more, will it not?"

And with that, he turned on his heel and marched swiftly away, disappearing into the shadows almost as if by magic. After what had just happened, I could not have been excessively surprised if he really had disappeared by magical means.

Saint-Germain was less impressed. "What a clown!" he exclaimed. "He's a good magician, no doubt about it—but surely not as great as he thinks he is, if I'm any judge. Independent scholars always go mad. That's the strength of the Society, you see—it keeps its members in balance. Dupin should join us soon, lest he go the same way. Mind you, if Breisz really does have a copy of the *Necronomicon*, it would be worth Dupin's while to accept his invitation. If that's where he found the spell he used to get rid of the shoggoths…but we ought to get out of here. If we're found with them, there'll be questions asked—and that bump on your head will make it obvious that you broke this fellow's nose. No one will blame you, as I'll give evidence that he was trying to rob you, but still…you know what *sergents de ville* are like."

I looked down at the unconscious footpads, who seemed very commonplace villains now that they had been disenchanted. Then I felt my forehead, were there was indeed a fluid bump that was bound to give way to a visible bruise.

"Come on," Saint-Germain urged, as he picked up the two parts of his swordstick and reunited them. "Recover your cane and let's be off—you need to get home. I'll walk you to the corner of your street, just in case. You have a message to deliver now, as well as the amulet. The plot's thickening, and no mistake—I'm deeply intrigued myself. Don't forget to impress upon Dupin that he's in my debt now, and that the merest glance at the medallion will incur an obligation."

I was completely out of my depth, and not only because my head had begun to ache as a result of my intemperate assault on the pickpocket. I was glad that Saint-Germain walked me home, for I would have been frightened without his presence. I was even glad to see Madame Lacuzon open the door; I felt that I had a better sense now of the true value of her protective presence.

CHAPTER EIGHT
A GENERAL HISTORY OF THE PYRATES

I HAD NOT THOUGHT that I had been absent for more than an hour, and had not been conscious of any bells chiming the hours, but when I checked my watch I found that it was past two. Leuret and Chapelain had both gone and Dupin was alone in the smoking-room. He seemed to be extremely weary, and was certainly not his usual incisive self. Ysolde Leonys had apparently gone to sleep again, although Dupin's concierge went to sit with her again as soon as she had let me in.

"I take it that the session was not a success," I said, as I sat down heavily in my armchair. The normality of the cushions seemed very welcoming, and I was glad of their familiarity.

"It was not," Dupin confirmed. "This time, she really did wake up fully, to all the agony of her condition. She was in great distress. Chapelain had to dose her with laudanum, and still had difficulty persuading her to go sleep again. There was no possibility of asking her any questions. Leuret did not seem overly disappointed about that. I fear that his opinion of me has gone down, and that he now thinks me even madder than Victor Hugo. What have you done to your head, my friend? That's quite a bump."

"I had a slight *contretemps* with a pickpocket. He came off worse than I did."

"I've glad that you've got safely home. I'll ask Madame Bihan for some hot water, so that we can bathe it."

"Don't bother," I told him. "It's nothing. It might have been a great deal worse, if Oberon Breisz had not come to our rescue."

That caught his attention, as I had known that it would. He forgot all about the bump on my head and the possibility that it might need attention. I had the rare satisfaction of seeing his eyes grow wider, with patent astonishment. "I only ever heard his surname," he murmured.

"It's not a coincidence," I said. "He asked me to give you a message."

"What message?" Dupin demanded.

"He says that if Ysolde wants to come home, she's more than welcome," I repeated, "and that you're more than welcome to visit his Underworld too. He says that it's time for you to remember who you really are, and to resume your study of the *Necronomicon*. Do you have the slightest idea what he means by that?"

Dupin shook his head in wonderment. "I've never seen a copy of the *Necronomicon*. I'm truly sorry that I didn't go with you, now—but I was so eager to discover what Chapelain might find out...and now it will have to wait until tomorrow anyway. We can't hope to decipher the puzzle until then."

"According to Saint-German," I said, "Oberon Breisz is a magician—but also something of a clown. I suspect that his judgment may be faulty, at least in the latter instance. At any rate, Breisz could certainly have taken this, had he wanted to, when the pickpocket had failed—but he didn't want to. He and Saint-Germain both seem strangely content for you to have it, at least temporarily. Saint-Germain was very insistent, though, that you'll be in his debt if you so much as look at it."

As I was speaking I took the linen parcel out of my pocket and handed it to Dupin, who took it without hesitation. "What is it?" he said, as he began to unwrap it.

"The Levasseur medallion," I said, bluntly.

If I had astonished him before, I had electrified him now. He actually started—but he completed unwrapping the wooden disk, and then stared at it in wonderment for two full minutes, turning it over and over, in silence. I could see the array of forty-nine tiny characters carved on the obverse, which seemed sinister now that I knew their possible significance, but might have been hardly noticeable to an ignorant observer.

"Is it the same cryptogram?" I asked, finally, to check Saint-Germain's assurance that it was not.

"No," he said, "it's a different one, but in the same script. With twice as much text, however, I'll have a much better chance of deciphering both."

"Do you really want to decipher the whole of the Cthulhu encryption?" I asked. "Is it even safe to try?"

He reflected for a moment, and then said: "Yes—but it probably isn't safe...especially if Saint-Germain wants me to do it. Whatever he told you will be a lie, of course, but did he tell you why he wants me to have it?"

"He said that it was a counter-spell, and that you'd need it if you succeeded in deciphering the last line of the other. Breisz, on the other hand, said that Ysolde ought to have it, because she might need protection. If the monsters that came after me as soon as I accepted it return, we might *all* need protection...but you'll have to figure out how to use it first."

His avid eyes were soaking up the strange array of symbols, squinting in order to make them out in the lamplight, but the mention of monsters snatched him back from his contemplation.

"What monsters?" he asked.

"Shoggoths," I said, succinctly, being in no mood for preliminary confessions of not-quite-certainty.

"You've seen the star-spawn?" he said, with more envy than horror in his tone. Then he made a further attempt to pull himself together. "Tell me *exactly* what happened," he said. "Every tiny detail."

I did the best I could, although my description of the two phantom monsters that had attempted to steal the medallion was inevitably vague.

When I had finished, he shook his head. "This needs further thought," he said, "But not now. I need a clear head. I need sleep—and so do you. Chapelain will come as soon as he can in the morning, and we must make every effort to capitalize on his expertise. This is far more complicated than I had anticipated."

My head was still aching, and I had probably never been in greater need of sleep, but I could not help saying: "Ysolde will not want to go back to Oberon, will she? She will want to stay with her beloved Tristan, now that she has found him again after so many years."

No matter how exhausted he might be, Dupin's inner pedant never became drowsy. "I am not Tristan de Léonais," he said, "nor is that poor woman upstairs in my bed the Queen of any Underworld. Nor is the person who is calling himself Oberon Breisz the King of any Underworld. He is probably not even a Breton. Perhaps he is a magician, with some skill in encryption and decryption…and perhaps he believes that he has been disinterred himself, like Saint-Germain…if Saint-German's assertions can be taken seriously. Whatever part Breisz is playing, though, I shall be glad to match wits with him. Now go to bed, my friend, and sleep. Tomorrow, we really *must* make progress in solving this puzzle."

I did as I was told, but I slept very badly, and not entirely because my head was aching. I dreamed, inevitably, about cephalopods and dragons, magicians chanting incantations of forty-nine incomprehensible syllables, and the Comte de Saint-Germain—who, in my dream. had not aged a day since they day that Olivier Levasseur was hanged in 1730, even though he had been buried in the interim, and still reeked of grave-dirt.

Even so, I did feel better in the morning, and even better when I had eaten breakfast. When I enquired about Dupin, Madame Bihan told me that he had been up for two hours already, poring intently over "a bit of wood and some bits of paper" in the smoking-room. Now, though, he had gone to sit with "the lady."

I was not unduly surprised that Dupin had risen before me; although he was a common mortal, and became tired when overstressed, he did not require much sleep to repair him, and often contrived to be an early riser as well as a night-owl, when he felt a sense of urgency.

"I'm very sorry for all this inconvenience, Madame Bihan," I said.

She seemed surprised. I thought at first that it was because, after a life in service, she was unused to having her employers apologize to her, but her reply suggested otherwise. "It is a matter of life and death, sir," she aid. "Antoine and I will not be found wanting, in such circumstances. Amélie has explained to us what is at stake."

It took me several seconds to realize that Amélie must be Madame Lacuzon's forename. "Really?" I said, wondering now much, and exactly what, Dupin had told the old gorgon.

"Don't be afraid, sir," Madam Bihan said, in a tone that was almost maternal. "She's a wise woman. Everyone is frightened of her, and rightly so, but she's not of the Devil's party. She has seen the Devil, in her time, but she sent him packing."

I knew that *wise woman* was a euphemism for *witch*, and I was not surprised to hear that suggestion being made, yet again, of Dupin's intimidating concierge.

"She sent Oberon Breisz packing as well as the Devil, it seems," I observed.

"She protects Monsieur Dupin," thee wise woman's cousin proclaimed, loyally—and adopted a more confidential tone to add: "He is a great and good man, she says…but he does not always know what is good for him."

I finished my coffee in haste and immediately went up to Dupin's old bedroom. The curtains were drawn to keep out the daylight, but there was a nightlight burning on the bedside table, and Dupin had obviously continued his intense study of the two cryptograms by means of its wan light, in spite of its unsuitability. When I came in, though, he laid two pieces of paper on the coverlet, where the wooden disk already lay, and looked up, blinking. He had evidently made a copy of the tiny symbols on the disk, magnifying them to the same degree as Leuret's sketch, and had been studying the ninety-eight symbols in careful juxtaposition.

I took hold of a chair and pushed it into a position beside his own, although I had to remove a book that was lying on the cushion before I sat down. I placed the book on the coverlet beside the medallion and the pieces of paper, after glancing at its title. It was a recent reprint of Captain Johnson's *General History of the Pyrates*, in English. I presumed that Dupin had brought it up, as it certainly did not seem to be the kind of reading-matter that Madame Lacuzon or Madame Bihan would have chosen.

"Madame Bihan just confirmed that Oberon Breisz has tried to see you at your apartment," I told him, in a conscientious whisper, "but that Madame Lacuzon would not let him in. She seems to think, as Breisz did, that your concierge is a witch, who has appointed herself your guardian angel since sending the Devil packing."

"Madame Lacuzon does have that conviction," Dupin admitted, also moderating his voice, although he would not condescend to whisper, "and she does not always tell me when she sends someone away. I never scold her for it, because her judgment is usually sound."

"You mean that her madness generally works to your advantage?" I said.

"She is not mad," he told me, sternly. "Indeed, she is he sanest person I know."

I was slightly hurt by the absence of an exception made for me, but I did not scold him for it. Instead, I asked: "How is Mademoiselle Leonys?"

"A little better, I think," he said, "although still under the influence of the laudanum. She was probably in dire need of deep sleep, after what must have seemed a hellish week in the pandemonium of Bicêtre, but a good bed can work wonders. Hopefully, by the time that Chapelain gets here, she'll be as ready as she ever will be to by obedient to his mesmeric authority, and to tell us what she knows. I hope so." His gaze strayed back to the medallion, as if magnetically attracted to it.

"You should not try to study characters as tiny as those in

this dim light," I told him, "or even the copies you have made. Ordinary print is not much better."

"My eyes are excellent," he assured me. "I really do believe that I might be able to work out the pronunciation of the unknown characters, given time—and I can't help feeling that the matter is urgent. As for the *History of the Pyrates*, it's set in comfortably large type—although I've only glanced at it, to refresh my memory, in case there was any information about John Taylor that had slipped my mind."

"Was there?" I asked.

"No," he said—but he did not seem unduly delighted about the implicit compliment to his memory. "There's very little said about him, and even less about Levasseur—Oliver de La Bouche, as a letter quoted by Johnson mistakenly calls him. The book was initially published in 1724, when both were still alive, but Johnson's record is mostly an exhaustive list of captured ships, with occasional supplementary comments from survivors of pirate attacks. The chapter in which Taylor is briefly mentioned is titled for Edward England, who was the more famous of the two at the time—but England disappears part way through, when Taylor is named as his successor. It's a rather pedestrian chapter, I fear, which cannot compare in melodramatic terms with the flamboyant account of the female pirates Anne Bonny and Mary Read and their adventures with John Rackham—but that, I suspect, is pure fiction."

"Mere travelers' tales?"

"Probably," he said, "Almost everything we think we know about many of the individuals whose stories are told herein, we owe to this one source. The dull passages drawn from official documents are presumably accurate, but the biographical additions regarding the pirates' personal affairs are probably as fictitious as the author's signature."

"Captain Johnson is a pseudonym?"

"Indeed. There's a rumor that the book was prepared for publication by Daniel Defoe, and that all the most readable sections are inventions cooked up by him—but I doubt that he added much to the chapter on Edward England, which is vague as well as tedious."

"But John Taylor is no fiction," I said, "and he and Levasseur really did capture *Our Lady of the Cape.*"

"That much is certain," he said. "But where legend takes over...do you know, by the way, what flag pirates flew?"

"The Jolly Roger," I said, promptly. "The skull and cross-bones."

"According to Captain Johnson," he said, "Ned Teach flew a black flag, and most of his Caribbean emulators copied him. John Taylor, however, *did* fly the skull-and-crossbones—but only after usurping command of his fleet from the device's inventor, Edward England."

"According to seamen's fabulations," I said, "it's still flown by many a ghost-ship—but if all the ghost-ships that seamen claim to have seen were gathered into a fleet, they'd put the Spanish Armada to shame."

Dupin had no interest in ghost-ships, so I changed tack. "If John Taylor really did maroon the commander he deposed in Mauritius," I said, "no matter how short or long a time elapsed before he was rescued, Edward England would surely have dedicated the rest of his life to seeking revenge on John Taylor." I had spent time on the Boulevard du Temple; I knew how melo-drama worked. "Wherever he was, he must have cursed Taylor with all his might when his usurper and Levasseur took the Portuguese galleon in his stead, and became fabulously rich."

"No doubt," said Dupin, looking down at the book on the bed, contemplatively. "But legend has nothing to say about that. In any case, the particular tale of *Our Lady of the Cape* is only a tiny part of the vast tapestry of pirate myth and legend: a tapestry whose principal anchorage is this tome...or tomb."

"Tomb?" I echoed, slightly startled.

"Legend is itself a form of encryption, as I've said before," he murmured, pensively. "It's a neutral zone in the borderlands of mundane history, into which exile all manner of dreams and delusions may be sent. Secrets may be buried there, hidden beneath symbols, and the unspeakable spoken there, albeit in code. Much of it, of course, is pure invention…if there ever was any such thing as *pure* invention…but there is hidden meaning in it regardless. If Dr. Leuret is correct, and the work of poets and arts is simply hallucination by another name, he's still wrong to call it madness—but he's right to recognize that the imagination underlies poetic creativity and legend-mongering, and that the processes of manufacture by which it works in those arenas is cousin to the manner in which it works in certain kinds of madness."

"Ysolde Leonys' madness certainly fits that description," I observed. "It's stitched together from the legacy of folklore and romance; there's nothing original in its fairyland at all… not even Cthulhu, since you say that the monster in question is legendary too, albeit in an esoteric sense."

"The legend of Cthulhu seems to be written in her flesh, not her dreams," Dupin reminded me. "Indeed, it's possible that her dreams might have been formulated to keep it *out* of her mind…perhaps deliberately, by someone other than herself, by means of what Saint-Germain would call magic. It's probable that the cryptogram that has been lying dormant in her flesh has emerged quite naturally, as a result of the climactic crisis of her disease, but that emergence is evidently not inconsequential. If there is a *scheme* in all this…."

"There *is* a scheme," I assured him. "A mad, incomprehensible scheme, no doubt…but a scheme of some sort. I think Oberon Breisz could tell us a good deal about it, if he were so minded. Perhaps your protective concierge should have let him in when he called on you, so that he could have explained himself."

"Amélie's instincts are sound," he repeated, in a faint tone that was *almost* a whisper.

"Have you made enough progress in your study of the two cryptograms," I asked, "to have any idea what the purpose of the one on the medallion might be?"

"You mentioned protection yourself," he said, "although I'd

be reluctant to take Saint-German's word for that…or Oberon Breisz's word. Did you examine the image on the other side of the medallion?"

"I never got the opportunity," I reminded him. "Faithful to my mission, I handed the object to you still wrapped. Is it an image of Cthulhu?"

"There can be no such thing as a two- or three-dimensional image of Cthulhu, whose being extends across three distinct and different universes—perhaps more when he was not encrypted—but there is certainly a suggestion in the carving of human-cephalopod hybrid, with a hint of something further and more alien. I'll continue my close study of the cryptogram once Chapelain has come and gone, in better light, but this mystery began with the patient, and I need to discover her story, if I can. Saint-Germain's treasure-hunt can probably wait a while.

"Treasure-hunt?" I queried.

"Certainly," he said. "Can you think of any other reason why a man like Saint-Germain would hand over an object like the Levasseur medallion? He has doubtless tried with all his might to decipher what he believes to be the guide to the treasure and failed, but he evidently hopes that I might succeed, especially now that I have the Chthulu encryption with which to compare it. I suspect, strongly, that he hopes that I might be able to lead him to Levasseur's treasure, so that he can steal it for himself."

"Do you think that Oberon Breisz has similar hopes and expectations?" I asked.

"I don't know—but Madame Lacuzon would have told me that he had asked to see me if she did not think his intentions more sinister than that. I wondered momentarily whether your entire experience last night might have been an illusion impressed on your mind by Saint-Germain, but I think not. As he persists in telling us, he's not really evil, merely greedy. Breisz, on the other hand…whose true name, we must remember, is neither Oberon not Breisz…."

"He saved me from the monsters," I pointed out.

"Apparently," Dupin conceded. He said no more, but I knew

what he was implying. If Breisz had sent the monsters he had then called off, he might simply have been introducing himself in a flamboyant manner. What, I wondered, would Madame Lacuzon have done if a creature like the ones in the church had turned up on her doorstep, whether at midnight or noon, demanding to see Monsieur le Chevalier Auguste Dupin? "Sent it packing," I presumed.

I heard the doorbell ring then, and could not suppress a chill at the thought of poor Madame Bihan opening the door to... but less than three seconds passed before I heard the faint but recognizable sound of Pierre Chapelain's voice drifting up the stair—to be followed, a few minutes later, by the man himself.

As the door to the bedroom opened and the mesmerist came in, Ysolde Leonys opened her eyes. It was exactly as if she had been waiting for a cue—and this time, she did not seem to have awoken to the agony of syphilitic reality, but merely to the fantasy with which she had cloaked herself before.

It occurred to me that if *she* had ever come to call at the house containing Dupin's apartment, the concierge would surely have sent her away too, just as I would have done to any syphilitic whore who knocked on my door...but here she was, lying in what I still considered to be Dupin's bed, in what was still, in every meaningful sense of the term, Dupin's room, monopolizing the great man's concern as well as his intellectual interest.

Her gaze went first to Dupin—her supposedly-beloved Tristan—and then to Chapelain, her faithful Merlin. Perhaps she would have spared me a glance too had her eyes not fallen on the three objects lying on the coverlet.

"My medallion!" she said, snatching it up. "Oh, Tristan, wherever did you find it? Thank you!"

Under other circumstances, I suspect that Dupin might have contended with her for the cryptogram's custody, but he had been forewarned that she might have an interest in it, and he had made a more easily-legible copy, so he let her have it. He picked up his two pieces of paper, though, and put them in his pocket for safe keeping.

Ysolde Leonys wrapped her hands around the wooden disk and then pressed them both to her chest, just beneath her neck—where the medallion might have hung had it been suspended from a chain.

"Thank you," she said again. "I thought that it was lost forever!"

I could see that Dupin was burning to ask her where she had lost it, and where she had obtained it in the first place, but he had a plan of procedure worked out, and that plan was to delegate all questions to the mesmerist, at least for the time being.

Personally, I had no doubt that she really did believe that the medallion was, in some mysterious sense, hers, even though it seemed impossible that any such entitlement could possibly exist...unless Saint-Germain had lied about it being in the custody of the Harmonic Philosophical Society since its foundation. Was it possible, I wondered, that Saint-Germain had stolen it from Ysolde Leonys? Was it possible that his pretence of handing it over to Dupin was a ploy to return it to her? If so, what could it all mean?

There is certainly a scheme here, I thought, *clever and convoluted as well as crazy. Pirate treasure is only one of the lures that have been set out to lead us through the maze...to meet the Minotaur.*

Such was the power of the scheme I had just invented that I immediately steered that train of thought into a brand new oasis, identifying not only the labyrinth but the myth of the labyrinth as a quintessential crypt, in which monsters and discomfiting ideas were safely confined and entombed in order to liberate the mind from their dire presence and free it for mundane and orderly intercourse with the everyday world.

Dupin had told me more than once that consciousness is a refuge, whose walls and moat protect us from the hazards of the dream-dimensions. It was a poetic image, but he did not mean it entirely poetically.

While these stray reflections were wandering through my mind, Dupin had supervised the rearrangement of the furniture, in order that Chapelain might be in the best position possible to commit Ysolde Leonys to a deeper mesmeric trance. I was obliged to retreat to the far side of the bed, and to do without a chair, but I took the opportunity to open the curtains and let a little daylight in.

It was a dull day, the sky being completely shrouded in grey cloud, although it was not actually raining. Although the window faced the south-east, the masked sun could not send more than a mild, soft light into the room, which seemed entirely appropriate for experiments in mesmerism. I supported myself as best I could on the windowsill, which was at the right height to serve as a misericord.

And the weak must go to the wall, I thought, taking what comfort I could from my knowledge of the true meaning of the phrase, which is the very opposite of the modern misinterpretation that condemns the weak to perish.

Dupin, again in his guise as Tristan de Léonais, did his level best to reassure his former lover Ysolde that all was well and that she must put her trust in the wizard Merlin and his magic, but when she asked for a potion to soothe her ills, he told her that she must wait until the spell was complete. Such is the power of imaginary love that she consented, although my hasty arithmetic suggested that it must have been at least eight hours since she had last been dosed with laudanum, and she would soon be feeling the commencement of the crawling chaos of withdrawal.

"This time," Chapelain murmured to Dupin, "I think we shall gain access to her intimate secrets."

You could have had access to her most intimate secrets for a gros sou *any time in the last twenty years,* I thought, reflexively—and was immediately ashamed of myself for having done so. I reminded myself, sternly, that streetwalkers are made by dire necessity, not by choice, and that it is their clients who are the pirates, the plunderers, and the exploiters.

Then I had to seal such casual thoughts away, in order to listen to the interrogation, and the narrative that it elicited.

CHAPTER NINE
YSOLDE'S STORY

"WHAT IS YOUR NAME?" Chapelain asked, when he was satisfied that the woman was in a deep trance.

"Ysolde Leonys."

"Have you ever had any other name?"

"No."

"Where were you born?"

"Callaba, in India."

"On what date?"

"Saint Sylvester's Day, 1722."

Chapelain looked at Dupin, but Dupin immediately shook his head, instructing the mesmerist not to challenge the impossible claim.

"Who was your father?" Chapelain continued.

"He called himself Mark Leonys of Cornwall, but that was not his true name."

"What was his true name?"

"John Taylor." There as only the slightest of pauses before she added the inevitable mantra: "Jack Taylor was a *bad man*."

"Who told you that Jack Taylor was a bad man?"

"Oberon."

Again, Chapelain looked at Dupin; again, Dupin shook his head.

"What became of your father, John Taylor?" Chapelain asked.

"He sailed for the South Seas. He never came back."

"Why did he sail for the South Seas?"

"To seek protection."

"Protection from what?"

"Angria—and the ghost."

Dupin raised his eyebrows at the mention of the name Angria, but did not attempt to deflect Chapelain from his course

"What ghost?" Chapelain asked.

"The ghost from the ghost-ship."

There! I thought. *I knew that it was relevant. I knew that there had to be a ghost-ship in this somewhere.*

"Whose ghost was it?" Chapelain hazarded.

No answer.

Another glance; another shake of the head.

"When did your father sail for the South Seas?"

"In 1731."

"When you were eight years old?" Because Saint Sylvester's Day is New Year's Eve, she could only have reached her ninth birthday on the very last day of that year, so Chapelain's arithmetic was accurate.

"Yes."

"Were you left alone with your mother."

"My mother was dead. I only had my ayah, and the Mahatma."

The Mahatma in question was presumably the original after whom she had named Leuret.

"Did you have any brothers or sisters?"

"No."

"Who took responsibility for you?"

Silence. Either she did not understand the question, or could not answer it. Dupin made a hand-signal to Chapelain

"When did you first go to Karla?"

That was the first question that seemed to disturb her. It surprised me too, even though I had heard her mention the name before. Dupin and Chapelain were obviously trying to draw upon everything she had let slip.

"I don't remember," was he answer she eventually gave. Presumably, she had been too young have any awareness of the date, or even her age.

"When was the last time you went to Karla?" Chapelain persisted.

"Before Oberon came."

"How old were you then?"

"Twelve."

"When did you leave India?"

"When Oberon took me away."

"And how old were you then?"

"Twelve."

"Where did you go?"

"To Oberon's home."

"What port did the ship sail to?"

"Le Havre."

"And by what means of transport did you leave Le Havre?"

"A diligence."

"Bound for where?"

"Caen."

"Did you stay in Caen?"

"No."

"Did you take another diligence?"

"Yes."

"Bound for where?"

"Rennes."

"Did you take another diligence from Rennes?"

"No."

"Did you stay in Rennes?"

"No."

"Where did you go, after Rennes?"

"To Oberon's home."

This time, Dupin had to reach out with his free hand to touch Chapelain's arm and attract the mesmerist's attention to his head-shake.

"Did Oberon have another name?" Chapelain continued.

"Yes."

"What was it?"

"He sometimes called himself the Ancient Mariner."

"Did he have any other names?"

"Yes."

"What were they?"

"He once called himself Captain Nemesis." This was becoming frustrating.

"Do you know the name with which he was baptized?" Chapelain demanded, trying to focus on the datum he wanted.

"He was never baptized."

"Do you know the first name he had, before he became Oberon, or adopted any other nicknames?"

Silence. Again, she did not understand, or could not answer.

"How old were you when Oberon made you Queen of his Underworld?"

This time, her face seemed to light up slightly.

"Thirteen,"

Thirteen! I thought. *That was when she had her fatal romance with Tristan de Léonais. In 1736, if her chronology can be trusted!* I did not suppose for a moment that her chronology *could* be trusted, objectively, although I was quite prepared to believe that she was not lying, and that she honestly imagined that she was well over a hundred years old.

"And how long were you queen?"

"A year and a day."

"Where did you go when you left the Underworld?"

"Paris."

"And when did you arrive in Paris?"

"During the Revolution."

"The Revolution of 1789?" said Chapelain, obviously surprised by the chronological inconsistency.

Mesmerized subjects do not usually respond to rhetorical questions, but Ysolde was an exception to the rule.

"No," she said. "The July Revolution."

The July Revolution had taken place in 1830, but this time Chapelain made the effort to swallow his incredulity.

Briefly slipping into the role of Thomas Linn the Rhymer, I was not surprised. According to folklore, a year and a day spent in fairyland can easily be the equivalent of a century in the mundane world. I carried out a rapid operation of mental arithmetic. If Ysolde had been thirteen when she went into Oberon's Underworld, she must have been fourteen when she came out, which meant that she was now, in terms of lifetime elapsed, thirty years old. Not nearly as old as she looked, in fact—but syphilis is a cruel disease, and if she had been walking the streets of Paris since 1830, she was fully entitled to look a great deal older than she really was...if *really* actually meant anything, in this context.

Chapelain changed tack. "Ysolde," he said, "Have you ever heard the name Cthulhu?" He tried to pronounce the word as Dupin had, but did not quite succeed in emphasizing every one of the name's seven elements as if it were a distinct syllable. The attempt was good enough, though; she knew what he meant.

The light in her eyes became strangely feverish.

"Yes."

"Where did you first hear the name?"

"In Karla."

"How old were you then?"

No answer—too young to remember, probably.

"Are you aware that there is an inscription on your back?"

"Yes."

"Do you know how it was put there?"

No answer—perhaps because the question was badly-phrased rather than because she did not know the answer. Chapelain did not attempt to repeat it, though.

"How old were you when was it put there?" he asked, instead.

Again, no answer. Very young, presumably.

This time Chapelain risked the direct approach. "*How* was it put there?"

"By magic."

"Has it always been visible?"

"No."

"When did it become visible?"

No answer.

Chapelain tried again: "When did you become aware that it was visible?"

"While I was in Bedlam." She obviously meant Bicêtre, but I was surprised by her substitution of the English slang term, which she must have known and used habitually before she committed herself to Leuret's care.

"Do you know what the inscription means?" Chapelain, persisted, doggedly. I knew, before he had even completed the sentence, that it was a mistake…that these were questions he ought not to be asking, no matter how much Dupin wanted to know the answers. He was stirring up something that would be better left undisturbed—but if he realized that, it was too late.

Suddenly, the sick woman was in desperate distress—but not because she was waking up. I think she actually tried with all her might not to answer the question, but she was in a mesmeric trance and was not the mistress of her own ill-treated flesh. She tried to remain silent, but she failed. It was, however, another voice—I am morally certain of it—that used her poor sore lips to say, or rather screech: *"Ph'nglui mglw'nat Cthulhu R'laiyeh wgah'ngl fhtaign."*

When she had pronounced the formula before, in Bicêtre, it had not seemed to have any manifest effect on our physical surroundings, although it had clearly disturbed the other patients on the ward. That had been a very bleak and rather gloomy room, though, and the awful fecal stench had drowned out more subtle sensory indications.

Now, we were in a pleasant, if slightly Spartan room, and the daylight, though no less grey, was coming into the room from a better direction at a more kindly angle. It would have been even brighter had I not been blocking it partially with my upper body. When Ysolde pronounced the formula, though, it seemed to me that the daylight *blurred*, that the room became distinctly chillier, and that there was a distinct whiff of rotting seaweed in the air. It might have been purely subjective, of course—an echo of the horror and terror of the night before.

If Chapelain noticed any change in the ambience, he did not

react. Nor did he stop following his script. Instead, he said: "Those are only the first six lines of the cryptogram. Do you know the seventh?"

"Nobody knows the seventh," she replied. "It is only to be pronounced in cases of the direst need. Angria judged that I would never need it, and should not be trusted with it." She was speaking in her own voice again, but she had become suddenly loquacious, in a way that obedient somniloquists were not supposed to do.

I knew that something was wrong—that among the things we did not know about her history there was something that made it dangerous to inquire about it. This time, Chapelain was puzzled, and looked at Dupin for guidance. Dupin pointed to her hands, still clasped around the medallion, holding it pressed to the top of her sternum.

"Do you know the purpose of the cryptogram on the medallion you are holding?" Chapelain asked.

"Yes," she said.

Don't ask her to pronounce it! My inner voice screamed, although not a whimper escaped my sealed lips.

When Chapelain checked with Dupin, however, the great man's reply was another insistent nod of the head.

"What is its purpose?" Chapelain.

"To protect me."

"From what?"

No answer—but she was disturbed again, and a visible frisson ran through her supine body.

I wanted to say "Please stop!" but my tongue seemed to be glued to the roof of my mouth. Dupin was frowning now, though, evidently disappointed and frustrated by the difficulty Chapelain was experiencing in making progress, but also anxious. He refrained from making any signals—but for once, Chapelain was not looking to Dupin for his lead. He had a question of his own that he had doubtless waned to ask for some time.

"Ysolde," he said, "Do you know where the remnants of the

treasure of the *Nossa Senhora del Cabo* are hidden?"

"Yes," she said.

Dupin looked furious, although I could not imagine why. I had heard him ask her where "the manuscripts" were on his own account. He shook his head furiously, but Chapelain could not be restrained.

"Where are they?" he asked, a trifle breathlessly.

"Some are in the Underworld," she replied, perhaps predictably—although it seemed to me to be useful information. If the mysterious Oberon who had brought her to France from India had taken her to somewhere near Rennes, then the Underworld, or its entrance, must be in Brittany.

I almost had to pinch myself to remind myself that the woman was dying, and mad, and that everything she thought she knew, about herself and everything else, was the product of pox-induced, or pox-encouraged, hallucination. Even the stigmata, striking as they were, were a product of her fantasy: what Leuret and Chapelain both called a "psychosomatic symptom." They were bizarre, but not impossible. The incantation was, it seemed, real—but probably only "real" in the sense that it had been written down in esoteric texts, available to be memorized by bibliophiles like Auguste Dupin…and bibliotaphs like Oberon Breisz.

That Breisz knew Ysolde Leonys, I did not doubt. That he had known her while she was a child, I did not doubt. But what he had done to her while she was a child, I could not imagine, and was not sure that I wanted to try. He had saved me from the shoggoth, apparently—but Dupin was certain that Madame Lacuzon's instincts were sure. If Jack Taylor had been a *bad man*, what was Oberon Breisz?

Again, I tried to remind myself that this was madness, and that anyone who tried to make sense of it was responding to a dangerous lure. I almost wished that Leuret was present, to remind us all that he would have taken a very different approach to the treatment of the dying woman. He would have tried to bring her back to reality. He would also have bought a priest into the ward to administer extreme unction, and hear her last confession, if she were capable of making one.

Perhaps, on the whole, it would be kinder if she were not.

Chapelain did not stop, but he reverted to what was presumably a further phase of the approximate script he had agreed with Dupin.

"Was Tristan de Léonais in the Underworld before you became its Queen?" the mesmerist asked.

Hesitation, then: "Yes."

"How did he come to be there?"

"He was one of Oberon's knights."

"How many knights did Oberon have?"

"I don't know."

"Were they all in the Underworld?"

"No."

"How many knights were in the Underworld when you were there?"

"Seven."

"Does that number include Merlin?"

"No."

"Does it include Tom Linn?"

"No."

"How many other people were in the Underworld, in addition to the knights?"

"I don't know."

"Can you tell me the names of the other knights."

"Huon, Gauvain, Roland, Lanval, Meliador and Lancelot."

Well, I thought, *at least she and Oberon had the grace to omit the saintly Perceval from their ironic roll-call. Their reading seems to have been conventional, though.* I wondered, however, whether Dupin was now regretting his readiness to stand in for Tristan of Léonais. If my growing suspicion as to the true nature of Oberon's mesmeric game and the roles played by the "knights" turned out to be true...but I did not feel able to voice it, even as a suggestion.

Perhaps Dupin had begun to conceive similar suspicions,

for he raised his hand, giving Chapelain a clear instruction to pause. He wanted a break in the interrogation, in order to confer with the mesmerist.

It was Chapelain's turn to shake his head and reply in mime. He, at least, had not entirely forgotten that this charade as supposed to be for his patient's benefit, rather than the satisfaction of Dupin's curiosity. He wanted to plant suggestions in Ysolde's mind that would ease her pain next time she woke up to harsh reality.

Dupin was not a cruel man, but he was obviously uncertain as to whether any such success might somehow prejudice his own enquiry. He repeated the gesture bidding the mesmerist to suspend the session and confer.

Whether Chapelain would have continued to be stubborn I do not know. He was interrupted.

Somniloquists are supposed to be utterly meek, entirely under the control of their inquisitor, but Ysolde Leonys apparently did not know that rule, and had already demonstrated that she was capable of loquacity.

Suddenly, she sat up in bed, and said, in her own voice: "They're coming. *This* is why I needed protection. *This* is why Angria gave me the amulet. He knew that the Mahatma had made me vulnerable, in making me useful."

Dupin and Chapelain could not have looked at her with more amazement and alarm if she had been a statue of Isis or Astarte who had suddenly taken it into her head to speak. All that Dupin could find to say, eventually—and I had never known him so stupefied—was: "Who is coming?"

"Not who, but what," Ysolde Leonys told him. "Pray that I can remember, for we are all in mortal peril—but it was so long ago!"

I would like to say that I did not know what she meant—but I did. Abruptly as they had arrived, before she reached the end of her sentence, there was no mistaking them.

CHAPTER TEN
THE SHOGGOTHS

THE FIRST TIME, when they had come in search of me—or, more probably, of the medallion—the shoggoths had used human carriers, and their actual presence had been removed in another dimension, perhaps to some neighboring universe or, more likely, to the encrypted borderlands that separate the universes. Those desert regions are haunted by the Dwellers of the Thresholds, but I doubt that the Dwellers ever try to scavenge *that* kind of carrion.

This time, the shoggoths arrived directly, not by moving through the intangible walls of the universe or the perfectly solid walls of my house, but rather by perverting space in such a way as to make the room in which our mesmeric séance was taking place *ambiguous.* They—or whatever was guiding them—*twisted* our reality, encrypting it in such a way that the loathsome predators could reach us without any intermediary of earthly space and time, let alone any vehicle of flesh and bone.

They had been so horrible before that I dare not say that they were any *more* horrible when they came again, but their presence was certainly more visible and more tangible, if no less easily describable. They were still unspeakable, still unthinkable—but whether I could speak or think of them or not, they were *here.*

Oddly enough, the most overwhelming accompaniment of their presence was the smell, whose faint preliminary echo I had earlier described, in the privacy of my mind, as "rotting seaweed." The impression of rotting remained, but if there was seaweed in the decaying morass, it was far from being alone; it was as if the life of an entire ocean had fallen into rapid putrefaction, concentrated by the lens of their advent.

If the stink made its impact more swiftly than any other sensory response, however, it did not hit harder. What I saw was what I had seen before: something like a cross between a squid and a sea-anemone, with more avid tentacles than I could ever hope to count, all possessed of a strangely intense viscosity that far was far beyond mere stickiness or sliminess, but seemed to be a partial liquefaction of space itself: a dissolution into some kind of primeval *urschleim*...which was, alas, far from being the worst of it.

The first time, I had only had a slight impression of the *other* aspect of the monster: the dragon behind the cephalopod; the thing with claws and wings and fiery breath. This time, I understood clearly enough that it was some kind of censor in my mind that had made me see the reaching entities as claws, the fluttering entities as wings, the fire as breath and the whole as a draconian worm. This time, the censor's kindly magic failed. This time, I realized how unrealizable the creature was, how lacking in anything authentically parallel to earthly substance it was.

The most fundamental aspect of the shoggoth that moved to possess me was not made of matter at all, even alien matter; it was made of something more akin to sound: harsh, cacophonous, obscene sound...but sound, however ugly, which as not lacking in rhythm, or, at least in a purely technical sense, harmony. It was in some strange, perhaps irrational and certainly transcendental, way *mathematically ordered*. In some bizarre way, it was alive...and because it was alive, it was deadly.

Apart from seeing into and through the shoggoths—for I remained aware of the others as well as the one that was focused on me—I had no visual impression of the room or its other occupants. It was not dark; it was simply that the part of my brain interpreting visual signals could not or would not see ordinary objects and individuals through that hideously twisted space. To the presence of Dupin and Chapelain, and that of Ysolde Leonys, not to mention the bed, the chairs and the fugitive copy of *A General History of the Pyrates*, I was now wilfully blind.

Would that I had been able to ignore my particular assailant as easily.

Paradoxical as it might seem, in view of what I have just written, I actually heard very little by means of my ears, except for a strange, high-pitched modulated *whistling*...but had I been younger, and had the kind of oral register that can hear bats in flight, I think I might have heard a great deal more, for most of the rhythmic sound of which the shoggoths were composed was undoubtedly beyond the spectrum of human perception.

The worst of it all, however, was what I felt and tasted.

This time, one of the shoggoths reached out to grasp me, not merely with its tentacles but with whatever reaching limbs its draconian aspect possessed. Those quasi-limbs reached *for* me, and they reached *into* me—and the first thing they reached for was not my brain but my tongue. Rumor has it that while carrion birds invariably aim for a corpse's eyes before savoring other flesh, marine predators attacking whales or other giant prey always go for the tongue before, and sometimes instead of, any other meat.

That my tongue was suddenly robbed of any power of speech, seemingly frozen into a solid, gnarled slab, seemed unworthy of anxiety, compared with the taste of the shoggoth, which was indescribably vile. Perhaps I should not be speaking in the singular here, although it seems inconceivable, in logical terms, that more than one shoggoth should have seized me, for the experience seemed somehow essentially *plural*. Perhaps, on the other hand, there never was any more than one shoggoth, and its seeming plurality was merely an effect of the twisting of space, like reflections in a mirror maze—but I can only repeat that they seemed plural to me, and that one in particular seemed to have singled me out for...for what? Possession? Consumption? Transfiguration?

Nothing harmless, at any rate—and certainly nothing pleasant.

I tasted it, or them, and it was worse than seeing it, or them, and perhaps even worse than feeling it, or them, although I was incapable of making much distinction, at that point in time, between tasting and feeing.

Was it a point in time, though? Was time any longer possessed of moments?

The previous night, I seemed to have lost an hour or so, somewhere between midnight and two, when I finally got around to feeling and noting time again. This time, I thought, I might lose days, or years, or an entire eternity. Indeed, I had the bizarre sensation of whirling through the entire cycle of time, to an end that was identical to the beginning, and back again, while there was nothing at the focal point of my thinking mind but that *taste*, that *feel*....

And then, if time was any longer possessed of a *then*, the febrile modulated whistling turned into a scream of agony.

I thought that it was mine. I thought that it was my death-agony—but it was not.

The shoggoths screamed, and the reason that the shoggoths screamed was that the twisted space-time was suddenly *full*, of a sound that was not the fabric of the worm-within-the-squid but the fabric of something even more powerful, even more predatory. I cannot say what sort of shape it might have had, had my brain been able to translate it into organically-understandable imagery, but I can say that it was organized mathematically and phonetically into forty-nine syllables, which were somehow arranged, in that convoluted space, into seven sets of seven, spoken simultaneously but in the correct order.

And the sound ripped the shoggoths apart.

Whether the shoggoths were actually destroyed, or were merely re-entombed in some mysterious encrypted space, I do not know—but I do know that I was suddenly free.

I collapsed, of course, falling off my slender misericord and instinctively coiling myself into a fetal position. Real time passed, in not insubstantial quantity. Five minutes, at least, must have elapsed before the echoes of unearthly sight and hearing, smell and touch and taste, finally consented to die.

Then I got up, slowly. Chapelain got to his feet at the same time. Dupin was already standing, looking with frank astonishment at Ysolde Leonys.

She was still recognizable—just. The syphilitic sores were no longer visible about her lips. Her skin was clear. Her complexion was no longer sallow. Her hair was raven-black, her eyes bright blue. She might have been thirty, for her beauty seemed maturely majestic rather than youthfully fresh, but surely no older. She was recognizable, but she was not the same disease-ridden individual that we had taken from Bicêtre. She was *healthy*. She was holding both her arms clasped hard to her breast. I could still make out the wooden medallion between her fingers, but they were no longer cupped around it; instead it was pressed to her flesh, with the encryption facing inwards.

I was unable speak as yet, and I suspect that Dupin was equally incapable, but Chapelain made the effort, because he had an urgent command to impart.

"Whatever you do," he whispered, hoarsely, "*don't wake her*. If she comes out of the trance now, the shock will surely kill her."

When Dupin finally recovered his voice, it was to ask the mesmerist, in an absurdly earnest whisper: "Have you ever seen this phenomenon before?"

"Only the faintest echo of it," Chapelain replied. "Mesmeric metamorphosis is a well-documented phenomenon—entranced individuals sometimes seem to take on new personalities, with new appearances to suit the alteration, and the most common shift is to a younger self, with an apparent rejuvenation of appearance, but there is nothing on record as extreme as this. She seems to have cast off her disease entirely."

"That's an illusion—mere glamor," Dupin muttered, "and there are precedents a-plenty in the lore of legend, if not in the records of mesmerism. Are you sure that she is still deeply entranced?"

"Absolutely certain," Chapelain said.

"And how long will the phenomenon last?"

"I don't know," Chapelain confessed. "There are reports of metamorphoses lasting several days...but they were far more trivial than this one. These are uncharted waters."

Ysolde Leonys' eyes had been open throughout this exchange, but she had not seemed to be able to see anything within the room. Now, though, she turned her head—not, as might be expected, to Dupin, but to me. "Would you fetch me a mirror, Tom?" she asked, politely.

Mechanically, almost as if I were a marionette on strings, I went to my dressing-room to fetch my shaving-mirror.

When I gave it to her, she studied her reflection with evident interest. "Is this who I am?" she asked, pensively—and added, without waiting for an answer: "Is this who I *might have been?*"

Then she laid the mirror down and turned to Dupin. "We must go," she said. "I do not know how much time we have, but certainly little enough that we must race against the clock."

"Go where?" Dupin asked.

"The Underworld," she said. "He might well try to imprison us when we get there, and all the advantages will be his, for he will be in his own lair, but we must go nevertheless. This needs to be settled, now, for the shoggoths will return again, and I doubt that I can hold them at bay on my own. We will be more vulnerable still in the Underworld, but that, at least, is ground on which we might resist, and ground on which we might be able to summon help. If we stay here, they will destroy us...or worse. I'm sorry that you have become involved in this, for it might have been wiser to let them take me from Bicêtre...or to let Oberon take me back directly, if he would consent to do so. Now, though, you're committed. There is no longer any safety in the world you know."

But it was a hallucination, I reminded myself, yet again. *It was not real.* It did not matter, though; real or illusory, the shoggoths would be deadly, if we no longer had the means to keep them at bay next time they came.

"The Underworld in Brittany?" Dupin queried, naively—but then, suddenly, he seemed to get a grip on himself, and added: "Yes, of course." He turned to me, suddenly self-composed. "Send Bihan to the *Messageries* to reserve five seats in this afternoon's diligence to Rennes," he instructed. "If that is not possible, get whatever seats he can on whatever coach is departing in the right direction, within the hour if possible." I did not have time to ask *why five* before the answer came, as he continued: "Send Madame Bihan to my house, and instruct Madame Lacuzon to come immediately. Find clothing and a cloak for Mademoiselle Leonys, then pack your bags with more spare clothing, and some food. Then summon a fiacre."

"You can't mean to race off to Brittany at a moment's notice," Chapelin objected. "I can't possibly...."

"Stay if you must, Chapelain," was Dupin's brutal reply, which I overheard as I was already hastening along the corridor to the stair-head, "but if you ever hope to clap eyes on what's left of Olivier Levasseur's treasure...."

Dupin knew how to frame a convincing argument. When the fiacre set off for the *Messageries*, less than an hour later, there were five of us aboard. Perhaps we were the strangest crew that ever undertook such a journey, thanks to the supplementary presence of the witch and the magically-awakened but rather ill-dressed beauty, but I could not help thinking that Dupin, Chapelain and I were the three musketeers, finally about to play our allotted roles in an authentic melodrama. This time, I had put my revolver in my pocket.

I could not help thinking, though, as I tried to slow my heartbeat and relax while the fiacre trotted across the Île de la Cité, that I had now seen the monsters that were pursing us in possessed-human guise, and in shoggoth guise. *Next time*, I wondered, *will I have to face the dragon directly? And if I do, can I possibly survive, no matter what enchanted amulets we have to hand, or magicians to pronounce their ugly incantations?*

CHAPTER ELEVEN
OVERLAPPING NARRATIVES

THERE WAS A DILIGENCE leaving for Rennes that afternoon, with an overnight stop in Alençon. Unfortunately, there had only been three seats left in the cabin, so two us had perforce to travel on the *impériale*. Fortunately, the cold weather was not yet so intense that we were in danger of freezing to death once the sun set. Dupin insisted that Madame Lacuzon should sit inside to guard the entranced woman—who was very definitely a somnambulist now rather than a somniloquist—and that Chapelain must sit with them too, in case of further developments in her condition. What the other passengers might have thought of that trio, I did not know or care; I was on the top of the coach with Dupin, sitting amid the luggage like two peasants going home from market, and begrudged them all their seats inside. Fortunately, there were no actual peasants going home from market to share our discomfort.

While waiting for the departure I had tried to bring my journal up to date, but it was impossible to write once the coach set off. Dupin had been studying his cryptograms, but even reading was difficult with the coach lurching on the muddy road, and he was afraid that the wind might snatch the papers from his hand, so he put them away again. By that time, however, they were probably so firmly engraved in his memory that he could continue their contemplation even in the absence of the models. His conversation seemed a trifle distracted, as if some partitioned part of his mind were far away, displaced in a different dimension where the inspiration of mediation could be given freer play.

"What do you expect to find when we get to Brittany?" I asked Dupin, once we were on the road and there was time to relax, at least to the extent that one can on the roof of a diligence.

"We need to get there first," he reminded me. "We have no idea how long Mademoiselle Leonys can hold herself together, and I am inclined to take Chapelain's word for it that reversion to her former state might be very rapidly followed by her death."

"But if she can survive long enough to do it," I said, "you believe she can guide us to this Underworld where she was held prisoner as a child, while mesmerized into believing that she was a fairy queen?"

"We shall see," was as far as he was prepared to commit himself.

"I am understanding the story that she told in the same way as you, I assume?" I said. "There are two overlapping narratives there, one of which can only be read between the lines of the fantasy. She really was brought from India, and she really was kept underground, if not for a year and a day then for some similar period. There she was compelled to take part in some elaborate charade, persuaded actually to believe that she was queen of a magical court, surrounded by characters from legend and romance, while she was actually...well, let us say that, if I'm interpreting her tale correctly, she began her career as a whore long before she reached Paris, without knowing what she was doing, poor child."

"That does seem to be a plausible interpretation," Dupin agreed, although his tone was dubious. It was the pedant in him that came to the fore, though, rather than the doubter. "There were not two overlapping narratives, however—there were three, of which the remotest of the three is the most puzzling of all."

"Cthulhu," I said, stumbling yet again over the improbable pronunciation.

"Cthulhu," he agreed.

"Personally," I said, "I can't see where the pirates fit in, let alone the encrypted monster from the dawn of time. The Oberon charade I can now comprehend, after a fashion, but not the constant refrain of 'Jack Taylor was a *bad man.*' I can see why Oberon Breisz might have felt obliged to provide his innocent captive with a revised account of an Indian childhood that she could hardly remember, and why he might have been tempted to persuade her that time had gone awry while she was in fairyland, but why drag in the pirates?"

"I don't know," Dupin said, frankly. Being the man he was, however, he could not help adding: "But there are one or two hypotheses I could frame, if I were prepared to risk being fanciful, and being led up the garden path."

"Go on," I said.

"Do you remember the other nicknames that Oberon attributed himself, for Ysolde's benefit?"

"The Ancient Mariner," I said. "Borrowed from the Coleridge poem, no doubt. Captain Nemesis."

"And who might those nicknames fit—as well as the continual assertion that John Taylor was a *bad man*?"

"The other pirate," I said, solving the puzzle almost instantaneously. "The one Taylor usurped and marooned—the one who must have been extremely annoyed when Levasseur and Taylor captured the fabulous prize that, in his eyes, should have been his. Edward…."

Momentarily, I could not quite bring the name to mind.

"England," Dupin supplied, "although that too was a pseudonym, of course."

"But Oberon Breisz cannot be Edward England," I said, "any more than Ysolde can really be the daughter of John Taylor the pirate, rather than some descendant namesake."

"Perhaps not," said Dupin, although he seemed to mean the *perhaps* literally rather than as a polite denial. "But even if we are dealing with descendants, the tradition of vendetta is not purely Italian. It is not unknown for quests for vengeance to be extrapolated to the fourth or fifth generation, especially when there is money at stake."

"You think that what Oberon Breisz did to Ysolde was a theatrical kind of revenge, visited by a descendant of Edward England on a descendant of John Taylor? In the great tradition of the Boulevard du Temple, they would have to be the only surviving descendants, and the treasure must have been stolen from the hapless child by the wicked villain."

"That is one possible construction that might be put on the superficial events," Dupin conceded.

"What's the other?" I demanded.

"Possibilities are always endless, my friend, especially in such phantasmagorical territory as this. If Saint-German is correct about Oberon Breisz being a good magician, and something of a clown, perhaps he really might be Edward England, in the flesh."

"I beg leave to doubt *that*," I said.

"And rightly so, my friend—but there were other items in Ysolde's replies to Chapelain's interrogation that recalled Captain Johnson's chapter on Edward England, and I suspect that we might only have glimpsed a corner of the pirate narrative thus far."

"What items?" I asked

"Ysolde named her birthplace as Callaba, and said that John Taylor sailed for the South Seas to seek protection from Angria, as well as a ghost. Callaba was Angria's fortress, not far from Bombay. Johnson calls Angria a pirate, but he was much more powerful than a mere robber. He was certainly a relentless predator of ships, though, and a serious thorn in the side of the British East India Company until he made common cause with them, at least for a while, against their rivals. It was partly on the Company's behalf, I suspect, that he went to war with the Viceroy of Goa, the Conde de Ericeira."

"The Viceroy whose treasure was plundered from the Portuguese galleon."

"The same. When I talked before about the difficulties that the pirates must have had in capitalizing on their good fortune,

I had it vaguely in mind that Taylor might have tried to form an alliance with the East India Company himself, but it seems more likely now that he actually took his share of the treasure to Callaba and made common cause with Angria—a common cause that eventually went sour. Perhaps that was only to be expected, given Angria's reputation...but there might have been another reason. We know that Taylor got rid of England while they were both associated with Levasseur, but we do not know how relations stood between England and Levasseur... or between England and Angria. If England really did escape, having been marooned by Taylor, and really was grimly intent on seeing revenge, he might have sought out Levasseur, or Angria, in the hope or expectation of remaking an old alliance."

"Which is all very interesting, from a purely antiquarian viewpoint," I said, "but does not help at all to explain how England might still be alive and calling himself Oberon Breizsz. That remains absurd. No man can live for more than a hundred and fifty years."

"Can he not? Personally, I feel compelled to maintain an open mind. After all, if our Comte de Saint-Germain really is the eighteenth-century Comte de Saint-Germain, as he now seems perfectly convinced that he is, it would become unlikely that there were not others in similar situations."

"I thought that Saint-Germain believed himself to be some kind of reincarnation of his notorious namesake, rather than an immortal continuation of the same physical existence?" I said, with a hint of contempt.

"I doubt that Saint-Germain knows exactly what he believes," said Dupin. "Given that he does believe it, though, and that he recognizes Oberon Breisz as a peer...."

"But you don't believe in immortality *or* reincarnation," I said, "Do you?"

"You know perfectly well that I try to avoid belief and keep an open mind," was his inevitable reply. But he added: "Besides, those are not the only possibilities."

"No," I conceded, sarcastically, "possibilities are always

endless. What's the third, then, in order of approximate likeli-hood?"

"That knots are being tied, or bridges built, in time. That the present is somehow being connected to the past, so that the narratives really do overlap."

Having seen, felt and tasted a shoggoth in the margins of space and time, that did not seem at all implausible, for the moment. "And that's how Cthulhu fits in," I said.

"Perhaps so," said Dupin, "given that it definitely fits in somehow."

"Those things have now attacked me twice," I said, "and the fact that their presence, strictly speaking, was no more than hallucinatory did not mean that they could not hurt of destroy me. Why? Were they trying to take possession of the amulet on both occasions?"

"Probably," Dupin opined. "It seems to attract them as well as having the power to repel them—but if the medallion really has been safe in the Harmonic Society's vaults since the Society's foundation, it must have been under some sort of protection there. It is only since Saint-Germain took it out and the symbols inscribed in Mademoiselle Leonys' flesh became visible that the star-spawn have become active...or become active *again*. She says that Angria gave her protection because he knew that she would become vulnerable when he made her useful...I must instruct Chapelain to ask her what she meant by *useful*."

"I can understand why Ysolde banished them, even though I have no idea how she was able to do so," I said, "but why did Oberon Breisz stop them the previous night, if he didn't want to take possession of the amulet himself?"

"I don't know," Dupin told me, apparently growing a little impatient with the necessity of confessing so much ignorance. "Perhaps he knows how dangerous possession of the amulet can be, but doesn't want it to fall into the control of Cthulhu's minions. Perhaps he is as enthusiastic to lure us to his den in Brittany as Ysolde now is to take us there—he implied as much in the message he asked you to deliver. If we're fortunate, time will tell. If not…we might never know."

He frowned, evidently wishing that he were inside the diligence, able to question Ysolde further, no matter what his fellow passengers might think. Chapelain, I felt sure, would be more discreet, He had a reputation to protect and a career to preserve, and might have been secretly recognized by one of those fellow passengers.

"But while we have the amulet," I said, "or insist on keeping company with the person who has—given that we dare not take it back from Ysolde in case it precipitates her return to normality, and death—we are perpetually in danger of a further assault, are we not?"

"In danger, yes—but we now know that Ysolde has the means to repel such assaults, as Breisz apparently also has. I think, now that I have heard the incantation inscribed on the amulet, that I might even be able to repel them myself."

"I'm sure that I couldn't," I said, a trifle piqued. "Whatever I heard—and I'm not entirely sure that I *heard* anything—was far too confused for memorization."

"But I was already familiar with six-sevenths of the other encryption," Dupin reminded me. "I really think, now, that I ought to be able to work out the seventh part, if I could just figure out the underlying theoretical pattern of the encryption, and its mathematical harmony."

"What is Ysolde's insistence that the amulet is hers supposed to imply?" I asked him. "Does it mean that the wooden disk is not the object that Levasseur threw into the crowd on his way to be hanged, or that Levasseur had no right of ownership to it in the first place?"

"Probably the latter," he opined. "If Saint-Germain can be trusted…." His skepticism on the latter point was so evident that he did not bother to finish the observation.

"Are you and Chapelain going to make another attempt to question her when we stop in Alençon?" I asked. "After all, she's still entranced."

"I hope so," he said, "but it's a decision I might be forced to leave to Chapelain's discretion. I shall consult him when we reach Alençon—if we survive the journey." The last comment was a perfectly normal complaint about the state of the road, and its effect on the *impériale*, where we felt every jolt as if it were magnified. Dupin was not a great traveler, save for blithely setting sail on the ocean of the imagination, so he very rarely had to endure such discomfort as he was now experiencing. I had had far more experience, although I always traveled inside a coach when I could.

"What do you hope to find in Brittany, Dupin?" I asked him. "You dangled the lure of Levasseur's gold in front of Chapelain, and you jumped to the conclusion that Saint-Germain has the same interest—but you don't care about that. Are you really hoping to find precious manuscripts looted from John Dee's collection?"

"What I hope to find," he told me, grimly, "is a little enlightenment—there is no other prize, I can assure you, that would tempt me to endure a journey like this one."

"Enlightenment about what? Cthulhu? The magic of encryption?"

"Yes," he replied, shortly.

After a few minutes' silence, I said. "I met a seaman named Pym once, who told bizarre tales of the South Seas. Poe based the longest of all his tales on the seaman's story, but could not provide a proper ending any more than Pym could. I gave you the book to read, if you remember."

"I do," he said. "I thought the ending quite appropriate, in its conscientious insistence on leaving the mystery incomplete and insoluble. The mysteries of the sea do not lend themselves to ready conclusion. I have met seamen myself who have recognized me as a sympathetic ear, as Pym evidently recognized Poe. Those who have had strange experiences are reluctant to speak of them in earnest to men who will automatically judge them liars and make fun of them.

"John Dee, who knew every captain that set sail from Elizabeth's England, might well have been the last man that was trusted wholeheartedly and universally in that regard. While mariners kept the secrets of his navigational tables and devices, he kept the secrets of their strangest tales. It was probably England's seamen, rather than Edward Kelley, who provided the most valuable raw materials of the *Liber Loagaeth*, the *Claves Angelicae* and the *Claves Daemonicae*.

"Dee was present when the British East India Company was founded, and was a key participant in its planning. If anyone ever knew what became of the three ships Elizabeth sent out in 1596, prior to the formation of the company—which were allegedly lost—Dee was in on the secret. Although he only crossed the English Channel on a handful of occasions, he probably knew more about the mysteries of the sea—including and especially R'lyaieh—than any other man who ever lived. Individual sailors only knew of individual encounters, but Dee caught a glimpse of the bigger picture."

"Which is?" I said.

"I wish I knew. He could not put it in the terms that we use today, but he undoubtedly knew that the boundaries between the universes are sometimes weakened in the deserts of the ocean, as they sometimes are in actual deserts and subterranean caves. How much more he knew I cannot tell—not without access to the lost manuscripts—but he certainly knew that there are crypts in the dream-dimensions, and that seers have access to the dreams imperfectly imprisoned within them. He also knew how direly unreliable seers can be, of course—although that did not prevent him from making what use he could of Edward Kelley, the most talented skryer he ever found…but a *bad man*, apparently."

"But why are the boundaries between the universes weaker in remote regions of the sea than anywhere else?" I wondered.

"I'm not sure. There seems to be something about the absence of humankind…or, perhaps more accurately, the absence of human civilization and self-confidence…that permits such flaws to appear and facilitates their growth."

"Growth?" I queried.

"Perhaps that's the wrong term—but such breaches can certainly increase, or deteriorate, either by virtue of blind and random processes—Nyarlathotep, the crawling chaos—or by deliberate effort that we are bound to see as malign."

"Cthulhu?"

"Among others…but in respect of the ocean, mostly Cthulhu. I don't know whether R'lyaieh, the earthly component of his transdimensional crypt, actually has a specific physical location on the deep sea-bed—if it has, it is probably somewhere in the South Seas—but I do know that its influence is not confined to that region. It extends across the Earth's surface, although it's mostly manifest beneath that surface, only emerging with difficulty. The tribes that know his name, and can chant the first six lines of the Cthulhu encryption, are mostly found on islands and in coastal regions, although some are troglodytic."

"But how do they know the name and the chant?" I asked.

"They discover it in their dreams. Our civilized culture makes rigorous attempts to forget dreams, or at least to exile their content from our view of the mundane world, using folklore, legend and literature as a kind of safety-valve or treasure-chest, but some tribal cultures take an opposite view, and search the dream-dimensions to which they have fugitive access, by means of shamans and other seers. Far travelers—especially seamen—often fall prey to similar kinds of madness."

"It is madness, then?"

"Oh yes—there's no doubt about that. But sanity is a refuge, far less of a stronghold than François Leuret would like it to be, and sometimes inaccessible even to the wisest of men."

"And where did *you* come across the name and the chant?" I wanted to know.

"Initially, in one of Bougainville's reports."

"I've read Bougainville's *Voyage autour le monde*," I told him. "I do not remember any such mention."

"He and his scientific collaborators made numerous reports," Dupin said, as if I should have known that. "The popular version is a selective summary. Some of the stranger details are known only to a limited number to scholars, having been rejected by the voyage's sponsors as products of ergot-induced delirium. That has become a virtual custom since John Dee's day. There is no worldwide conspiracy of silence demanding the hiding of such reportage—it hides, as it were, if its own accord, following the logic of the situation. Once one knows where to dig, it is not so very difficult to unearth it, in dribs and drabs. The bigger picture, however...."

"Remains elusive."

"Indeed—and perhaps will always remain so, given that scholars are mortal, and tend to die almost as soon as they begin to get a grasp on any subject whatsoever. Those who claim to be immortal or reincarnate seem to do no better than commoner men, alas...and they also tend to be the ones who forsake sanity altogether, to cast themselves adrift on seas of madness."

"In brief then," I said, "we are following a madwoman to the lair of a madman, in the hope that we might discover some shreds of enlightenment regarding the farther shores of madness?"

"You have an admirable talent for synopsis, my friend," he said. "And I'm glad that you're with us, for we might yet find a voice of pure sanity useful."

"But *you* are the sanest man I know," I protested. "And you told me last night that Madame Lacuzon is the sanest person *you* know. I'm surely superfluous to requirements, and far too vulnerable to bad dreams."

"Never superfluous, my friend," he said, "and not as vulnerable as you imagine."

I was flattered by the compliment. "And we have Chapelain too," I added. "All for one and one for all—like the three musketeers, Athos, Porthos and Aramis."

"More like Ethos, Pathos and Logos," he muttered, drawing his cloak around him to protect him from a sudden gust of wind. He had named the three components of classical rhetoric, from which Dumas had presumably derived two of his three musketeers' names, but not the third. Chapelain, I presumed, was Ethos or Athos, and I was Pathos or Porthos. I hoped that the adventure confronting us was one in which a Logos would, after all, prove more useful than an Aramis.

CHAPTER TWELVE
THE INN AT ALENÇON

WE WERE ALL HEARTILY glad when the diligence finally reached the outskirts of Alençon. We had stopped to change horses on several prior occasions, but express coaches do not linger over such necessities, and we had not had more than five minutes to stretch our legs at any of those relay stations. I had not even bothered to get down from the impériale, knowing that I would only have to climb up again and not being the most agile man in the world, but Dupin had got down every time to check on Ysolde Leonys.

He reported on each occasion that she was now as rigid as a statue, almost as if she had somehow stopped time within her body, but that Chapelan has assured him that she was still very much alive. Her heart-rate was slow and she was cold, but she was in better health now than she had been before her strange metamorphosis.

"Perhaps she's saving herself for her impending revenge on her persecutor," I suggested, in one of my more whimsical moments, when Dupin climbed back up after our penultimate stop before Alençon.

"I hope so," he said. "That is to say, I hope she's saving herself—I'm not yet convinced that she's seeking revenge on Oberon Breisz for the kind of sexual exploitation to which you imagine he must have subjected her."

"I don't suppose you are," I said. "We're always reluctant to see such things in our own culture, preferring to scapegoat foreigners. In Paris they call child prostitution an English vice, like flagellation, but in London they think it a continental affair. In the same way, the French call syphilis *the Italian disease*, while Englishmen call it *the French disease* and the Italians *the Spanish disease*."

"Whereas Americans have no such delusions?"

"About themselves, certainly. About Europe, none."

When we reached the inn where we were to spend the night in Alençon, Dupin was quick to jump down again, to help Mademoiselle Leonys out of the coach. After what he had said about her being as frigid as a statue, I half-expected that he and Chapelain might have to carry her, but she stepped down in a lady-like manner, and thanked her loyal Tristan kindly. She even favored me with a brief smile, but it seemed to come from a long way away. She was obviously capable of speech, but I doubted that she would respond meekly to any sort of interrogation.

The inn was large, and moderately comfortable; the innkeeper came out into the courtyard to make arrangements for our feeding and accommodation, and I was able to hire two rooms upstairs for our exclusive use during the hours during which the coach was due to pause. Once we had sorted out our luggage, while my companions were still preoccupied with our enigmatic guide, I stepped into the inn's dining-room to investigate its comforts. The dining-room and pot-room were both very quiet, but not quite deserted. A few local drinkers were gathered in the pot-room, while a lone traveler, who must have arrived not long before on horseback, was enjoying a hearty meal in a corner of the dining-room.

He looked up as I came in, and our eyes met. Strangely enough, he seemed more surprised that I was. It was the Comte de Saint-Germain.

"My God!" he said, when I had moved forward to confront him. "You're at least twenty-four hours ahead of schedule. I had no idea that Dupin was capable of solving the puzzle as quickly as this. I expected him to be running around Paris for at least a day, digging up all the information he could find regarding Oberon Breisz, and poring over the medallion for hours on end."

Feebly, I could think of nothing better to say than: "What are *you* doing here?"

"Going to Britanny, of course," he replied. "I expected to wait for you in Rennes, with plenty of time in hand to make my preparations, and then to follow you clandestinely…assuming, that is, that Dupin knows where to…." He broke off suddenly, having seen something over my shoulder. I looked back, and saw my four companions making their way up the stairs, moving swiftly but not surreptitiously.

The President of the Harmonic Philosophical Society had been surprised to see me, but now he was flabbergasted. "Is that…," he said, weakly—and then stopped in order to swallow. When he resumed speaking, it was to mutter: "I always *knew*, in my heart of hearts, that Dupin was a secret magician, only posing as a skeptic as a means of self-concealment—but I had never thought him capable of anything like *that*."

He was referring to Ysolde Leonys' transformation, of course, and had completely mistaken the manner in which it had occurred. I did not feel that I was under any obligation to correct his error. To tell the truth, I had occasionally suspected myself that Dupin was a secret magician, only posing as a skeptic for reasons of concealment. The conversation we had just had on the roof of the coach had done nothing to counter that suspicion.

A few minutes later, Dupin came downstairs again, and immediately came forward to stand beside me.

"I fully expected you to follow us," he said to Saint-Germain, "but I did not expect you to ride so hard as to get here ahead of us. I pity your poor horse."

"Actually," Saint-Germain said, stiffly, "I came at a very leisurely pace, allowing my mount to rest at regular intervals. I would *never* abuse a fine horse. I know what kind of man you think I am, but you really ought not to keep hurling these careless slanders at me whenever we chance to meet. I see that you've brought your gorgon along—not to keep me at bay, I hope?"

Dupin turned on his heel and went to speak to the innkeeper, presumably to arrange for Ysolde, Madame Lacuzon and Chapelain to be served with food and drink in their rooms. I did not know what his own intentions were, and thought that he might intend me to take exclusive responsibility for dealing Saint-German, since I was the one who had gone to meet him at Saint-Sulpice. Thus, when the self-styled Comte invited me to set down at his table I did so, meekly.

"I suppose I still owe him a debt of gratitude for helping me to recover my stolen Guadagnini," Saint-Germain said, with a sigh, "so I ought to be generous in regard to his rudeness, even though I have paid him back in triplicate by lending him the medallion. I do wish we could be friends, though. Imagine what the Society might accomplish if he and Oberon Breisz would consent to join it! We really are all on the same side, in the quest for enlightenment. We are scientists now, and ought to work together, in the common cause...not that the members of the Académie des Sciences are free of churlish rivalries and the hoarding instinct, of course."

"How much do you know about Breisz?" I asked, conscious of my duty to play the interrogator, if Dupin really was going to leave that job to me.

"Very little, alas," the Comte replied, contriving another sigh. "Not enough, obviously, else I'd not have been so astonished by his appearance last night. Who could have anticipated that he'd intervene on our behalf—and not even with the intent of taking possession of the medallion? I could have dispelled the hallucination myself, of course—but perhaps not in time to save your sanity as well as my own. Given that he's been searching high and low for documents relating to Levasseur and other pirates of the Indian Ocean for many years, it's difficult to imagine why he didn't demand the amulet when he had the chance. I confess that I don't understand the game he's playing. Obviously, he doesn't know where the treasure is, but...perhaps he's pinning his hopes on Dupin's ability to solve the cryptogram too. *Has* he solved it?"

"I don't know," I said, evasively, but could not resist the temptation to add: "But I don't believe he's looking for the kind of solution you seem to be expecting."

"Really? You mean he doesn't believe that it's the key to Levasseur's treasure?"

"No. I think he'd be bitterly disappointed if that was what it turned out to be. Indeed, it certainly seemed to me that what is inscribed on the medallion is the spell that Ysolde used to get rid of the shoggoths when they attacked us in my house."

"The shoggoths came back?"

"More forcefully than the first time."

Saint-Germain pulled a face. "I'd like to say 'that's strange'— but I know too little about such hallucinations to know whether it's strange or not. I have magic enough to ward off things of that sort...but you might be in more danger than you think, even with Dupin to shield you."

"I haven't the slightest idea what to think," I admitted.

"Very wise," he said, sarcastically. "It's always best to keep an open mind. I wish I were better at that myself. Knowledge is sometimes a burden, don't you think?"

"It can drive you mad," I replied.

He laughed. I was oddly pleased—Dupin so rarely laughed at my quips.

"*You* should join the Society, you know," he said. "I think you'd find it very interesting. I don't issue very many invitations."

"Mostly to people a good deal richer or more gifted than I am," I retorted. "I'd be flattered, if I didn't think that the invitation was just a ploy on your part, to annoy Dupin."

"The last thing I want to do," he told me, "is annoy Monsieur Dupin. I'd love to join your little expedition—and I really do believe that you might find my help useful. Breisz is only one man, however gifted a magician he might be, but he's far from being the only man in France who'd like to lay his hands on what's left of Levasseur's loot."

"If anything *is* left," I put in, conscientiously.

"There is that possibility too," he admitted. "Sometimes, when you chase wild geese, that's all you end up with. There was a lot of gold, though, and I doubt that anyone with a heart could have bought himself to melt down the Flaming Cross of Goa. Angria probably ended up with every last penny of John Taylor's share, but Levasseur came to France in order to keep his portion safe from that particular threat…ironic, isn't it, that he was then arrested in the Seychelles?"

"Ironic," I agreed. "Why did he go back, if he'd already brought the treasure to France?"

"I don't know. Breisz might, given that he's been hoarding as many documents as he can for longer than even Père France can remember, but I haven't been able to find out, even with the resources of the Society behind me. If only I'd got to meet Levasseur face-to-face…at any rate, there was something he had to do—some obligation he couldn't dodge…which, given that he was a pirate, and treachery was his business must have been an unusually heavy obligation."

"An obligation to whom?" I asked, curiously.

"Come on!" he said, "You're giving me nothing. You can't expect me to tell you what I know, or even what I can guess, unless you're prepared to do the same."

I was about to make some cutting remark about working in a common cause, but I was interrupted by the innkeeper, who transferred two brim-full soup-dishes from his tray to the table, setting them down side by side, along with two spoons and a basket of bread. I was still looking at the second dish, feeling slightly puzzled, when Dupin sat down beside me, and immediately started spooning the hot liquid into his mouth.

"Eat," Saint-Germain said to me. "Warmth is its chief virtue—if you let it go cold, you won't enjoy it at all." Then he turned back to Dupin to say: "Now that we're breaking bread together, are we friends?"

"No," Dupin said, succinctly.

"I lent you Levasseur's medallion—surely I'm due some

credit for that?"

"It wasn't yours to lend," Dupin told him. "Nor was it Levasseur's. It has now been returned to its true owner, apparently. I suppose we owe you some thanks for that—but an honest man would regard it as his simple duty."

"But it *was* Levasseur's," Saint-Germain protested, "and now it's mine. It can't possibly be *hers*. *La Buse* gave it to me himself, and I can account for its whereabouts ever since. I've tried everything I know to solve the cryptogram, but I have to admit that I failed. If you've succeeded, you're a better man than I am."

That was a temptation hard to resist, and it brought a compromise from Dupin. "I can't yet claim the credit for deciphering it," he said, "but I think I can recite it for you, if you wish."

"Do you know where the treasure is?" Saint-Germain asked, bluntly

"Alas," said Dupin, between mouthfuls of soup, "I don't. I fear that you might have been harboring unrealistic expectations with regard to the significance of the cryptogram, which probably contributed enormously to your failure to decipher it. It's not a set of instructions as to how to find the treasure—it's what you would probably call a magic spell."

"Which does what?" Saint-German asked, suspiciously.

"It re-encrypts stray shoggoths—which is to say, it dispels a certain kind of malevolent hallucination."

Saint-Germain looked at me. I had already told him that, but he had not believed me. He was a little less certain as to whether the claim could be dismissed when it came from Dupin. "Oberon Breisz already knows how to do that," he murmured, pensively

"Which is probably why he did not think it worthwhile taking possession of the medallion yesterday night," Dupin said.

"So why has he been searching for it?" Saint-Germain wanted to know.

"I don't know," Dupin said, "but I suspect that he hoped that the search might somehow lead him to Ysolde, who certainly seems to believe that it is hers, and who appears to have given him the slip in 1830. You doubtless heard the message that he asked my friend to deliver to me."

"He's been looking for the whore all along? Why? Does *she* know where the treasure is?"

"I think she might. What I don't know is why *he* doesn't, if, in fact, he doesn't—or, if he *does* know where the treasure was, and has been in possession of it for a very long time, exactly what it is for which he is still searching."

"You think Breisz already has the gold?"

"Probably. I certainly suspect that he has the manuscripts. Given Père France's evaluation of the man, I assume that he'd be just as inclined to hoard gold as he is to hoard books. Do you evaluate him any differently?"

"No," Saint-German admitted. "I'd only met him twice before last night, although some of the older Society members have had dealings with him before my...return. Everyone agrees that he's a miser, though. I suppose that if he did have the cross...."

"If he does," Dupin opined, "you won't find him an easy man to rob."

"Rob!" Saint-Germain protested. "I never had any such intention. I thought he didn't know...that the treasure was hidden by Levasseur, and would belong to anyone who can find it. That's what Levasseur told me...." He broke off there.

"I think you might be misremembering, Comte," Dupin suggested, dryly. "Your memories of the eighteenth century have always been a trifle hazy, have they not?"

Saint-Germain wasn't about to answer that. "You're trying to trick me," he said, resolutely. "You're trying to persuade me to give up and go home—but you must know that there's no possibility of that. I intend to see this through...and if Breisz really does have the gold, I'll redouble my attempts to bring him into the bosom of the Society."

"If he had wanted to join," Dupin said, "he would probably have done so at its inception, as one of the founders."

"You really think he's that old?" Saint-Germain said, warily.

"You don't?" Dupin countered, provocatively.

Dupin had finished his soup now, and the two of them were staring at one another, matching their mesmeric authority as well as their wits.

It was Saint-Germain who capitulated. "I gave you the medallion," he said, "and nearly lost my life doing so. You aren't prepared to give it back, it seems, so I really do think that you owe me better treatment than this. I'd like to join your party, if I may."

"I can hardly stop you following the diligence," Dupin said. "If you want to keep company with it, you're at liberty to do so."

"You know that's not what I mean," Saint-Germain said. "I want to be party to what you know."

"I don't *know* anything at all," Dupin told him, tiredly. "Either that, or far too much. I really do believe, though, that Levasseur's treasure, if any of it still exists, is irrelevant. The point is that at least one, and probably more, of his former acquaintances and rivals tried to make what they probably thought of as a pact with the Devil, in order to further or protect their ends...the Devil, in this instance, being Cthulhu the dread dreamer, the terror of the seas: the most dangerous and treacherous ally imaginable. I don't suppose for a moment that any such pact could really be made, but I do think that attempting to make contact with, and issuing invitations to, creatures of that sort can have dire consequences. It seems to me, in view of recent visitations, that the consequences of any particular contacts that were made in the 1720s have still to be fully worked out. *That*'s the important matter at stake here, not the question of whether any gold coins still lie buried in some Breton bog."

Saint-Germain still seemed skeptical, but he was clearly wavering in the face of Dupin's persuasiveness. "I'm not afraid of shoggoths," he said defiantly.

"That isn't important," Dupin said. "Whatever the human actors in the drama wanted—or still want, if some of them really are still alive—is irrelevant to anyone but them and a few greedy gold-hunters. If the ultimate result of their in-fighting, however, is that Cthulhu gains any more purchase on human dreams and madness than it already has….let alone the possibility, however remote it might be, that it could actually succeed in becoming decrypted, the consequences will be dire. That's the situation as I see it—and I hope it's payment enough for the surrender of the medallion you believe, probably falsely, to be your property."

Saint-Germain's brow was furrowed in concentration. "I believe you," he said, finally. "I can see the situation a little more clearly now. I think. You and I *are* on the same side, you know—against Cthulhu, at any rate. I'd love to have a long conversation with you some time about exactly what you know about the Great Old Ones. You really ought to join the Society first though—all of that's strictly Inner Circle stuff, shielded by every layer of secrecy we have. Do you suppose Breisz has that sort of information too?"

"Far too much of it, I fear," Dupin opined.

"He's made a pact, you mean?"

"I mean that he's fully possessed by that form of madness," Dupin replied.

"Let's not argue about terminology. He has power—what I'd call magic power?"

"Apparently."

"And he'll use it against us if he doesn't get whatever it is he wants?"

"He's already using it *on* us, in order that we'll bring him what he wants, now that we've happened upon it…Ysolde, that is. What I don't know is what will happen if and when we reach the mysterious Underworld. Ysolde is eager to return, but she's not operating in circumstances of her own choosing, and perhaps not according to her own will. My friend thinks she's in search of revenge for sexual abuse suffered as a child, but I strongly suspect that there's some vital element of the scheme of which we're still unaware, and haven't even hypothesized as yet."

"There always is, alas," Saint-Germain muttered. "Well, I'm glad that you caught me up—and glad, too, that you've decided to play fair. If Breisz does have the cross…not to mention any spare coins and gems that might still be with it…but there's still a possibility, is there not, that at least some of the treasure is buried, awaiting a discoverer?"

"There is," Dupin agreed, with a sigh. "And if that's all that interests you, Monsieur le Comte, I wish you the best of luck in finding it. I must ask you to excuse us now, though. The diligence will make an early departure in the morning. You may follow it or not, as you please."

CHAPTER THIRTEEN
INTO THE WOODS

THE DILIGENCE DID indeed make an early start, and none of our party required hurrying along in order to get aboard, although one or two of our fellow-passengers had to be encouraged. They, apparently, thought that their journey so far had been a trifle nightmarish, and some of them had had bad dreams—probably occasioned by nothing more serious than keeping company with Madame Lacuzon inside the coach. Neither of the gentlemen who had seats inside volunteered to change places with Dupin or myself, though. However intimidating the proximity of an apparent witch might be, it is insufficient to make any sane man elect to ride on top of a fast coach in chilly weather.

There was no sign of Saint-Germain, but Dupin only had to ask a brief question of the innkeeper to ascertain that he was not sleeping late. He had made an even earlier start, and would certainly reach Rennes ahead of us—but he would surely have to wait for us there, if he hoped to exploit what Ysolde Leonys apparently knew about Oberon Breisz's whereabouts. Doubtless he would do what he could to locate Breisz without our assistance, but I did not think it likely that he would succeed.

"Have you obtained any more information from Mademoiselle Leonys?" I asked Dupin, once we were perched on the *impériale*.

"None," was the curt answer Dupin supplied. Apparently, rejuvenation did not give rise to unlimited endurance; Ysolde had fallen into profound unconsciousness as soon as she had eaten her supper, and had woken up in the same deep somnambulistic condition, completely self-enclosed. She was, apparently, saving her meager reserves of energy for her return to the Underworld...or, to be strictly accurate, to the physical equivalent of the Underworld of her dreams, in which she had once been a queen for a year and a day.

"So you have no idea whether our journey will conclude in the city of Rennes?" I said to Dupin.

"I'm sure that it will not," he said. "She has already told us that there was a further stage to the journey she made when she first came to France. We will be heading further west, I imagine. We shall need to hire a coach, and at least two spare horses."

"Let's hope that Saint-Germain is waiting for us, then," I murmured. "He might consent to share the expense."

If he perceived the reproach, he ignored it. "It will be best if Chapelain travels in the coach with the two women," he said, "but you and I ought to ride, to lighten its load. It might be wise if we were each to lead a spare horse. I don't propose to ride all night, but we might as well go as far as we can before we pause."

It occurred to me that I had never seen him astride a horse, but he was obviously not intimidated by the idea.

"I hope that your book collection comes to no harm in Paris while the dragon that normally guards it in your absence is with us," I said, a trifle maliciously. "If it takes us three days to get to our destination, we shall probably be away for an entire week."

He looked at me a little sharply, but all he said was: "Madame Lacuzon has made arrangements for her replacement. My fellow tenants will not be lacking a concierge, nor my books a guardian."

"We might all feel a little foolish," I observed, "if it turns out that Breisz is still in Paris, rather than on the road ahead of us."

"That might be the better alternative," he said. "Assuming that Mademoiselle Leonys can find this mysterious Underworld, I would not be averse to investigating it at my leisure, undisturbed."

"Saint-German doubtless feels the same," I said. "If it

comprises the cellars of a house, though, there are likely to be servants in attendance. On the other hand, Brittany is full of ruined châteaux and megalithic monuments, so we can at least hope for a more romantic alternative."

"I'd prefer a well-kept wine-cellar," he said, pragmatically. "Subterranean spaces that seem romantic attain that status in being ominous and dangerous. Whatever was done to Mademoiselle Leonys as a child to bind the Cthulhu encryption into her flesh was almost certainly done in the remoter caverns of Karla. The larger chambers have been used as a Buddhist Temple for centuries, but—like many a modern temple—the Buddhists almost certainly took possession of an arena that had previously played host to other cults."

"No one knows who constructed the megalithic structures of Brittany," I remarked—I had been to the region before, on holiday—"but it certainly wasn't the Bretons. They didn't arrive until the Romans left. Before the Romans, there were only the barbarian tribes of Armorica. The monuments are said to be thousands of years older than that."

"Indeed," Dupin agreed.

"It's possible, of course," I continued, "that there were civilizations of a sort long before our history commenced, and that the legend of the drowned city of Ys dates from remote times rather than having been imported by the Bretons. Léonais, on the other hand, and all the legends associated with it, was certainly imported by the Bretons—the short-lived province was named for one of their dialects, which might have originated in Scotland."

"The history of tribal migrations is less significant here than the transference of legends," Dupin told me, warming to the conversation as his scholarly expertise was lured forth. "The forms in which we know them only date back to Norman times—it was the Normans who romanticized feudal behavioral codes as chivalric mythology, in the form that is typical of Medieval romance. Tristan de Léonais, as we know his story, was a Norman invention, as were Merlin, Lancelot and the other names cited by Mademoiselle Leonys—save for yours. The Oberon who befriended Huon of Bordeaux and made him heir to his kingdom, however, is a more enigmatic figure than the others: a dwarf and a powerful magician, able to read human thoughts and transport himself from place to place instantaneously. The man you saw in Saint-Sulpice was, I assume, of ordinary height?"

"Yes—but Shakespeare's Oberon was not a dwarf. That image would be more familiar to an Englishman than the one from French romance...if Ysolde's Oberon really is an Englishman."

"True," Dupin admitted. "All the more so, perhaps, since Mademoiselle Leonys evidently has English ancestry herself. Not that she is likely to have seen Shakespeare performed on stage before concocting her own long dream."

"She is a magician herself now," I observed. "At least, she has a magical object in her possession."

"So it seems," Dupin agreed, thoughtfully. "She has the ability to repel shoggoths...although that might only be necessary because her treacherous flesh, spoiled by disease, seems also to attract them. She obviously did not issue the invitation to Cthulhu herself—she is a victim in this, though probably not the kind of victim you suspect."

"What do *you* suspect?" I demanded, resentfully.

He did not answer. He was still distracted, as he had been the day before, only giving me half his attention. A part of his mind was still working, obsessively, on the Cthulhu encryption. I could not help wondering whether that very fact might make him something of a magnet for dangerous hallucination. There is, after all, more than one way to issue an invitation, or open a breach where reality is worn thin.

After a long pause, however, the pedantic Dupin showed through again. "Bougainville was wrong, I think," he opined, pensively, "to conclude that his South Sea islanders were *worshippers* of Cthulhu, who chanted the incomplete encryption as a kind of homage or glad anticipation of an apocalypse to come. Their primary motive, I think, was self-protection. The ritual repetition of the partial encryption is surely intended to reinforce the imprisonment, or at least the concealment, of the entity, and not to break the seals of encryption. It is a shield, of sorts, like the other spell, which wards off Cthulhu's minions whenever they contrive to manifest themselves, however tangentially, in this universe The encryptions were not initially devised by humans, though; they have merely been handed down to us, awkwardly by necessity, as a kind of legacy— an angelic legacy, if you wish, to oppose Cthulhu's demonic legacy. John Dee certainly thought of the matter in those terms, and encoded his *Claves* accordingly, presumably intending to keep the darker element of the power strictly between himself and Edward Kelley."

"It's a pity he wrote them down at all, if they're so dangerous," I observed.

"He was a scholar," Dupin said, as if that explained everything. In fact, it did. Scholars cannot bear to obliterate knowledge; they are often inclined to bury what they know as deeply as they can, but they can never bear to leave it to oblivion.

"But if the Cthulhu encryption is intended to keep Cthulhu at bay, not to let its disturbing power loose," I said, "why is the last sequence of seven syllables omitted from its vocal version?"

"Presumably because it is only to be used in cases of dire necessity, when some manifest loosening of the crypt's seal has already taken place. It is the true word of power, whose possession probably exacts a price...just as Mademoiselle Leonys' inheritance has exacted, and is still exacting, a price."

"Do you know how the last set of syllables is pronounced?" I asked.

"Not yet," was his telling reply. He was a scholar.

"You're unlikely ever to need it," I said. "Saint-Germain is surely right when he says that we're all on the same side where Cthulhu is concerned...even Oberon Breisz. All humankind is united in *that* defiance."

"Let us hope so," Dupin said. "Like you, I can hardly imagine that it might be otherwise—and yet, men have sometimes attempted to make pacts with the Devil, for their own petty advantage. The legend of Faust assures us that scholars are more vulnerable to that kind of temptation than common men…and suggests, too, that scholarship in itself might be an instrument of evil, no matter how well intentioned its seekers might be."

"Perhaps," I suggested, whimsically, "the entire human race and all of its history is no more than a hapless instrument of patient evil."

"Perhaps it is," Dupin agreed, a little too soberly for my liking.

We reached Rennes in the early afternoon, and hastened to find a carriage and horses as soon as we had made a cursory meal. At first, when Dupin presented himself at the hirers and listed our requirements, the hirer said that it was quite impossible to provide a carriage and six horses at such short notice, but when Madame Lacuzon emerged from behind her master, the hirer only had to glance at her to be persuaded to think again, and to promise that he would assemble what we needed within the hour, even if he had to go cap-in-hand to his competitors. The old woman had not said a word, and the hirer had never seen her before, but the power of her presence seemed to have increased further now that she was back in her homeland.

"It's wonderful what a heart of gold can accomplish," I commented to Dupin, while we waited for the hirer to fulfil his task.

"You may mock," he said, "but I assure you that Amélie is on the side of the angels, in spite of her appearance. No matter what legend might imply, ugliness is not contiguous with evil; nor beauty with good."

I remembered the shoggoths, and was not so sure about that—but I made no explicit comment.

When we eventually rode out of Rennes, heading westwards, there was still three hours to go until sunset. The light carriage we had hired, pulled by a pair of horses, sat three people abreast in reasonable comfort on its hooded bench. Madame Lacuzon took control of the reins, but disdained the whip. I had the impression that the horses might have obeyed her even without the reins, but she was prepared to use orthodox methods when convenient. Ysolde Leonys sat between the concierge and Chapelain. Dupin fell in behind the vehicle and I brought up the rear, each of us with a second horse attached to our saddle with a leading-rein. The animals were all practised and docile, and we made reasonable speed without having to push them too hard.

There was no sign of Saint-Germain; presumably, he had decided not to wait for us after all, having found information by himself to indicate the direction he should take.

The day was as grey as the one before, but the light drizzle that was falling when we left the city was sporadic, and did not increase in intensity until the gloom was quite intense. The sun had not yet set, but it was obvious that the twilight would be not far short of pitch dark, and so we began to look out for an inn in advance of its setting. None materialized, perhaps because we were passing through a dense wood, which was not nearly as inviting to human construction as the heathland occupying the greater part of the Breton heartland, which was known collectively as the *Grand'Lande*.

Extensive woods are uncommon in Brittany today, although legend has it that the whole region was once heavily forested, and that is almost certainly true. Centuries of felling and erosion by the weather have left much of its lowlands barren, the heath competing in many areas with boggy marshes, while its hills have frequently reduced to rugged crags, but the forest whose remnants are still called Lyonesse was once part of a vast pan-European wilderness that still has a legendary echo in the alternative name of Broceliande.

The deforestation must have happened long before the Bretons came, let alone the feudal dukes, and the forbidding crags that appealed as fine locations for castles were ready-made for any and all Bronze- and Iron-Age invaders. The castles in question could never have been comfortable homes, though, and they had mostly been vacated as soon as their defensive capability no longer seemed a desperate necessity. A few had been besieged and sacked, but the majority had simply been abandoned for more modest châteaux built in the heart of farmland domains. My exploits as a tourist in the region had assured me that there was not a single one that was not haunted, usually by some woeful Medieval knight unjustly dispossessed of his wealth, his lady love or his honorable reputation…or all three, the melodramatic impulse being somewhat incompatible with modesty.

A few woodlands still survive, though, including one or two that are optimistically called forests, and we had not ridden a mile into the one that had temporarily swallowed us up before I was wishing that there were fewer still. We lit the two lanterns that were attached to the carriage's hood, but their light did not extend far enough forward to give the horses confidence, even on a well-marked road, and our pace slowed to a walk—which inevitably had the effect of making the wood seem interminable, even though we knew full well that it had to be small in strictly geographical terms. The foliage kept the rain at bay, though, and there would have been no moonlight or starlight in any case, so it was not entirely an inconvenience or a hindrance.

I heard Chapelain arguing that we should stop, and make what camp we could in the trees, but he did not win the argument—not, if my judgment was correct, because Mademoiselle Leonys roused herself sufficiently overrule him but because Madame Lacuzon was stubborn.

In the end, her stubbornness paid off, because we did eventually come through the wood, as had always been inevitable, and we found a hostelry of sorts just beyond its end, positioned in the first spot that was convenient for the erection of a building made mostly of stone.

By comparison with the coaching-inn in Alençon, the roadside establishment in question was a poor one, with only a single storey and no private rooms at all. Chapelain opined that it had better accommodation for the horses than for us, but he was a Parisian through and through, unused to rural privations. Madame Lacuzon inspected the floor where we would have to sleep, and the larder from which our dinner would be supplied, and judged them satisfactory. I had every confidence that the master of the house and his wife would make sure that we got the best of whatever there was to be had, for they were clearly more respectful of the crone than they were of the rest of us.

The tenant of the hostelry built a blazing fire in the main room, in order that we would be able to dry ourselves before lying down to sleep. We had time in hand before we went to bed, however, and Dupin and Chapelain were equally enthusiastic to question Ysolde Leonys one more time, if she could be persuaded to reply.

At first, I thought that she was now quite impervious to Chapelain's suggestions, but he persisted in his attempts, and eventually she seemed to weaken—or to least to relent.

"Is the Underworld nearby now?" Chapelain asked, once we were convinced that she might be co-operative.

"Not far," she said. We were in a region now where all distances were habitually described either as "not far" or "a long way," and she seemed to be adapting to local custom.

"Will we get there before noon?" Chapelain asked.

"Probably."

"What will you do when we get there?"

"Find Oberon, if I can."

"What will you say to Oberon, if you find him?"

"That will depend on what he has to say to me."

"And what will you do if he is not there?"

"Wait."

Chapelain checked with Dupin; there was an exchange of whispers.

"How were you able to read the medallion that Tristan gave you two days ago?" Chapelain asked, when he resumed.

"I know how to read." That was an obvious evasion, but it was quite casual. She was a somniloquist still, but she was no longer as meek as she had been when first questioned in that manner.

"Who taught you to read symbols of that kind?"

"The Mahatma."

"Angria's Mahatma?"

"The Mahatma in Callaba."

"Was this Mahatma a magician?"

"Yes."

"Was he a worshipper of Cthulhu?"

"No."

"But the magic he worked upon you was to do with Cthulhu?"

The question was phrased rhetorically; there was no reply. Dupin was making hand-signals.

"When Oberon took you away from Callaba," Chapelain resumed, "was it by stealth?"

"No."

"Did Angria allow him to take you?"

"Yes."

"Did Oberon pay some kind of price for you?"

Silence. Not understood, or not known.

"Why did your father leave you with Angria?"

Silence.

Another swift conference between Chapelain and Dupin. Then: "What did Oberon do to you, Ysolde?"

"He made me his queen."

"Yes—but what did that entail?"

Silence.

"Did Oberon ever hurt you?"

"Never."

"Then why did you run away from him?"

"I betrayed him."

"In what way?"

"I fell in love with Tristan."

"Did you and Tristan run away together?"

A hesitation; then: "Yes." *Why the hesitation?* I wondered

"Who first told you Tristan's name?"

"He did."

"Where was Tristan in the years before you saw him again, three days ago?"

"I don't know."

"Why did he desert you?"

Hesitation. Then: "I was punished."

"By whom?"

Silence.

Another swift conference; then: "Why does Oberon want you back now?"

Silence, unsurprisingly.

"Has he forgiven you for betraying him?"

Silence.

"Or does he want to exact revenge?"

A slightly disturbed silence—but not a fearful disturbance. I had the impression that she thought that time was being wasted, and that she did not want to waste precious energy on such trivia.

"What do you want from Oberon?" Chapelain persisted.

No hesitation this time: "I want to be his queen again."

"Why?"

I expected silence; presumably we all did. In fact, we got an answer: "Because I don't want to die."

"Do you believe that Oberon can prevent your death?"

"Yes."

I thought she was overly optimistic. So did Chapelain, but he was not about to say so. After a pause, Chapelain asked: "How old is Oberon?"

"Very old."

"More than a hundred years?"

"Yes."

"More than two hundred?"

Hesitation, then: "I think so."

"Did you ever hear the name Edward England?"

"Yes."

"When?"

"When I was a child."

"Who first spoke the name in your presence?"

"Angria."

"When?"

"I was five."

"What did Angria say about Edward England on that occasion?"

"*I can't protect you from Edward England—you have to go away.*"

Chapelain hesitated, and Dupin was quick to whisper in his ear.

"To whom was Angria speaking when he said that?" the mesmerist asked.

"My father."

"John Taylor?"

The rhetorical question must have slipped out, but it brought a predictable response: "Jack Taylor was a *bad man*."

"Is that when John Taylor sailed for the South Seas?"

"No."

"Where did he go, on that occasion?"

"Poona."

"Who first spoke the name of Olivier Levasseur in your presence?"

"My father."

"You told us that the medallion that Tristan returned to you was not Levasseur's. Whose was it?" He was just checking; we already knew the answer.

"Mine."

"Who gave it to you?"

"Angria."

"How did you lose it?"

"Levasseur took it."

"When?"

"Before he returned to Brittany, the first time."

"How many times did he return to Brittany?"

"Twice."

"Did you tell Angria that Levasseur had taken the medallion?"

"Yes."

"What did he do?"

Silence.

Chapelain opened his mouth to ask another question, but it was too late. The somniloquist had lapsed into a deeper sleep, in which speech was no longer accessible.

Madame Lacuzon whispered something in Dupin's ear, and he nodded. "Go to sleep," he advised us. "If we're fortunate, we shall find out more tomorrow than Mademoiselle Leonys can tell us in this state. If she can guide us to her Underworld, and her Oberon, answers will surely be far more freely available there than they are here."

CHAPTER FOURTEEN
IN THE MIST

I WAS NOT ENTIRELY unused to sleeping on a stone floor, but it was not an experience I could relish now that I was no longer young. I was, however, quite exhausted; it is surprising how tired a day in the saddle can make a man, given that he only has to sit while his mount carries his burden. I was sore too, in spite of having ridden on a regular basis since I was a boy, but that only added a further edge of discomfort to my dreams, which were hardly in need of the assistance. Fortunately, I still possessed the invaluable faculty of forgetfulness, and was able to dispel my visions as soon as I awoke, without magical aid. Once I had stretched and shaken my limbs, I felt fully human again—and I say that because it describes exactly how I felt, although I couldn't quite imagine how I had been less than fully human while I slept.

Primitive as the hostelry was, the mistress of the house had flour and a good oven with which to bake bread, and goat's milk heated almost to boiling-point to warm us up—which we needed, for the floor, in spite of the straw we had used as makeshift mattresses, had grown very cold once the fire had lapsed into sullen embers.

Plain as the fare was, I felt sufficiently repaired once I had eaten my fill. I even contrived to feel optimistic at the prospect of reaching journey's end before another day had run by—at least until I stepped outside, and walked into a wall of mist.

The rainclouds had cleared overnight to leave clear skies and allow the temperature to fall sharply. The result of that, as the

Chevalier de Lamarck has taken care to explain in his tedious text on the fledgling science of clouds, had been that all the water saturating the atmosphere close to the ground had turned to crystalline vapor. This was not the foul fog of Paris, which is impregnated with smoke and other by-products of industry, so that it retains a faintly organic texture and a nasty odor; this was a pure, unsullied mist, more silver than white or grey—but still, it was exceedingly dense mist, and although I could still see my hand clearly enough when I stretched out my arm to its full length, everything further away was cloaked and hidden.

The master of the lodging-house assured us that we would have no trouble, provided that we stuck to the road, which was clearly marked and still in reasonably good condition in spite of the seasonal mud. Besides, the optimistic fellow assured us, the sun still climbed high enough in the sky in October to dispel mist of this sort by noon at the latest. Not until December would entire days pass without the fog clearing, so that the korrigans would have free rein upon the heath. We would reach Loudéac with no difficulty before sunset, he assured us.

Which as all very well, except that—so far as I knew—we were not going to Loudéac. We had no clue as to exactly where Ysolde Leonys might be leading us, but wherever it was, it was unlikely to be on the Rennes-Loudéac road. If she expected to arrive there before noon, she would presumably take us away from the main road very soon, on to some ill-trodden bridle-path. Would the carriage, light as it was, be able to cope with the final phase of the journey, I wondered—and what would we do with it if it could not?

That was probably a matter of little relevance to Mademoiselle Leonys, and not a question to which Auguste Dupin would deign to pay attention, but I was the person who had hired the carriage and horses, and I was the man who would be accountable if we could not return them safely. I did not suppose that a relatively bleak stretch of road leading into the Breton heartland would be replete with highwaymen, but there are brigands everywhere; even heathland has its hamlets, its cultivated fields, its mills and cider-presses…and wherever there are peasants there are opportunistic horse-thieves.

Nevertheless, we set off. I took what reassurance I could from the fact that I could ride close enough to Dupin not to lose sight of him, and that he could ride close enough to the carriage not to lose sight of its rear wheels. I also took some comfort from the fact that I still had my revolver in my coat pocket, tucked behind my journal, with five bullets loaded.

I do not know how long we were on the road before leaving it. By the time a seasoned traveler is on the third day of a journey, his mind is easily dulled, so that the passage of time loses all urgency and all measurement—all the more so when he is in an underpopulated region where the traffic is thin and one cannot even hear the occasional clanging of cracked church bells ineptly attempting to sound the hours.

The traffic was exceedingly thin. I cannot swear to the number of pedestrians we passed, for a few might have slipped by unnoticed in the mist, but I know that we did not encounter a single laden cart, let alone a horseman or another carriage. Perhaps that was not unusual, the last of the harvest having been brought in and redistributed some while before, but to someone accustomed to the relentless crowds of Paris, it seemed positively eerie.

The road was not straight, because the heathland was far from flat; it wound around in shallow curves and I became so used to the meandering course that I would not even have noticed when we left the road had it not been for the noticeable change underfoot, of which my mount was certainly conscious and did not entirely approve. At the time, I was astride the largest of our animals, which had broad hooves and heavy shoes, and it did not appreciate the more glutinous mud.

Fortunately, the worst of the mud lasted less than a mile, for we soon began climbing a slope. That did not suggest to me that we were getting closer to any kind of underworld, but it did offer the hope that we might climb out of the mist and be able to see our way again. That optimism lent a slight alleviation to the dullness of my patience…but again, tedium soon numbed it.

We paused twice to change the horses round, but I did not even bother to take my watch out and check the time. It did not matter what the instrument said—which was, in any case, still adjusted to Paris time and not to local time. All I knew, and all I needed to know, was that we were somewhere between where we had been and where we were going, and that—barring accidents—we would eventually arrive…hopefully before the invisible sun reached its incalculable zenith.

And we did arrive, after a fashion.

The path we were following petered out, although the carriage rolled on for a further hundred paces or so. In the meantime, I was able to glimpse two huge slabs of stone to either side of our course, and knew that we were among a cluster of megaliths. I was not surprised when the carriage stopped thereafter.

Dupin dismounted; so did I. The mist *was* clearing, finally. As the passengers in the carriage got down, and we all gathered together, I perceived, vaguely, that there was an entire circle of standing stones, and that we were in the center of the formation. There was, I knew, a great abundance of such monuments scattered throughout Brittany. No one knows why they were constructed. In many of them, fearful of pagan echoes, Christian latecomers had raised crosses or established saintly shrines—but there was no sign of anything of that sort here, so far as the silver mist permitted me to see.

I thought at first that we were pausing yet again to rest and water the horses, and to take some food from our luggage, but as soon as I looked at Ysolde Leonys at close range, I knew that our situation had changed. *Her* situation had changed, and ours was entirely dependent on hers.

Chapelain had told us that if she woke up from her somnambulistic state her metamorphosis would melt away and she would likely fall down dead. I did not doubt that he had been correct, in Paris; but we were not in Paris any longer. We were now in a place where she was able to awake, not as her direly mortal, pox-ridden self—her true self, as I stubbornly persisted in thinking of it—but in her present one. In a sense, she had now completed her metamorphosis, which was not, after all, merely from almost-hag to almost-beauty, but from human to…what?

Fairy? Enchantress? Ghost?

She was still solid, though, and just as ill-dressed as before.

It was to Chapelain that she addressed herself first.

"Thank you, Doctor," she said. "In another age, or another world, you would have been a great magician…but I think you can be well content with your work as a physician. I could never have come home without your help."

Then she turned to Dupin. "Thank you, Monsieur Dupin," she added. "Your help was as valuable as Dr. Chapelain's, if not more so—and you recovered my medallion for me."

I felt a twinge of envy at that, for I thought that I was entitled to the lion's share of any credit not due to Saint-Germain, but I made no protest.

"Am I not Tristan de Léonais any longer, then?" Dupin asked Ysolde, in a perfectly level tone that refused all astonishment.

"I fear that I was lost, for a while, in an old dream," she said. "I sought comfort there, because I had obtained comfort there before…before things went awry. I have been mad lately, and by no means myself—but I'm home now, thanks to the four of you. I don't know how Oberon will receive me, but if he is disposed to be generous, there is a chance that I might live for some time yet. Thank you all."

I looked around, at the megaliths half-hidden in the magical mist, and could not imagine anything further from "home". The bare ground within the stone circle seemed very solid, and I could not imagine that any of the massive blocks of stone could be moved without tremendous effort and very sturdy levers.

"Where, then, is the entrance to the Underworld?" I asked. "Where is Oberon Breisz's lair?"

"Why, this is the Underworld," she said, "or at least its threshold. Oberon's house is on the hill. We shall have to walk from here, but it is not far."

This time, I was prepared to believe that it really wasn't

far—but that did not make the prospect of the approach any less intimidating.

"We seem to have mistaken the sense of the prefix *under*," Dupin observed, with scholarly scrupulousness. "The limitations of three-dimensional thought, I suppose."

"Why?" I asked. "Have we somehow stepped out of the world, into some other universe, displaced in a dimension other than three we measure with Cartesian co-ordinates?" I knew enough about his theories to pose as something other than a complete novice.

"No," he replied. "We have not gone nearly as far as that, and certainly could not have crossed the barriers that separate material worlds as easily. We are still in Brittany, and if we have been displaced at all, it is by means of some petty trick with time, not the dimensions of space…but we have been encrypted, after a fashion."

"Are we dead, then?" I asked, alarmed.

Ysolde Leonys laughed. "Quite the opposite, my friend. That is not dead which can eternal lie…and here, no matter that it *is* a lie, one might indeed be eternal, if Oberon will permit it. He will probably send you packing though…you and Chapelain, and the witch. To Monsieur Dupin, on the other hand…you might not know it yet, Monsieur Dupin, but you and he have business to settle. If you cannot remember of your own accord, he will help you."

"Remember what?" Dupin asked.

"You're in the Underworld now, Monsieur Dupin—you can remember, if you wish. It isn't always easy, at first….oh, how difficult it was when I was still a child, in Karla! But I remembered, in the end. I forgot again…but dreams are so hard to maintain, are they not, when there are others intend on guiding them?"

"Can you tell us, now, who you really are?" Dupin asked.

"Oh, but I told you all of that, when Dr. Chapelain held me in thrall. I'm Ysolde Leonys, daughter of Mark Leonys of Cornwall, alias John Taylor the pirate…although I have other, further memories, just as you have, if only you can reach them. Once, I was another Ysolde, who really was beloved by Tristan. Once, too, I was a demoiselle in Ys…so this really is my home, you see. My roots are here. I could have been a seer even in Karla, but to reach into eternity, I had to come here. Oberon knew that. Angria accepted it. All Indians are fatalists—even kings. Especially kings."

"By Oberon," said Dupin, "you really mean Edward England?"

"Not at all," said a new voice—that of a man, certainly no dwarf, who had just emerged from the mist, between two of the standing stones. "By Edward England, Monsieur Dupin, *you* really mean Oberon…unless, of course, you can remember the name I had when we last met, to which I will answer gladly enough."

Dupin turned to face the newcomer, and looked him up and down. "We have never met," he said, confidently.

"It was a long time ago," conceded the man that the Comte de Saint-Germain had identified to me as Oberon Breisz. "I apologize for interrupting you, but I really had grown very impatient, even though I did not complete my return from Paris until yesterday. I had hoped that you might demonstrate more urgency, and more cleverness…but you are here now, and you must come to the house without further delay, where you can wash and change your clothes, while my servants prepare a meal. You'll have to leave the carriage and horses here—there are steps that only human feet can climb—but they'll be quite safe. No one dares steal so much as a rabbit or an apple from my land."

Dupin was about to ask another question, but Oberon Breisz had already turned away from him, to confront Ysolde Leonys. He made no move to embrace or kiss her, or even to greet her with a polite bow.

"You shouldn't have run away, my child," he said.

"I know that now," she replied, "but I *was* a child, was I not, in spite of my years? I was foolish…and there was something within me that moved me to revolt. If I had only kept the medallion…but even you could not keep my dream unsullied, while you were ambitious to direct it to your own ends."

"That's true," he admitted. "It wasn't your fault—not entirely."

Personally, I thought that she should have left out the last two words; the fact that he had felt obliged to include them was revealing of his character. He was a vain man, and not a forgiving one, although he knew how to keep a straight face.

"Can you save me, my king?" she asked. "Can you still make use of me?"

"I believe so," Breisz replied. "I'm a magician, after all—more powerful now than the old Mahatma. Besides, you were my queen once…together, we might accomplish anything. Provided that you are obedient…."

He left it there. Arrogance again—but if he really was a powerful magician, perhaps arrogance was unavoidable, if not forgivable.

Madame Lacuzon tugged at Dupin's sleeve very urgently, and he was forced to listen to a whispered speech longer than I had any I had ever seen her utter before. I studied them closely, hoping to pick up the thread of their conversation, and was slightly startled to find Ysolde Leonys suddenly beside me.

"Don't be afraid," she said, in a low voice—perhaps addressing Chapelain as well, since he was also close by. "You're under my protection. You'll get back to Paris safely, I promise you—even if I have to summon help. I believe that I can do that…if the old man is still able to come." She dropped her voice even further, and leaned close to my ear, to add: "Oberon doesn't know everything."

I looked at Chapelain, wondering how long he would grant his patient to live now, in his expert opinion. The physician was evidently troubled, but he said nothing, contenting himself with a slight bow by way of response to her promise. He knew as well as the rest of us that we really were standing at some kind of boundary, neither wholly in the world we knew nor wholly in

Oberon Breisz's curiously mislabeled Underworld.

"Thank you, Madame," I said, on behalf of both of us.

Dupin finally looked up again. "Madame Lacuzon will stay here, with the horses," he said. "The rest of us will be pleased to accept your invitation, Monsieur Breisz."

Oberon Breisz bowed to the gorgon. "I'll have some food and wine sent down to you, Madame," he said. "I harbor no hard feelings over the fact that you would not let me see Monsieur Dupin in Paris. That was your home after all—and I delivered my invitation regardless."

As Oberon Breisz turned away to lead us out to the stone circle and up the hill, I made haste to fall into step with Dupin and whisper to him in m turn. "What should I do?"

"Be polite," he murmured. "We have been invited to visit this man's house—let us do so. Perhaps it is not quite as fully in the word we know as any other dwelling we have ever visited, but I doubt that he intends to hold us prisoner within his crypt. I don't know what business he thinks he has with me, but I dare say that we can settle it like gentlemen."

The way up to the house was steep, and the crude stone steps that wound around the hill were chipped and crumbling, but the mist was clearing now, and I had no fear of missing my footing by virtue of poor sight. There were brambles growing on the hillside—which, was, in truth, more like the face of a cliff, and at one point there was a rickety wooden bridge over a mysterious torrent that had no obvious source, but no more than a quarter of an hour had passed when the house appeared.

I had been half-expecting a vast Medieval edifice with turrets and battlements, but it was far more compact that that, and if any of it was genuinely old, the building had certainly been renovated to modern standards. Its windows were square and neatly glazed with the aid of sturdy wooden frames. Its roof was tiled and pitched to accommodate mansards to serve as servants' quarters. The edifice did have rounded corners, but they only gave the illusion of towers; that was an affectation, such as one sees in the more pretentious town-houses in every city. It undoubtedly deserved the title of manor-house, perhaps that of château, but it was no quasi-Medieval fortress or relic thereof. The perron leading up to the front door was in much better condition than the steps leading up the hillside, and the brass fittings on the door were brightly-polished.

When he reached the perron, Oberon Breisz paused, and so did we. He turned and gestured expansively with his arm, inviting us to look back the way we had come.

We did. We were above the mist now, but it still filled he valleys between the various hills stretching away to the east and south. There were, however, plenty of ridges and crags looming up above the silver ocean. Many of those peaks, I knew, should have had human dwellings on them: not merely ruins of ancient feudal holds but farmhouses and cottages. There should have been roads looping over the shallower hills. Somewhere, between my station and the distant horizon, there should have been towns and cities, whose church spires and high flagpoles, at least, ought to be projecting from that silent silver sea.

There was nothing—except for a few single standing stones, like gorgonized sentinels keeping watch on a deserted land. Much of it was heath, but the entire horizon seemed to be ringed by a vast, illimitable forest.

"We really have stepped back in time," I murmured to Dupin.

"Nothing so extreme," Oberon Breisz interjected. "Civilization is still there...my powers of encryption don't go as far as projecting my house back in time, alas...but the view is another matter. To play with light...that kind of magic is mere illusion. Think of it as a kind of picture...a landscape in the wild Italian style."

The servant who opened the door when our host rang was not dressed in livery. He seemed little different in age and bearing from my own Bihan, and might even have been a distant relative.

There was nothing reminiscent of Perrault or Charlemagne in the furniture, either. Some of it was certainly old, but no older than the furniture accumulated in any aristocratic house in the environs of the Faubourg Saint-Germain, and much of it was a good deal plainer. There were armchairs in the drawing-room into which we were initially taken, but no sofas and no rugs; the principal item was a huge Breton dresser laden with crockery. There were no sideboards or bookcases, nor was there very much ornamentation on the walls in the traditional forms of paintings, tapestries or the kinds of panoplies that serve as conventional souvenirs of voyages to India or Africa. There was, however, one item of decoration suspended over the fire-place that was as impressive as it was sinister.

It was a flag, torn and tattered now, but still bright enough in the whiter design superimposed on a black background. The design depicted a skull and crossbones. It was what modern legend called a "Jolly Roger." Indeed, I strongly suspected that it was *the* Jolly Roger: the very one invented by the pirate Edward England.

CHAPTER FIFTEEN
THE PIRATE
NARRATIVE CLARIFIED

IT WAS A LARGE enough house, although we were not given a tour, but merely shown to the rooms where we would be sleeping that night. We had one each. The beds seemed comfortable enough, but the furniture was otherwise sparse and the walls undecorated. Better that, I thought, than to sleep beneath the pirate flag.

I was provided with a basin of hot water in a small dressing-room annexed to the bedroom, so I took the opportunity to wash myself thoroughly and change into cleaner clothes. Dupin and Chapelain did likewise before we made our way back to the drawing-room into which we had first been introduced.

When I arrived there, I had the impression that the hollow eye-sockets of the skull painted on the flag were staring at me in a curiously knowing fashion.

Oberon Breisz offered us each a glass of red wine, which we accepted gladly. Ysolde Leonys came in while the glasses were being handed out, but Breisz did not offer to pour her one. She was still wide awake, but was, I thought, still somehow in thrall. I wondered whether her wakefulness might be illusory—a matter of glamour, like her fresh skin and sleek hair. She had undoubtedly recovered a measure of self-consciousness, and probably thought herself free, but I had a suspicion that, as soon as she had stepped into this encrypted space, she had also stepped back into Oberon Breiz's possession. He had said that he wanted her back, having somehow lost her more than a decade before, but now that he had her, he almost seemed to have lost interest in her. At the very least, he was taking her future compliance with his plans for granted.

Among other things, I thought, that confidence in her total possession probably meant that her promise of protection was worthless. Here and now, we were all at Oberon's mercy.

Fortunately, the renowned bilbiotaph did not seem to have the slightest shred of animosity toward any of us. He was playing the host gladly—which surely implied that he must want something from us. Obviously, he did not want it from me, or from Chapelain. But what was it that he wanted from Dupin—badly enough, perhaps, to have planned and mounted this entire charade?

"You must have a great many questions to ask, Monsieur Dupin," said our host, when we were all seated. "I'm sure that Ysolde has done her best to answer the ones you have asked her, but she probably has a great many questions herself, now that she is finally coming round from her long nightmare. That was Angria's doing, I fear. The British eventually sacked Callaba, as I had known that they would, in spite of any pact made in the past, but he was bound to escape—and they never recovered the Flaming Cross of Goa, as they doubtless hoped to do. With the Buddhists firmly in possession of Karla again, I thought that he would probably head north for the mountains and lose himself there, but the sea had got into his blood too. He did not stay long in Paris in 1830, although it's possible that he's come back again, if he's still alive. It has occurred to me that it *might* have been his presence that mobilized the shoggoths, although I doubt that they needed his mediation. In any case, it seems more likely to me that he followed poor Jack Taylor's example, if he's addled enough to think that he can draw any advantage from R'lyaieh. *That* kind of madness, mercifully, I've always been able to stave off."

What kinds, I wondered, *can he not stave off?* It was a silly question. He was as deeply enmeshed in his own madness as Ysolde Leonys…and his madness, I suspected, extended much further than hers. She was merely a fly caught in his spider-web.

"Taylor, at least, must be long dead," Dupin observed.

"I certainly hope so, although I've heard rumor that he's encrypted too, on a ghost-ship. It's probably nonsense, as most such rumors are. I was the one entitled to vengeance, but you understand how these things work, Monsieur Dupin."

Does he? I wondered.

"If my crews had only let me make a deal with Captain Mackra while we were fortunate enough to have him in our custody," the man who had once been Edward England continued, "we'd all have been far better off—but that snake Taylor convinced the men that I was selling them out to John Company for my own selfish profit. If Jack *were* still alive...well, what a *bad man* he would be by now! Fortunately, Monsieur Dupin, men of our sort are rare...and those who need to come back, once having died, have a hard road to follow to remembrance. Few accomplish it without help...but I can help you, if you'll let me."

Dupin ignored the bait. "I hope you'll forgive me, Monsieur Breiz...Mr. England...but I still haven't quite grasped all the details of the pirate narrative. Would you be prepared to fill in the gaps for me?"

Breisz shook his head, not in denial but in mock-commiseration. "I do hope you're not still thinking in terms of finding Levasseur's legendary treasure," he said. "I had not suspected you of such vulgarity. There's still a little of it left in my cofffers, mind...most of the gold is spent, but some of the gems remain. *La Buse* had to take the cross back to Angria, though, along with a weighty tribute. He should never have imagined that he could get away with keeping a prize that was not really his."

"But he and Taylor did capture *Nossa Senhora del Cabo*, did they not?"

"They boarded her, it's true—but they did not cripple her and they certainly did not destroy her escort. They were merely the carrion crows, descending on to the bloody field when the battle was over—and what a battle it must have been! I would have played my part in it had Angria let me, but...well, I was his guest, after all. He rescued me from the island where Jack Taylor left me to die, and there was some justice in his notion that he had the right to command me...and some justice too, in his claim that I was then too precious to be risked in mere pirate enterprises, since I was operating as his go-between with the Company. At any rate, It was Angria's fleet that found and fell upon the *Lady*'s guardians, and engaged the in the fiercest conflict the Indian Ocean had ever seen. The *Lady* escaped, after a fashion, but she would certainly have had to put into port somewhere for repairs. She was dead in the water, ripe for the plucking—but Jack and *La Buse* should never have imagined, even for a moment, that they'd be allowed to keep their booty.

"Jack was the more cunning of the two—he went to the British first, knowing, as I did, that John Company would be obliged to root Angria out eventually—but they weren't yet ready to try, even though his naval capacity had been badly dented, and Mackra still had a powerful grudge against Jack. Instead, Jack had to go to Callaba, simply to avoid being sent home to hang—but he dared not go there until he knew that I had put to sea. Angria would not let me play my part in the battle for the *Lady*, but he knew that I was the best man to chase and make a deal with *La Buse*.

"As things turned out, I had to follow Levasseur all the way to Brittany, and then convince him of the necessity of making his peace with Angria, which wasn't easy, once he was on home ground and thought himself safe. The mere fact that the French wanted to hang him wasn't intimidation enough; the Bretons have never considered themselves French, and they make their own assessments of a man's criminality. In fact, it wasn't until *he* had seen shoggoths that the inclination to treachery finally deserted him. Eventually, he agreed to go back, albeit very reluctantly, taking all the manuscripts that Angria wanted but insisting on leaving the gold and gems hidden, for the sake of further leverage—that was in '25.

"I went back too, as I had promised—but I went back equipped to make a new deal of my own. Jack Taylor fled to

Poona before I arrived, else I'd have killed him. *La Buse* and I came back to Brittany again in '27, and Taylor returned to Callaba. Levasseur had no alternative but to take the flaming cross and the greater part of the gold and gems to Angria, but he never made it back here, and I can't say that I'm sorry. I suspect that Angria betrayed him to the French, but I don't know for sure—*La Buse* wasn't short of enemies, any more than Jack or I was. Men like us are never short of enemies, are we Monsieur Dupin? I stayed here when *La Buse* returned for the second time, and didn't get back to Callaba until '31. Taylor fled again to escape me. It wasn't easy persuading Angria to let me return, let alone to bring the girl with me, but the Mahatma hadn't made much progress with her, so he gave in. I had no choice—I needed her, if I were to make progress in my own endeavors. I broke some of the promises I made to Angria, of course—but we were all pirates then, no matter what we had been before and were ambitious to become again. I knew that the British would smash him eventually, and that I only had to play a waiting game. There's a price to be paid for immortality, even though it's a slippery prize at best."

Again, Dupin refused to take the bait—but he was pensive now, as if he were trying furiously to work out what Breisz could possibly mean.

"What possible need could you have had for Taylor's thirteen-year-old daughter?" I asked our host—although I have to admit that I was risking disobedience of Dupin's injunction to be polite. "Were you intent on exacting your revenge on her, since her father had fled?"

Oberon Breisz met my gaze frankly, and laughed. "Do you imagine that I debauched her?" he said. "She was far too precious—and anyway, I'm not the sort of man to hold a child guilty of her father's crime. He betrayed me; she had not...not then, at any rate. No, I had very different plans for her, far more ambitious than mere rape, and my need had little to do with her being Jack's daughter—if she was offered as a tribute, that was in response to Angria's demand, not mine. I've been a bad man in my day—as bad as Jack Taylor, some might say—but I'm not a *vile* man, no matter how history paints me. I've cherished that child like a true father, and made a better job of it than Taylor or Angria could ever have done."

"But you *have* used her," I retorted, unwilling to be fobbed off so easily. "She is in your possession now, is she not?"

"I have kept her alive," Breisz retorted in his turn, showing a little intemperance. "Had she not run off with the ghost that Angria sent to worm his way into her dream, she'd have avoided a great deal of pain and suffering. Do you really think that she'd rather be dying in Bicêtre than here with me? Ask her, if you doubt it."

I didn't have to ask; she had already told me the answer. Even if she hadn't, I would only have had to look at her. Reflexively, I did look at her. She met my eyes, and said: "I'm better now. I've been punished enough. I didn't want to die." There was a hint of a strangeness in her lovely blue eyes, though, as if she were asking silently for forgiveness, for bringing us here. I was convinced, at least, that she *wanted* to protect us, even though I wasn't sure that she could.

"You still haven't answered my question," I said to Oberon Breisz, stubbornly. "Why did you want her, and how have you used her?"

"I wanted her," he replied, looking at Dupin rather than at me, "because of what Angria had made her."

"What was that?" Dupin asked, this time answering his cue mildly.

"A skryer."

"And what did that involve?" I said, attempting to take back the initiative—but my question overlapped Dupin's, which was: "And how did Angria do that?"

Perhaps unsurprisingly, it was Dupin's question to which Breisz elected to reply directly—although, in fairness, he did eventually clarify both.

"You have to understand," he said, "that the British and Portuguese view of Angria as a pirate or petty warlord does him little justice. Indeed, it was precisely because he had begun his career as a common bandit that he conceived ambitions that would never have occurred to any hereditary maharajah. He became determined to master the secrets of Indian magic, and undertook that quest as a serious scholar. You have doubtless heard traveler's tales about the magic of the fakirs, including their ability to grow fully mature plants from seeds in a mater of minutes, and their ability to climb ropes and vanish—but the most significant of all those abilities, witnessed on numerous occasions by British observers, is that of suspending animation, to the extent that they can be buried alive for months on end.

"Because they continue to live, their bodily needs are merely slowed down, not halted, so there is a limit to their endurance in that state, but the suspension also slows down the aging process drastically. Fakirs who make frequent use of the ability are able to live for as much as two hundred years—nor is the hundred and fifty years they spend entranced wasted, for it frees their consciousness to undertake explorations in the dream-dimensions. The dreams in question are admittedly slow, but they're nevertheless enlightening. The most enlightening of all are the ones that are least frequently interrupted—which can be contrived, provided that the individual whose animation is suspended can be fed while still entranced. The magicians working in the more exotic Eastern monasteries place partic-ular value on the hallucinatory explorations experienced by an innocent, unquestioning soul. Rumor has it that there are chil-dren concealed in such institutions who have reportedly been in such a state of suspended animation for centuries, directed in their explorations by suggestion and delivering their findings by somniloquism, but rumor always exaggerates. At any rate, that's what Angria attempted to do with Jack Taylor's daughter—with Jack's full, if somewhat reluctant, co-operation."

Dupin took a few moments to digest that. For once, however, I was quick on the uptake, immediately seeing the consequence of what had been said in the context of my own question.

"You mean," I said, aghast, "that she really is more than a

hundred years old—but that she has spent eighty years of that life *in a deep trance*?"

"It was only a year and a day, subjectively speaking," Oberon Breisz told me, coldly. "And it was only in dreams within the dream that she did my specific bidding. She was as pliable as I could have hoped, and built her own fantasy to occupy the primary level of her decelerated consciousness: a confabulation compounded out of stories that she had been told and books she had read. You mustn't blame me for her fantasies of living as a queen in a legendary court, surrounded by knights and magicians. That was her own doing: a concoction cooked up with a little assistance from tales Jack had told her, when he was in a fatherly mood…and perhaps more than a little from the tales *La Buse* told her while he and I were in Callaba together in the mid-twenties. He took quite a shine to her, in his own crude way, and Taylor had run for the hills. The poor child only got to see him once in more than two years. Levasseur tried to take his place, after a fashion.

"In fact, Levasseur even tried to weaken Angria's control by taking away the medallion that Angria had given her before we set sail for Brittany in '27, but he had misunderstood its purpose. The amulet was intended to protect her while she was in suspended animation, for that kind of encryption can render a sleeper vulnerable to leakage from R'lyaieh. *La Buse* was no ready-made scholar magician, any more than Jack Taylor was… but they didn't have my advantages. I could have taken the amulet back from Levasseur, but there seemed to be no point— Angria could have given her another had he thought it worthwhile, and by the time I took her away from Callaba, I was sure that I could provide protection for both of us without the aid of toys of that sort. I went looking for the medallion after Levasseur was hanged, of course, but I never found it, any more than I could pick up Ysolde's trail. I went back to Paris periodically, using different pseudonyms, discreetly putting the name about, but it wasn't until…well, you know the rest."

"You must have spend a good deal of time in a trance yourself," Dupin observed, evidently having taken that inference from Breisz' reference to periodic returns.

"Not as much as you might think," Breisz replied. "I have other ways to preserve myself from aging—but yes, I *have* spent abundant time in crypts of more than one sort. I've carried out my own explorations of that dangerous kind. So should you, Monsieur Dupin, if you want to know who you really are, and to come into your full intellectual inheritance."

"I think I have a sound grasp on my identity," Dupin told him. "Sounder, at any rate, than the Comte de Saint-Germain."

"You shouldn't mock the Comte," said Breisz. "He has a long way to go yet, but he shows promise. I'm thinking of joining his Society. Cagliostro invited me once before, but I was too preoccupied. Now…perhaps it's time. It would then be *my* Society, of course, and the Comte my apprentice. It might be a useful resource, for its library is not uninteresting."

"But not as good as yours?" Dupin was quick to say.

"Perhaps not," said Breisz, with blatantly false modesty. "Is there some particular text about which you want to inquire."

"Do you have John Dee's copy of the *Claves Demonicae?*"

"I have Edward Kelley's copy of the *Claves Demonicae,*" was Breisz's corrective counter to that.

"And the copy of the *Necronomicon* that Dee inherited from Roger Bacon?"

"Yes, I have the Latin version—but not the original Sanskrit text from which the Arabic translation was made. I had to cede that to Angria. What use he has made of it since, I cannot tell."

"Do you have…?" Dupin never revealed the third title he had in mind, however, because the old manservant came in just then to announce, with ostentatious formality, that dinner was served.

According to my watch, it was rather early—but I was ravenously hungry, and did not mind at all. Besides which, what did Paris time have to do with the encrypted time of Oberon Breisz's lair?

"When we have eaten, Monsieur Dupin," said our host,

graciously, "I shall be very happy to reintroduce you to those two books, and many more of similar interest. There is a great deal more that might be gleaned from them, by two minds such as ours, working in collaboration again."

Again? I thought—but Dupin did not query the assertion, which was merely part of a teasing pattern by now.

CHAPTER SIXTEEN
THE DEMOISELLE D'YS

As CONVENTION DEMANDED, the specific interrogation was suspended while we ate—but Chapelain, perhaps attempting mischief, asked Oberon Breisz whether he paid any attention to recent developments in the diagnosis, analysis and treatment of madness.

"I fear not," Breisz admitted. "I confess that I had never heard of Dr. Leuret until rumor reached me—belatedly, alas—that Ysolde was in his care. I would be glad to hear your opinions on the subject, however, when we have time. I hope that you won't rush back to Paris in to much of a hurry—you're welcome to enjoy my hospitality for as long as you wish. I'm grateful to you for the help you have been able to give Ysolde."

"I fear that I can't accept," Chaplain told him. "I really should not have left the capital at such short notice, for it will cause distress to several of my patients, with whom I had appointments. Mademoiselle Leonys' need seemed urgent, but now that she's safely home, I really must start back tomorrow—early in the morning if that's possible."

"Of course," said Breisz. He could presumably see that Chapelain was not as firmly resolved as he alleged, partly because he was still anxious about Ysolde. The physician was still studying her intently, and I was not at all surprised by that, for her present wakefulness was surely as odd and disturbing as her previous somnambulism had been. She was forever touching the table, her chair and the wall behind her, as if savoring some precious texture—although I could not imagine anything more ordinary. When she breathed in, she seemed to be breathing some intoxicating perfume, and one could easily have imagined, from her silent reactions, that she was dining on ambrosia and nectar rather than plain food and mediocre wine.

In spite of Ysolde's quasi-ecstatic responses, the banality of the occasion was bizarrely oppressive, eerie in its utter lack of distinction. The food, which included blue trout and jugged hare, was as acceptable as the nourishment routinely served in Paris restaurants, so Breisz's cook was clearly competent, but it wasn't gourmet fare. Breisz seemed well aware of that when he asked us, a trifle anxiously, whether the food was too our liking, just as any host who rarely entertained at home might have done. Indeed, but for the assurances I had received that Oberon Breisz was a powerful magician, who had contrived to encrypt his entire dwelling and the pinnacle on which it stood, so as to remove into some private margin of the world, I could easily have believed that he was a commonplace provincial gentlemen, awkwardly aware that he was a foreigner by birth, anxious to win the good opinion of cultivated Parisians.

Chapelain was suitably complimentary in response to enquiries about the food, although he was clearly distracted by his puzzlement regarding his patient's evolving condition. Dupin made no effort to conceal his indifference, and seemed so guarded in his own attentiveness that he seemed almost to be in some encrypted psychological retreat of his own.

Absurdly I found myself asking our host how many servants he had, and whether they all lived in. He told me that he had five, and that they did indeed all live in. He didn't say anything about their attitude to what must be a very peculiar lifestyle, so he obviously wasn't pricked by the same sorts of anxieties that I had, even though he had surely not been nobly born. He had been a pirate captain once, and was well accustomed to the habit of command.

Coffee was served in the drawing-room—the house, in spite of its modernity, apparently had no smoking-room—but Breisz was quick to excuse himself in order to invite Dupin to his library. He didn't invite Chapelain or myself, and seemed eager to have Dupin entirely to himself, but I think that the mesmerist was glad to have the opportunity to remain with Ysolde Leonys, and I had no objection to the arrangement.

Ysolde did not take coffee, and did not remain seated once Breisz had left the room. She got to her feet and wandered back and forth, sometimes pausing to look out of the window at the starry sky and the vast black shadow of the land, but sometimes also pausing by the dresser, or even the black walls, to run her fingers over them, affectionately. Once, she paused on front of the pirate flag, seemingly meeting the skull's mocking stare.

"Angria flies it now," she murmured. "My father added it to his fleet, before Oberon took it back...but Angria was not a man to give up his possessions easily, even when he had made an agreement."

"They were *all* bad men," I told her. "Products of their time and place."

"I understand that *now*," she said.

"The other walls are a trifle bare, though," I remarked, when she passed on from the flag and paused to run her finger over the whitened plaster. "I can understand why Monsieur Breisz has no ancestral portraits to hang, but he surely might have invested in a few tapestries and mirrors, if not Oriental carpets and screens."

"Can you not see how artful it is?" she asked, seemingly surprised. "Can you not feel the thrill of the space itself? I felt it even in the stone circle, which lies on the very edge of his domain, but here...there is magic all around us. Can you not see what a palace this is? If you were really my Tom Linn, you would. My knights understood how precious space becomes— how strangely taut and curved—when time slows."

Automatically, I took out my watch, as if I might somehow be able to perceive an unnatural slowness in the passing moments, even though the naked eye cannot really perceive the normal movement of a minute-hand.

"You seem to be feeling quite well now, Mademoiselle Leonys?" Chapelain observed.

"Very well indeed," she assured him, moving back to the window but keeping her back to it in order to face Chapelain as she spoke to him. "I was very ill in Paris, was I not?"

"Very ill indeed," Chapelan confirmed, echoing her own formula. "I feared for your life."

"I thought that I had lost my life," she said. "There were moments when I wished that I were dead—but you saved my life, my faithful Merlin...oh, don't look at me like that. I know that you're Dr. Pierre Chapelain, of Paris...but for a little while, you were my Merlin, my wizard, my protector. Now I shall be yours, if I can."

Exactly what are we in need of protection from? I wondered. *Can she really provide it, if we are?*

Chapelain was following a different train of thought. "I would love to claim the credit for such a miracle," the mesmerist said, "but it seemed to me that you saved yourself, with the aid of the medallion. It isn't the first time that I've seen talismans used to focus and concentrate a somnambulist's powers of self-healing, but I never saw anything nearly as spectacular as your own transformation."

"I was very glad to see the medallion again, after such a long time," she said. "It was given to me for my protection, and it seems that I recovered it just in time, else those monsters would surely have claimed my soul."

"Had you ever seen anything like those monsters before?" I asked, swiftly.

"When I was a child," she said. "I had almost forgotten them, and the danger they pose—but I had forgotten so many things. Angria tried to conjure them, but they will not be conjured. They come readily enough when they are summoned, but also when they will, and there are no bargains to be made with them, no matter how one tries. Angria shielded me, and gave me the means to protect myself, but that was because he had plans for me...I never truly belonged to Callaba, though, and there were always bargains to be made with Angria. I'm beginning to remember everything, now—and to understand my memories. Oberon isn't my father, but I was always his child…always. I think I shall be safe here now…at least for a little while." She sounded far less than certain.

"Even if Oberon puts you back into suspended animation again?" I asked.

"I shall have to go back to the dream, of course," she said, "but I can do that, now—and I know now *where* to go. I can't go back to my knights, for that was a childish dream, and I ruined it by falling in love with Tristan and answering the ghost's seductive call…but there is so much magic in these walls, in the very air I breathe, that I know that I can go further now, far beyond the dream I created for myself. That really was a childish yearning, beautiful but transient. I'm older than that now, and…I've been punished for my weakness."

"What do you mean by *going back further*?" Chapelain wanted to know.

"I can find other selves now, just as Oberon has. I was a demoiselle in another court once, in Ys, before it sank beneath the sea. When I dream again, I shall go back there, far away from Oberon and Tristan. If I could take anyone with me, I think it would be you, Tom Linn, for the sake of your songs, but I cannot—and you must not worry, Tom, for I would never try to take you from your own world…and if he or anyone else should try, I will defend you. I know what I owe you, now."

She was looking at me, but I wasn't at all sure that she was talking to me, rather than to some ghost of her own imagination. I had some faint inkling of what she might be feeling; I had had occasion, in the past, to speak to ghosts of my own imagination

Chapelain was still pursuing his own agenda. "You believe that you have lived other lives, in the distant past?" he queried. "Other mesmerists have claimed to be able to enable patients to remember past incarnations—and when I first questioned you, I thought your answers reflected something of that sort—but I've always been skeptical about metempsychosis."

"What's metempsychosis?" she asked.

"The Pythagorean notion that the soul is eternal, moving from one incorporation to another in an endless sequence. I believe the Buddihsts and Hindus of India have similar notions."

"I don't know about an endless sequence," Ysolde said. "If that's so, than I still have a great deal more to remember...but I do have access to other dreams. Perhaps they're fabrications, like my dream of being queen in Oberon's court. Perhaps Ys never existed either, and is merely a further phase of my own slow maturity...or my own inescapable madness. If so...well, better that, I think, than murderously brutal reality. I have only ever been happy in dreams."

How could Chapelain or I challenge that assertion? How could François Leuret ever have contended that she would be better sane than mad, given what reality and sanity had cost her in the past? But I didn't need Leuret to tell me that she was a very rare exception, and that madness was usually far less kind—cruel enough, in fact, to make sanity a very welcome refuge, for those who can attain it. Even in Ysolde's case, tragic as its Parisian episode had been, I couldn't help suspecting that a calculated retreat into sweet enchantment in the mythical drowned land of Ys might not provide the release she hoped and expected. Her present condition was ominously reminiscent, in some respects, of a kind of fever—a delirium that could not last, and might yet prove a brief stay of execution.

Chapelain presumably thought so too—but he still had other things on his mind, in addition to his patient's precarious well-being. "In Paris," he said to Ysolde, trying to seem casual, "you said that you know where the residue of Levasseur's treasure is. Is it in this house?"

A strangely sly expression stole across her previously-innocent face. "Some of it," she said.

"You mean that some is not?" Chapelain promptly inferred.

She put her finger to her lips, suddenly seeming very child-like. "Oberon doesn't know everything," she said. "Levasseur was cleverer than he thought."

"You mean that Levasseur told you where the treasure is?"

"Not exactly," she said, in a hurried whisper. Again, she leaned close to my ear in order to continue, forcing Chapelain to lean over too. "I'd never been here when he used to tell me stories, and I didn't realise what he meant at the time…I was only five years old. He liked me—although I didn't like him, after he stole my medallion. I didn't know, until much later, that he thought he was protecting me—poor fool—and it was later still that I worked out what he meant by telling me the story of the buried treasure. He was foolish to do that too…but then, he was never as clever as Angria or Oberon, even though he was cleverer than they thought. Oberon thinks that he recovered all the gold and jewels, but Levasseur set some aside, and gave me he clues that told me where it was without my realising what he was doing. He had to take the cross back, though—whatever is in the box, if anything still is, the cross isn't. Perhaps nothing is—I never had a chance to dig. It's possible that Oberon knew too, and took possession of it long ago…but I don't think so."

An inspiration suddenly struck me, which immediately bubbled over, as sudden surges of enlightenment are prone to do. "When Levasseur told the man to whom he consigned the medallion that it held the key to his fortune," I said, "he didn't mean that the inscription was a code to be deciphered. He meant that if the recipient could find the owner of the medallion—you, that is—you could tell him where the remnant of his share of the treasure was hidden. Saint-Germain—if it was, in some sense, the Saint-Germain I know—misunderstood him, and didn't have an opportunity to correct his misconception. When he gave the medallion to me, hoping that Dupin might be able to decipher it with the aid of the encryption inscribed on your back, he was barking up entirely the wrong tree…but he obtained the right result by accident."

By accident? I wondered as I spoke the last words. *Has any of this been accidental?*

"I don't know anything about that," said Ysolde, "but I was very glad to get the medallion back…even before its magic took effect."

Chapelain evidently wanted to question her further about the hidden gold, but as soon as he opened his mouth, she put her finger to her lips again, insistently. I could see that he was still having second thoughts about returning to Paris in the morning.

"Do you know what Oberon wants with Dupin?" I asked her.

"He wants to use Dupin as he has used me."

"He wants to put Dupin into suspended animation—to use him as some kind of seer?"

"Yes."

It was on the tip on my tongue to ask: *Why Dupin?*—but there seemed no need to voice the question. Dupin was the sanest man I knew, and the most knowledgeable. What a seer he would make, if there really were a kind of magic that might give him the visionary reach!

I was convinced, though, that Dupin would not agree to any terms that Oberon Breisz might offer. If ever he undertook any such experiment, he would want to do it by himself.

The door opened then. I had not expected Breisz and Dupin to come down again so soon, but I presumed that Breisz had only offered his guest a teasing glimpse of his library, as yet another lure, another diabolical temptation.

"I'm sure that you would be glad of the opportunity to study here at your leisure," Breisz said to Dupin, as he went to the dresser in order to pour his guests a liqueur from a decanter that must have been set there by one of the servants. It had the color and distinctive odor of Benedictine.

"It might be interesting," was all that Dupin would concede.

Breisz frowned slightly at Dupin's lack of enthusiasm. "Don't be so coy, my friend," he said, as he handed Dupin a glass with his right hand, and gave another to Chapelain with his left. "You would give your right arm to have those books in your possession again—and you know what a sacrifice it is for me to offer you the opportunity to possess them, for I know what the booksellers of Paris whisper when they mention my name. Literary miser! Biliotaph! Yes—and proud of it. But they were *our* books once before, Monsieur Dupin, and can be ours again…and what use we shall be able to make of them, now that we and civilization are a little older, a little more mature!"

"I'm sorry to repeat myself yet again," Dupin said, "but I really have never seen those books before—nor you."

"You have owned and treasured them," Breisz retorted, letting impatience make his voice shriller as his vanity took offense, "if you will only make the effort to recollect the memory. I really can help you remember, if you still cannot do it unaided, but I must admit that I had expected better of you, once you were here."

"I can assure you that I have never seen the *Necronomicon* before, Monsieur Briesz," said Dupin, with scrupulous politeness, "although I have read several second-hand reports of it."

"You, of all people, need not call me that," said our host, handing a glass of Benedictine to me and offering to pour another for Ysolde, who shook her head. He poured one for himself instead.

"I apologize, Mr. England," said Dupin, serenely, having taken a sip of the liqueur. "I do not mean to offend you with my inability to tell you want you want to hear."

"You always used to call me Edward," Breisz told him, reproachfully, "and you know full well that England is no more my true name than Breisz."

"I do know that," Dupin admitted, "but I confess that I have no idea what your true name is."

Our host sighed deeply, finally tiring of his game. "It's Kelley," he said, after a pregnant pause. "Edward Kelley."

CHAPTER SEVENTEEN
THE SLEEP OF REASON

THAT WAS SOMETHING of a bombshell, I admit, but Dupin did not seem shocked, nor did he laugh. I think he must have guessed some time before, and had been teasing Breisz as Breisz had been teasing him. They were, after all, as arrogant as one another.

"Are you implying that I am John Dee reincarnated?" Dupin asked, calmly.

Why not? I thought, remembering the enthusiastic way in which he had talked about his hero—and his determination to construe Dee, not as the deluded wizard that legend painted him, but as a man very much like himself: an inquisitive and thoroughly rational bibliophile and scholar. Except, of course, that I did not believe in metempsychosis any more than Chapelain did—and Dupin's open mind would never yield to the conviction of a man like Oberon Breisz, no matter what games the magician could play with space and time.

"You *are* John Dee," our host affirmed, with a certainty that had to be based in hope rather than reason. "If you would only let me help you, you could remember. If you would only consent to help yourself, you would remember. You have lain idle too long, my friend, while I have made progress. We achieved great things once, you and I—but circumstances were against us. We shall achieve greater things, now that I may play the guide and you the skryer. Innocence has its value, but childhood dreams are too easily corrupted by confabulation. The best skryer of all would be a man with vast knowledge, but an open mind. I think you know how rare that combination is."

"A knowledgeable man with an open mind can hardly help but be skeptical about the possibility, and the wisdom, of skyring," Dupin observed. "Innocence has the virtue of generating childish confabulations—what nightmares might an educated mind produce?"

"If that is an accusation, my friend, it is unworthy of you. I played my part in the generation of the *Claves Demonicae*, it's true—but the *Necronomicon* existed long before Edward Kelley was born. I wish you could have set your hand on the Sanskrit version...but even that cannot really have been the first. All the texts attempting to render its peculiar wisdom in human tongues are mere shadows of the book the angels could have written, had they been able to write instead of merely dream."

"The Edward Kelley that John Dee knew," Dupin said, thoughtfully, "had been convicted of forgery—a crime whose penalty, at the time, was the amputation of the ears. Your ears, Monsieur Bresz, seem to be in very good condition."

Our host's immediate response to that was a wry smile. "You're determined to resist the truth," he said. "It will not matter. You're in my domain now, where I am in command. I make no threats, mind—but this is not your little nook in Paris, and even though you have carefully left your dragon on my threshold, there's no escape. This is Fate, John...it has been determined since the dawn of time. None of us really has a choice, or ever had. You'll play your part, as I am playing mine."

"There is no Fate," Dupin replied, soberly. "Even Cthulhu, which has moved heaven and earth in the attempt to play that role, cannot fully control the dreamers it has made, even in the absence of the defenses bequeathed to us by the entities you call angels. We *are* free to choose, Monsieur Breisz—but not alas, to choose who we are, merely in answer to a whim. The sad truth is that we are far more impotent in the face of circumstances than our self-made dreams urge to be believe...but still, we *are* free; there is no Fate to force our capitulation."

Oberon Breisz did not seem annoyed, or intimidated, by the contradiction, although I could not imagine that he liked it. "It's getting late," he said—inaccurately, according to Paris time. "We will all benefit from sleep…and you might see things differently in the morning."

Dupin let him have the last word. Coupled with the enigmatic anxieties that Ysolde had generated, it seemed a distinctly ominous last word to me.

On the stairway, as we went up to our rooms, I said to Dupin: "Should we leave now, do you think? Perhaps it would be better to gallop away into the night than to risk sleep in this strange domain."

"No," he said. "If we flee, we shall invite pursuit—and he who invites pursuit is half way to being caught. A challenge has been laid down, and is better met head on. I'm not entirely certain that I can resist the pressures that might afflict our dreams, but I feel obliged to try—and you must try too. Reason may sleep, but it does not die; it remains available to us, even in the worst of nightmares, if only we can remember how to find and use it. I have confidence in you, as I have in Chapelain. We are sane men, and we know the value of our sanity. Oberon Breisz is not, and does not understand the treacherousness of his madness. He cannot seduce us, and has no wish to hurt us, as yet…and we might still save him, if we have time enough"

"*As yet?*" was the phrase I elected to echo. It implied that the time might comes, and soon, when Edward Kelley reincarnate *might* want to hurt his former mentor, and those associated with him

"He seems uncommonly robust," Dupin said, "but dreams are brittle, and ever wont to shatter. When they do, wrath often burst forth."

"I'll keep my revolver under my pillow," I decided.

"It might be direly ineffective weapon, in the heart of a nightmare," he said. "Don't allow its possession to make you forget that you have others."

The bedroom, as I have observed, was as ordinary as any

guest bedroom, save for its total lack of decoration. The bed, however, was capacious and comfortable, very conducive to sleep—and that seemed a useful luxury, after the hard floor of the inn on the road to Rennes. I was tired, and I do not think that I could have stayed awake even if I had determined to try. At any rate, Dupin had said that he had confidence in me, and I was obliged to live up to that expectation. I did not undress, though, and I did place my gun beneath my pillow, just in case.

How much of what followed as real, I cannot tell for certain; nor can I even specify very clearly what *real* might mean in the circumstances in which I found myself. I know that I went to sleep, which certainly licenses the belief that it was all the merest kind of hallucination, and that is definitely the preferable interpretation—but I did not wake up where I went to sleep, so, at the very least, it was a somnambulistic adventure. Nor was it only *my* adventure, for I was not alone for very long, and there were other survivors of the dire dream to confirm at least some of its details.

Did Oberon Breisz intend to take action while we slept? Did he believe that he could risk some magic to entrap us, and draw us by degrees into his fantasy? I believe so. Did Ysolde Leonys have her own agenda, her own vague plan to exploit the dream-conducive environment to build a new safe haven to replace the one she had lost sixteen years before? I am certain of it. Neither plan, however, came to fruition. Whatever contribution those pre-hatched schemes made to the hallucination we actually experienced was a minor one, usurped, perverted and altered out of all recognition by a much-superior force. Even minor contributions can be vital, though; they can determine the difference between life and death.

Was it Cthulhu that invaded all our dreams, and almost destroyed us all? In a manner of speaking, yes it was—but not in the sense that the creature encrypted in the borderlands of the earthly ocean had any particular interest in the petty affairs of half a dozen human beings. It was not bent on any kind of piracy, predation or revenge. It was not really *acting* at all, but merely *being*...waiting and dreaming, as it had been condemned to do, in the immeasurable past, by the unimaginable angels who had imprisoned it, in order to protect the coherency of the plenum. It was not malevolent, in the sense that it wished specific ill to any particular individual, world or universe, although humans, and other thinking beings, cannot possibly regarded it as anything but utterly inimical and implacable destructive. It was simply *being what it was*...and it was our misfortune that some among us, and people with whom they had had contact in the past, had deliberately involved themselves in its being, trying to summon its phantom aspects in the hope of drawing power therefrom, or even to make some kind of pact with the vast whole—a futile endeavour, given that it was not at all the kind of Devil that they imagined the Devil to be, but something far more horrid.

As I had anticipated, the sequence of my own involvement continued to progress. I had seen the shoggoths in semi-human guise, and I had seen them, as it were, naked. On both occasions, I had been aware of the superficiality of what I was seeing—that the furthest removed and most abstract of their multi-dimensional aspects was, in some sense, the core of their being, the heart of their dream.

On both occasions that I had seen then, I had assumed that they were trying to take possession of the medallion, or at least to remove it from our possession, in order to nullify its repellent authority, but now I think that such an interpretation was overly anthropomorphic—Dupin, as a pedant, would probably prefer the term anthropopathic, since the familiar term is to do with matters of form. Anthropo*pathy*, if my Greek can be trusted, is falsely to credit unhuman creatures with human purpose, human endeavor and human feeling. If, instead of partially humanizing them as malevolent marauders, one thinks of the star-spawn as drifting fragments of random hallucination, unthinkingly and unfeelingly following unnameable and incalculable tropisms, that might be a little nearer to the unspeakable, unthinkable truth—but perhaps that too is a futile endeavour, and the words "unspeakable," "unthinkable" and "unnameable" really do go to the heart of the matter.

Whether or not Cthulhu perverted Earth's native life so as to fabricate the human race, in order produce a legion of dreaming minds that might one day forge the key to its release, either by accident or design, I cannot tell. The logic of the situation, however, suggests that it *does* have an innate interest in dreaming, thinking minds, and in the shapes of their dreams and thoughts—to which its instruments respond, reflexively or instinctively.

Our involvement with Ysolde Leonys had attracted the shoggoths twice before; it was inevitable, I suppose, that it should attract them again, in greater force—and doubly inevitable that they should find us all the more easily in a tiny cranny of space and time that was itself encrypted, where their force might be multiplied tenfold, as if they were in their own element.

In all probability, they could not have done anything without a bedrock of human dreaming to work with—but there was no shortage of human dreams and nightmares in our company, on that night of all nights. Oberon Breisz had made an exception to his reclusive habit by inviting guests into his home, gladly and eagerly—but perhaps recklessly.

At the merest suggestion of the cephalopod aspect of the invaders, I sat up in bed and took out my revolver—but this time, the tentacles did not reach out for me, and there was no embrace to taste. This time, they made no move to seize or enter into me at all. This time, they were in the walls of the house, and the fabric of the pinnacle on which it stood.

I did see the ultimate form of the monsters, and felt that presence, after a fashion, although I cannot quite explain the dream-logic that allowed me to see and feel through solid matter, perhaps curving my lines of sight and extrapolating my sensations of touch through higher dimensions. I saw the dragon-worms more clearly than before, like abstruse mathematical and musical sequences writhing in the guts of the earth and flowing into the walls of the house.

Microscopists tell us that there are worms everywhere—

that if all the substance of the Earth were to vanish, save for the worms, a hypothetical observer would still be able to see the ghostly outlines of people animals and trees, buildings and rivers and mountains, by virtue of an infinite host of tiny white eelworms, both parasitic and free-living. The dragon-worms comprising Cthulhu-dreams are not tiny and not white, however, but vast and multicolored, in all their algebraic glory. Nor are they mere blind tapering cylinders of flesh, undifferentiated in their ultimate simplicity, but eyed and mouthed and scaled and winged and clawed, and hideous in their ultimate geometrical complexity. Nor are they patient parasites, lying docile in their hosts, absorbing aliments while creating the absolute minimum of disturbance, but impatient trigonometric aggressors, utterly careless of disruption.

No sooner had I perceived them, in fact, than they began to digest the house, dissolving it in unearthly acids and equations, liquefying and differentiating its solidity—and I could feel the floor becoming treacherous beneath my feet as the house and the hill on which it stood began to sag and sink.

Is this, I wondered, *how legendary Ys sank, before being covered by the sullen waves? What became of its poor delicate demoiselles?*

I ran, then—out of the room and down the stairs.

I heard the echoes of other running feet, but could not see whose feet they were. All I could see were the worms, writhing and coiling, like an immeasurable and irrational Gordian knot, not merely inside everything solid but *instead* of it, more real, for the moment, than the cold and brittle solidity of mere matter, or the active, bloody warmth of flesh.

I could hear, though, and what I hard was the angry voice of Oberon Breisz, pronouncing the now-familiar formula: *"Ph'nglui mglw'nat Cthulhu R'laiyeh wgah'ngl fhtaign."*

It had no effect. He tried another formula, and then a third, his voice becoming louder every time—but the shoggoths were on safer axiomatic ground this time, from their own transcendental point of view, and were not to be so easily dislodged.

The formulae undoubtedly had their effect, for I saw ripples of agony flowing along the bodies of the worms, and their horrid red eyes bulging, and their vicious jaws chattering—but they were determined to do their work no matter what, and they were working with terrible rapidity.

I knew that I had to get out of the house—by leaping through a glazed window if the door was firmly locked—but I knew before I reached the bottom of the stairs that I could not even hope to reach the vestibule. The shoggoths were not assaulting my flesh directly, but they were stealing all purchase from it. My feet were sinking ankle-deep into the substance of the floor, and the air that I was sucking into my lungs was decaying into unbreathability.

I brandished my revolver, but did not fire. I might as well have fired at a tempest, hoping to cripple a thunderbolt.

I contrived to reach the ground floor, but I could get no further. I was thigh-deep now in the worm-infested slime, and now the worms were in my flesh as well, surging up within my limbs and bowel, aiming for my heart and brain. I put the revolver back in my pocket, in order that I could use both hands to support myself against the wall—but the wall had become treacherous, and when my hand touched it, I had difficulty tearing it free again. I began waving my hands in the air and I twisted my body, trying to pull my legs free from the slime without the aid of any authentic leverage, and therefore hope-lessly.

I felt the tide of alien flesh welling up inside my own, and knew that I was within a second of death—but then a hand reached out, as if from nowhere, to grasp my flailing wrist, and a dazzling white light appeared amid the multicolored chaos, resolving the series of my distress into reassuring finitude. That light spelled out two cryptograms, back to back, each inscribed in letters at least an inch across—but it was evident in the way that the symbols moved that they were inscribed on a invisible human body...a female body.

Ysolde Leonys was not pronouncing the cryptograms—the

only voice I could hear was that of Oberon Breisz, chanting spell after spell—but their incarnation fore and aft of her heart was a protective cage, extending throughout her own flesh and any flesh she touched. The moment I made contact with her, the worms within my lower body disappeared, in hectic retreat and division. She transferred her grip from my wrist to my hand, so that the clasp was mutual.

"Reach out," she whispered—and I could hear the whisper perfectly, in site of Oberon's chanting.

I reached out, and felt another hand grasp mine. It was Dupin's; I recognized it.

"I have Chapelain," he whispered in his turn.

The symbols of the encryption moved past me then, heading for the door, and the human chain they drew behind them followed in their train.

The door was locked, but it did not matter. The encrypted symbols passed through it, and so did everything they encaged.

That was not the end, though—not by any means. The hill was still dissolving, and the steps that had been crumbling even when they were humbly material had already been crudely subtracted from the sum of all things. The whole enclave was still sinking, as if ambitious to become the Underworld that Ysolde had named it, in every sense of the word. The steep crag was becoming a glutinous mass, flowing away in every direction.

The starlight was very faint, and the surrounding landscape was profoundly steeped in shadow, but the symbols incarnate in Ysolde's flesh were not the only things glowing. In the distance—a *very* long way away, it seemed—there was a circle of rough-hewn lights, roughly oblong in form, standing on their ends.

It was, I realized, the megalithic circle: the threshold of Oberon Breisz's perverted domain. And between the stones that formed the gate through which we had entered the heart of that domain the previous day were two human shadows, already reaching out for us.

There were two because Madame Lacuzon, Dupin's faithful gorgon, was not alone. The Comte de Saint-Germain was with her, having succeeded in following us to our goal. They were both waiting for us now, ready to pull us from chaos if they could...but they were so very far away, that I could not believe that we could reach them before the earth swallowed us up and plunged us into its bowels.

The worms could not get inside us while we were caged by Ysolde's magic, but they did not have to. They merely had to suck us down into the slimy morass of their digestive chyme, from which there could be no escape.

There was still a battle in progress, though, for the house was not dissolving as rapidly as the hill. Indeed, as I looked back, it was not obvious that the uppermost floor of the house was dissolving at all, although it was slowly descending into the protoplasmic prenumerical *urschleim* that the worms were making of the lower floors.

Oberon Breisz was visible, at least in silhouette, behind the lamplit casement of what I assumed to be his library, where he was raging still against the threat. He was doggedly determined to hold chaos at bay, at least from his books and his own precious person.

In the meantime, Ysolde kept moving forward, heading for the megaliths, drawing me behind her, while I drew Dupin after me and Dupin drew Chapelain after him. The glow of the symbols in her flesh was fading, though, and when I heard her sob, I knew that she had no more faith than I had that we could actually reach the megaliths.

"Would that you really were Tom Linn," she murmured, plaintively "for at least you could sing us a song while we die."

But I wasn't Tom Linn, and I couldn't sing.

"I wanted to be in Ys," she said, then, to herself rather than to me, "but not like this. Not like this." It occurred to me then that she thought that she had brought this fate upon us, by means of a careless dream.

"It wasn't you," I told her. "It's not your fault—not at all."

"So you *can* sing, after all," she murmured.

She had not stopped moving; she was still striving with all her might—but it was obviously hopeless. We had sunk too deep to walk or wade, and we could not swim in that dense, worm-infested subatomic soup. The symbols were almost extinct now, and their protection could not last much longer.

"You should have gone to the library," I said to Dupin. "There, at least, you would have stood a chance, even if you could not have given him the help he wanted and expected from you. He might yet succeed in preserving that corner of his domain."

"I hope he can," said Dupin. "We three are only human, after all, and a dozen infants will be born in Paris at the very moment of our death—but there are books in that room that are irreplaceable. The two lost volumes of Sanchuniathon alone...."

I was shoulder-deep in slime by the time he finished, and thought that there was nothing left to do but look up at the stars, and try to take what comfort I could from my own utter irrelevance within the universe, let alone the plenum.

I felt the worms writhing inside my flesh again. This time, they reached my heart.

I felt Ysolde's hand slip out of mine, and Dupin's too.

I could not hold on. There was no longer anything to hold on to. I was disintegrating, in body and mind alike.

CHAPTER EIGHTEEN
THE JOLLY ROGER

AS MY MOLTEN HEAD went under the surface of the now-oceanic liquid, and the flesh of the worms flooded my mouth, squirming through my lungs and brain, I raised my arms instinctively, as drowning men do.

Incredibly, both wrists were instantly gripped, and I was suddenly hauled out of the morass again, spitting and spluttering, by strong arms, regaining my solidity and integrity as I came. I was hauled up and up—further than seemed probable, if merely human arms had reached down to grab me—and was dragged over a bulwark on to a wooden deck. The wooden deck seemed to be sucking the worms out of me, although that might have been an illusion. In all probability, they were simply losing their purchase again.

The help that Ysolde had promised to summon had arrived. No matter how impossible it seemed, even in terms of dream-logic, help had arrived, gliding through the margins of the world as certain mythical entities can.

Cthulhu had not yet triumphed over human resistance, no matter how easily other matter had yielded to its dread tide.

With that thought in mind, I rubbed my sticky eyes—which had closed reflexively as I went under—and opened them gingerly, peering into the darkness in search of some cryptogram of white fire.

There was white fire a-plenty, but it was in the form of a flaming cross, mounted on a mast. Above the flaming cross was a flag, whose silver symbols stood out clearly, inscribed by reflected light. They depicted a skull and crossbones. My rescuer was flying the Jolly Roger.

Angria flies it now, Ysolde had said. The scholarly warlord had given the original back to Edward England, after taking it from John Taylor, but he had not surrendered the symbolism, or the right to deploy it.

My *rescuers*, I should say, in the plural, for Angria was far from being alone—and I should also have said *our* rescuers, for I was not alone either. I had not been the first to be hauled out of the ocean of uncanny flesh, nor was I the last. Ysolde helped me to my feet while the two men who had hauled me out did the same for Dupin, and then for Chapelain.

The ship seemed to be fully crewed, with a captain and a mate—or perhaps two captains. Although one seemed to be a wraith compounded out of unnaturally sturdy mist, the other apparently still owned his flesh, albeit that he was as thin as a rake, seemingly on the brink of starvation, and clad only in a loincloth.

"Not such a bad man, after all," I said to Ysolde, who was staring at the wraithlike ghost, trying to remember who he was.

Jack Taylor was looking back at her, with eyes of mist that held more expression than any eyes of flesh and fluid I had ever seen. He had been dead a long time, but something of him still survived, perhaps by courtesy of Indian magic. Having been born into a Protestant family before lapsing into agnosticism, I had never believed in the Roman notion of purgatory and post-humous repentance, but this, I knew, was a penitent soul—not under the pressure of any repentance forced by torture or divine bullying, but of his own free will.

Ysolde had called for help, but I think he would have come anyway, had he been able to do so.

That he was able to do so was surely due to Angria, the captain of the ship—who was, I suspect, not dead yet, and still endeavouring to find his way in life, through a treacherous laby-rinth of negotiation and deception. While his henchman looked at Ysolde, he kept his eyes on a different prize—save for one belief glance in my direction.

I only imagined that I could read minds, taking the gift for granted as one can in a dream, but I still think, even at a long removed, that my intuition regarding John Taylor's thoughts was accurate. Angria's dark eyes were far more opaque, and even though they actually met mine, for a split second, there was still a mystery behind them. He too had come of his own free will, though, glad to have been summoned, glad to be able to make a small payment on a debt that he had carelessly incurred when he was a younger and more reckless man. He, I think, probably did believe in metempsychosis, and in *karma* too, and knew that there were moral accounts to be balanced before it would be safe to die.

Then I got to my feet, steadied myself on the cluttered deck, and turned to Dupin. "For a moment there," I said, "I almost believed that this was not a dream, and that I was actually going to die."

"This is most certainly a dream," he told me, grimly, "but that does not mean that we have an automatic entitlement to wake up. I suspect that better men than us have died in dreams of this dire sort."

It was Angria, not John Taylor, who screeched orders at the crew and brought the ghost-ship around—headed, not for the island of the megaliths, which seemed more distant now than it had been while we were still making progress toward it, but for the remainder of the house, which now seemed an island itself, consisting of nothing but the second storey, the mansards and the crumbling roof. I could see the heads of people in the mansards through gaps in the tiles. I tried to count them but could not be sure that there were five.

The principal intention of our rescuers, I was convinced, was to save the man they had known as Edward England. They had been direly treacherous men in their time—pirates as blood-thirsty as any that had ever committed mass murder—but they were working on the side of the angels now. They wanted to save England, his servants, and perhaps the books too.

Oberon Breisz did not see matters that way. He undoubtedly thought that Angria and John Taylor both had old scores held against him, and were coming to settle them while Cthulhu had weakened him. It was Taylor who shouted out to him, trying to reassure him, but it would not have made a difference even if his old mentor John Dee had instructed him to be calm and trusting. As Dupin had observed, there comes a time when broken composure turns entirely to emotion—usually to uncontrollable wrath.

Breisz paused in the tiresome work of keeping Cthulhu's agents at bay long enough to curse the ship, and everyone sailing in her. Perhaps, in that reckless action, the shoggoths lent him a little of their own force, but I doubt it. Cthulhu's agents were not really agents, in a pedantic sense, because Cthulhu was not the kind of entity that was possessed of agency, in a pedantic sense. At any rate, the core malevolence of the curse was Edward England's, and his alone. A storm wind ripped through the sails and rigging of the ghost, and might have shattered her masts and hull had it not been for the glaring cross, which soaked up much of the blast.

The ship survived the maleficent formula. Had I ducked, I would have stayed safely on her deck. As it was, however, I was tumbled backwards into the bottom of a small, shallow jolly-boat tucked into a covert between the foredeck and the bridge. As the ship lurched, the angry wind snatched the jolly-boat into the air, and dropped it overboard.

Fortunately, it landed bottom down, and floated. Unfortunately, I had no oars—no means of propulsion, or of steering.

The jolly-boat was whipped away from the ship by a wayward current, and tentacles immediately began reaching up from a surface that now seemed much less viscous, groping for me and forcing me to flatten myself out in the bottom of the boat. I took my gun out of my pocket again, intending to blast any tentacle that contrived to wind itself around me, but none did while I stayed low, even though bulky shadows rose up and fell back to either side of the boat.

I had given up all hope of saving myself from the nightmare by waking up, but I told myself that it could not last forever, and that I was far from being alone in the conflict.

If the tentacles could not quite contrive to grasp me, though, they could certainly grasp the boat, and they had strength enough to crack and splinter the hull. I could almost feel the little craft coming apart, and risked raising my head to see where the ship was, in the hope that some further rescue might be possible from that direction.

It was not. I could see the shining cross and the skull-and-crossbones lit from below, but they were a long way off now. I could also see Oberon Breisz's lighted window behind it, but the voices that carried to me over the tortured surface were distorted in passing, and bore more resemblance to he muttering of demons that human beings engaged in urgent but constructive negotiation.

By way of compensation, however—and I felt entitled to a measure of compensation, by now—the hectic flight of the boat from Angria's ship and Breisz's unsteady island had bought me a great deal closer to the megaliths, where Madame Lacuzon and the Comte de Saint-Germain were still waiting, eager to help if their assistance ever became practicable. I could not hope that the seething and swarming sea would deliver me to within their arms' reach of its own accord, but now that the liquid was indeed authentically liquid, I wondered whether I might be able to swim through it in spite of its deadly infestation.

I had no time to reflect at length; if the boat split open beneath me I would surely be doomed, so I pocketed my revolver yet again, leapt to my feet, ran the length of the jolly-boat—which was not, alas very far—and dived into the water, poised to swim as fast as I could as soon as I surfaced.

Tentacles and eel-like entities immediately tried to capture me, but they were clumsy as well as blind, and the greater danger came from the mathematical omnipresence beyond those crude artefacts, which was ambitious to get inside me again. Once more, I felt the algebraic worms invading my flesh—but this time, instead of starting at the legs and working their way up, they struck directly at the head, and dug into my defenceless brain.

As soon as they made contact with my thoughts, they seemed to metamorphose into something even less imaginatively graspable, but far more inimical. There had been a moment during my second encounter with the shoggoths when the most distant aspect of them had seemed to be musical as well as mathematical, and now that aspect became foremost in its insistence, mounting a full frontal attack on reason itself—but I had heard demonic music more than once, and my reflexive reaction had been educated, at least to a degree. It hurt me, but it did not damn me.

In was on the very brink of madness and annihilation—but then, in addition to my own resistance, I heard shouting of a peculiarly rhythmic kind, and I realized that there were two voices nearby, howling in unison. It was not mellifluous, by any means, but it was virtuous music, not merely to my ears but—more importantly—to my fugitive consciousness. As another castaway might have clung to a spar of driftwood with all his might, I clung to that barbarous shanty with all the force of my sanity—and I truly believe that it literally pulled me to the shore, where the two singers seized me avidly and dragged me from the glutinous waves on to the solid ground within the ancient circle.

Saint-Germain howled with triumph—not so much because he thought my life worth saving but simply because the victory really had been a triumph of his magic over malign circumstance, of which he might be proud, even if he had been forced to join forces with the wise woman to achieve it.

Madame Lacuzon said nothing; I was not Dupin. Saint-Germain, on the other hand, pulled me to my feet and demanded: "What in Heaven's name is going on over here?"

"It's a ghost-ship," I said, "come to redeem a little of the debt its crewmen owe to human kindness. The repentant pirates will save everyone if they can—but I'm not sure that Oberon Breisz, alias Edward England, alias Edward Kelley, will consent to be saved. When I was blown overboard, he still seemed very intent on going down with his library. Dupin will save the books if he can, though—you may depend on that."

"What about the gold?" the Comte demanded, intemperately. "Is that the Flaming Cross of Goa on the ghost-ship's mast?"

"Very likely," I said, "since Angria is the ghost-ship's master, and Olivier Levasseur had to return the cross to him—but I doubt that you'll ever get your hands on it, or even the meager fraction of the treasure that is still somewhere in the house... unless, of course, you volunteer to join the ghost-ship's crew. Mind you, they might refuse to take you, as you're no mariner. There are conventions to be observed, after all."

"Damn it!" he said. "Hell's bells and buckets of blood!" He seemed to be practising what passes for pirate parlance on the Parisian stage, but if he was momentarily tempted to pursue the golden cross even on to a ghost-ship, he rapidly abandoned the idea. "So the treasure *was* still here, after all," he murmured. "To get so close and then to have to stand and watch...what exactly am I watching?"

"Don't worry," I said. "It's just a hallucination: a stray madness that was wandering the winds of the world in search of victims, and found us. It will all be gone in the morning... if we live that long, and can contrive to wake up. And you didn't really get close—I'll wager you only got this far because Madame Lacuzon was desperate for whatever help she could find, in the hope of pulling Dupin from the quagmire."

"She certainly didn't try to keep me out, for once," Saint-Germain admitted. "If that ship doesn't turn away soon, you know, the monsters in the sea will have them all. Can ghost-ships perish, do you suppose, or will it simply reappear in some distant ocean if it founders here?"

"In this arena," I said, "I suspect that it can go down with all hands...except perhaps for Angria, who might still be alive and asleep, somewhere else in the great wide world, still capable of finding his way home if he loses his dream-vessel."

The ship did not turn away. I saw the shadows, at least, leap from the windows of the mansards on to her deck—but so far as I could tell, Oberon Breisz's window was still firmly closed. I think he was still chanting—but he was alone, with no one to form a chorus.

And the remains of the house did eventually *go down*, dragged into a vast whirlpool.

The ghost-ship immediately began circling the vortex, whirled helplessly around by the furious water. Silently, I began counting the seconds while it battled against the avid mouth, and had reached thirteen before Angria's loyal crewmen contrived to steer it clear of the rotating funnel, with the aid of a seemingly-haphazard gust of wind.

Then the ship set a course for us—and seemed to be skimming over the waves, with all the speed expectable of an artful pirate. The monsters were helpless now, or seemingly so. The ghost-ship had the upper hand, even though its pickings had been thinner than its captain hoped.

It reached us within minutes, and crewmen threw ropes by which we were able to make it fast to the megaliths. Then people began leaping down from the deck on to the solid ground.

I was there beside Madame Lacuzon to catch Dupin when he landed, and prevent him sprawling on the ground in an ungainly fashion. He was overjoyed to find me. "We thought you were lost!" he said

"Did you get Breisz away before his house finally sank?" I asked, in case my impression had been mistaken.

"No," said Dupin, "and he took the books with him, alas. We saved his servants, though. That's something, I suppose." It was an unusually generous concession on his part. I knew how devastated he must be by the thought of the lost treasure, far beyond the price of gold and diamonds in his eyes.

We found Chapelain then, and checked that he was uninjured—but he was looking up at the deck of the pirate ship, and had no time for us. He was looking at Ysolde Leonys, who was poised on the balustrade of the forecastle.

"Don't jump!" he yelled. "Stay aboard!"

John Taylor's ghost was clambering up on to the forecastle, evidently with the same thought in mind—but Ysolde took no notice. She jumped—perhaps because she was foolish, and perhaps because she felt that she had no choice. She had summoned help for us, because we were under her protection; she had not summoned it for herself, because she did not believe that she had any entitlement to rescue.

Dupin and Madame Lacuzon ran to help her, and succeeded in preventing her from slipping back into the water, although she could not stand up. Dupin retained her on her knees, and she gripped his hand convulsively, clasping it to her upper torso, as once she had clasped her stolen medallion. The medallion was long gone, having served its purpose and used up its residual power.

"Read me, Monsieur Dupin," she croaked. "Read me, for Heaven's sake—I will pay the price."

Then she collapsed; his efforts to hold her up were unavailing.

Chapelain knelt down beside her, but he must have known that it was hopeless. He picked her up and carried her into the circle, and there was still enough life in her to allow her to whisper something in his ear—but that was as much as Dupin and I saw, for we whirled around as a fearful clamor went up from the deck of the ghost-ship.

Beyond the ship's figurehead—which was shaped as a bare-breasted woman with snakes for hair and claws for hands—the water of the sea was seething, as if another whirlpool were about to open up. Then a head burst through the surface, and a gigantic body began to rise up from the sticky waves. It was humanoid in from, but its flesh was compounded out of the flesh of the thousands of shoggoths—or the single shoggoth reflected thousands of times—that had digested and excreted Oberon Breisz's encrypted enclave on the margin of reality.

It was, in terms of its form, not much different from the

shoggoth-possessed footpads who had attacked me in Saint-Sulpice—but when it had risen fully from the water, it was thirty feet tall. It could probably have stepped over the ghost-ship, if it had been so inclined, but in fact it walked around her prow, shattering the figurehead with a casual flip of its left hand. With its right forefinger, it stabbed one of the glowing megaliths that had previously barred the way to its smaller brethren—and the megalith shattered, forcing everyone within the circle to duck the flying splinters.

The gap was wide enough for the giant to step through, but it seemed to be in a mood for destruction, and it flicked another megalith with the index-finger of its left hand. That one shattered too.

The giant bent down then, and stared at us with its baleful eyes: human eyes in which we could see all the slimy tentacles in the world, and, beyond them, the draconian entity that that was numerical and symbolic magic not-quite-incarnate.

The giant's face was the one that had belonged to Oberon Breisz. Nor was it only Breisz's face that the monster had: it had his wrath, too. The shoggoths that had destroyed the enclave had been blind, devoid of any real purpose, merely following the dictates of their nature. This one was different. This one had *human* malevolence.

It was all unnecessary. Breisz could have been saved. He could have taken advantage of the ghost-ship, accepted the assistance of his old comrades and adversaries—but there was too much bitterness in him, too much gall, and too much vanity. Centuries of life had dried up all the humility that had once been in him, and had left him a creature of arrogant obsession, a miser in every sense of the term.

Now, he was all wrath, all resentment, all chagrin. He wanted revenge on the person he believed—falsely—to be responsible for the death of his dreams. He wanted to kill Auguste Dupin.

Now that the protective circle had been breached, it seemed that nothing could stop him, no matter how loudly Dupin's guardian might howl her spells, in company with Saint-Germain.

In fact, though, Saint-Germain had backed away very hurriedly. The gorgon was alone in her defiance—except, of course, for her master himself...and me.

Glad, at last, to have an unambiguous opportunity, I took out my revolver and fired, five times.

The shots should have been effective; the giant was solid, after all, and the bullets ripping through his flesh did material damage. Alas, the giant was *too* solid. The bullets lost impetus within its mass, lodged in its blubber, unable to reach any vital or vulnerable point of its perverted anatomy.

The giant simply *soaked up* the bullets. It did not even deign to recognize me as a nuisance, let alone a threat, so intent was it on reaching the object of its ire.

Madame Lacuzon would have stood her ground; the giant would have had to trample her to get to Dupin—but Dupin did not want that. He stepped swiftly in front of her, and in a loud but perfectly steady voice, he recited: "*Ph'nglui mglw'nat Cthulhu R'laiyeh wgah'ngl fhtaign....*" And then he added the seventh set of seven sounds, which I shall not reproduce, because they are not to be written down in any form but the one in which they were hidden.

I remembered what he had said about there being a price to pay for such usage—but I remembered, too, what Ysolde Leonys had promised him with her dying breath.

Dupin assured me, later, that he had been working on the problem incessantly, in his mind, ever since he had first seen Chapelain's copy of the cryptogram, and that he had solved the mystery by means of logic alone. He had not needed to read it in Ysolde's magical flesh, even had he been able to do so—which he could not, for he was a rational man, even in his nightmares. For once, I did not believe him. It seemed more likely to me that Saint-Germain was right, and that he was really a secret magician, posing as a skeptic in order to put potential rivals and adversaries off the scent. But what do I know?

I know, at least, that the complete formula stopped the giant in its tracks, re-encrypting Oberon Breisz and the shoggoth with whom he had fused.

The giant did not *go down*, but it froze, and then slowly dissolved into oily mist, while the ghost-ship cast off its moorings and sailed away. It had to go, I imagine, while it still had a sea of sorts on which to sail. Its captain did not want to run aground on the *Grand'Lande*.

Then I lay down and went to sleep—again—extremely glad that the danger was over at last.

CHAPTER NINETEEN
LEVASSEUR'S TREASURE

WHEN THE COMTE DE Saint-Germain finally succeeded in shaking me awake, I was not at all surprised to find that I was lying on the ground at the foot of one of the surviving megaliths in the stone circle. I would have been extremely astonished to find myself back in my bed in Oberon Breisz's house, having been summoned to breakfast. I would have been equally astonished even to see Obern Breisz's house, perched upon the summit of its steep hill. Even the hill was not there now. Instead of rising ground there was a rounded depression, at the bottom of which was a sullen stretch of water. I suspected that it was one of those deceptively small lakes that rumor would one day call bottomless.

"Chapelain says that we should bury the woman here," Saint-Germain told me. "Fortunately, I brought a spade with me, in case I had occasion to dig for buried reassure. You'll have to take your turn, for the ground is stony and more than a trifle recalcitrant, and none of us has hands hardened to such labor by long experience in the fields. Breisz's servants have all decamped, alas, else we could have paid them to do the job with a little silver."

"Is there no better ground to be found?" I asked. "Surely the soil is softer nearer to the lake."

"Apparently," sad Saint-Germain, with a sigh, "she told Chapelain before she died exactly where she wanted to be buried. Like all physicians, he's well used to burying his mistakes, and seems to have a code of conduct with regard to honoring their last wishes."

The spot that Ysolde had allegedly chosen was in the shadow of one of the unbroken megaliths. It was slightly different from the others, in being slightly thinner and top-heavy. It was, I suppose, as worthy a tombstone as many I had seen.

Someone had laid a sheet over hr body, but I lifted it briefly to look at her. She was exactly as I had seen her the first time, in the ward at Bicêtre: ugly, old before her time, with sallow skin, thinning hair and syphilitic sores around her lips. All glamour had gone.

"What will you tell Leuret?" I asked Chapelain, when I had the chance.

"That she died," Chapelain said, simply. "He will not be surprised—and he will not think it matters in the least whether she passed away in Paris or Brittany, or where she is buried. Better here, I think, than in an unmarked ditch outside the walls of Paris, with a dozen assorted whores and lunatics for company."

"If the story she told us was really true," I observed, "then she had a truly remarkable life."

"If it was not true," Chapelain replied, "it was hardly less remarkable for its falsehood...but I certainly shall not report it to Leuret as an instance of infectious madness. I cannot, in all honesty, tell him that she died sane, or even at peace...but I shall refrain from going into detail."

"By the time we get back to Paris," I said, "we shall all be taking comfort in the knowledge that it was, after all, merely a hallucination...one whose like, with luck, we shall never experience again."

"Amen to that," he said.

By the time it was my turn to dig, there're was not much further to go, and the ground had become a little easier, free of pebbles and grass-roots. The worst problem was that I had to throw the earth that I shifted out of the deepening hole, which required considerable effort. I was soon sweating, and cursing the dirt that was spattering my clothing. My spare clothes had, I assumed, gone down with the impossible house. At least I had transferred my journal, my purse and my portfolio to the jacket I was wearing, along with the revolver that had proved, in the circumstances, to be impotent.

I was just about to give up when the spade hit the box.

As treasure-chests go, it was nothing very spectacular—not the kind of decoratively brass-bound chest one seen on stage in the Boulevard du Temple, but merely a rectangular wooden box, already soft with rot. It was locked, but I smashed it open with a single blow once Saint-Germain and I had lifted it out of the grave. It was small, but it was heavy.

When we had sorted out the contents from the wooden shards, we counted forty gold pieces and twenty small diamonds.

"Is that all!" Saint-German complained. "Legend spoke of millions!"

"Legend always speaks of millions," Dupin observed, softly. "Talk is cheap—but those sad remains, I suspect, were dearly won."

"But forty coins, damn it!" Saint-Germain complained. "That's only ten apiece!"

"Eight," Dupin corrected.

"You can't...." the Comte began, but stopped when he looked around, met Madame Lacuzon's eyes, and decided that we could. He shrugged his shoulders, and muttered: "It's as well there weren't thirty-nine, and nineteen diamonds, else we'd have been haggling over them for hours."

I contemplated suggesting that we should deduct the costs of the expedition before making the split, but decided against it. As Saint-Germain had said, the arithmetic was too convenient to warrant that kind of petty disruption.

"But if she really did know that it was here," Chapelain said, "why did she leave it where it was? Why live as a common street-walker in Paris, when she knew the location of a treasure—a treasure that is certainly enough for one person's needs, even if it seems less than a fortune when split five ways?'"

"She did not dare come back, until the spur of imminent death left her to choice," I said, simply. "Besides which, she felt that she deserved her punishment. She was little more than a child, after all, no matter when she was born."

Dupin, of course, was utterly miserable, having found nothing but gold and diamonds.

"Not a single manuscript saved," I observed, sympathetically. "The *Necronomicon*, lost. The only existing copy of the *Claves Demonicae*, lost—and hundreds more. To see them, and touch them, and then to lose them…it must be hard."

"It feels hard," he admitted. "But we are wiser for the experience, and must be content with that. We're alive after all…and a little richer." The gold and gems were, of course, a great deal more significant in the context of his economic condition than they seemed to Saint-Germain…and to Madame Lacuzon, they must, indeed, seem a veritable fortune.

"We should complete the burial," I said. "Which of us will stand in for the priest?"

No one rushed to volunteer; after a moment's hesitation, Chapelain decided that the duty was his, and improvised as best he could.

When the makeshift ceremony was complete, Dupin took me aside, and said: "Are we entitled to keep this treasure? Are we not pirates ourselves if we do?"

"I suppose the Portuguese ambassador would be happy to take it off our hands," I said, "but where does the chain of piracy begin and end? Who really has a legitimate claim of ownership? And we have undergone a trial by ordeal, have we not? Why not take your prize, and use it wisely?"

He stiffened himself then, and said: "You're right."

"It's an all-round victory for reason and piracy," I said, supportively. "We win the treasure, even if we do have to share it with Saint-Germain—and you now know the whole solution to the cryptogram, in case you should ever require it again."

"God forbid," he said.

"The problem is," I said soberly, "that He doesn't seem to."

"No," said Dupin, "and that is why we must strive to live as best we can, within the laws of nature as we find them."

* * * * * * *

MUCH LATER, LONG after our return to Paris, I had a dream. In the dream, I was back on the ghost-ship, with Angria and Jack Taylor. We were all three standing on the bridge, with the skull and crossbones fluttering overhead, looking toward the prow, where the misty figure of Ysolde—the beautiful Ysolde, not the wreck—was standing in company with a ghost that I knew to be the Tristan de Léonais of her dream. I could not see the expressions on their faces, for I could only see them in profile, but I knew that they felt serene as they looked out over the infinite ocean.

It was only a dream. It meant nothing. I can't help hoping, though, that when I am dead and gone, somewhere in the world, someone else will still be capable of dreaming the same dream, uncomprehendingly but accurately, thus preserving and protecting it from its ultimate decay into oblivion. I have done my part by writing it down, albeit in a language that will one day stand in need of deciphering before it can be understood, if it ever is, by other-than-human eyes.

ABOUT THE AUTHOR

BRIAN STABLEFORD was born in Yorkshire in 1948. He taught at the University of Reading for several years, but is now a full-time writer. He has written many science-fiction and fantasy novels, including *The Empire of Fear*, *The Werewolves of London*, *Year Zero*, *The Curse of the Coral Bride*, *The Stones of Camelot*, and *Prelude to Eternity*. Collections of his short stories include a long series of *Tales of the Biotech Revolution*, and such idiosyncratic items as *Sheena and Other Gothic Tales* and *The Innsmouth Heritage and Other Sequels*. He has written numerous nonfiction books, including *Scientific Romance in Britain, 1890-1950*; *Glorious Perversity: The Decline and Fall of Literary Decadence*; *Science Fact and Science Fiction: An Encyclopedia*; and *The Devil's Party: A Brief History of Satanic Abuse*. He has contributed hundreds of biographical and critical articles to reference books, and has also translated numerous novels from the French language, including books by Paul Féval, Albert Robida, Maurice Renard, and J. H. Rosny the Elder.

www.ingramcontent.com/pod-product-compliance
Lightning Source LLC
Chambersburg PA
CBHW031405250626
47155CB00004B/1423